Taming the Earl

The Earls of the North
Book 3

Elizabeth Heights

ARE YOU SIGNED UP FOR DRAGONBLADE'S BLOG?

You'll get the latest news and information on exclusive giveaways, exclusive excerpts, coming releases, sales, free books, cover reveals and more.

Check out our complete list of authors, too!

No spam, no junk. That's a promise!

Sign Up Here

www.dragonbladepublishing.com

Dearest Reader;

Thank you for your support of a small press. At Dragonblade Publishing, we strive to bring you the highest quality Historical Romance from some of the best authors in the business. Without your support, there is no 'us', so we sincerely hope you adore these stories and find some new favorite authors along the way.

Happy Reading!

CEO, Dragonblade Publishing

Additional Dragonblade books by
Author Elizabeth Heights

The Earls of the North Series
Gambling with the Earl (Book 1)
Forced to Marry the Earl (Book 2)
Taming the Earl (Book 3)

Chapter One

Year of Our Lord 1301.
Wolvesley Castle, North-east England

A HIGH-PITCHED WAILING noise summoned Angus from the comfort of rare slumber. The noise came again, slicing through his body like a freshly-sharpened blade and echoing around the tapestried walls of his bedchamber. He flung away the blankets and sat up in bed, his fumbling hands reaching out for the tinder on the nightstand.

God's Bones, what was that dreadful sound?

The desperate shriek reverberating through the second floor of Wolvesley Castle could have been summoned directly from the fiery depths of hell itself. It was keening infused with both terror and terrible grief. Much more of it would send a man mad.

The flame struck and Angus lit his candle, casting quick eyes around the spacious room to ensure all was still before rising from the bed and striding to the doorway, chill night air wrapping itself around his nakedness. The sound grew louder as he flung open the panel and a hot wave of dread washed over him when he realized where it was coming from.

His mother's bedchamber.

This was grave indeed.

Angus hesitated no more. He reached for a fur-lined mantle, belted it tightly and closed his oak wood door behind him. Shadows jumped around the vaulted corridor as he covered the distance to his mother's room. He had been right to insist the guards be repositioned from this part of the castle at night; else the de Neville family secret might have finally been exposed.

He knocked sharply and twisted the handle, but the door was bolted on the inside. Angus put his mouth close to the wood and spoke softly.

"Mother, it's me, let me in."

Rapid footsteps sounded, although the wailing did not let up, and Angus straightened as the bolt was shot back. The door opened slightly and a blaze of light spilled out of it. He blinked and found himself looking into the wary grey eyes of his mother's loyal lady's maid.

"My lord," the elderly woman said, her voice trembling. "I am sorry to have disturbed your sleep."

Angus folded his arms and flashed her a reassuring smile. The servant had failed in her duties tonight, but Angus was not quick to blame. "Forsooth, Nella, I do not believe it is you who woke me."

Nella pulled a faded shawl over her head for decency, just as another wail of anguish came from behind her. "Your mother has had another nightmare but I will tend to her, my lord."

Relief tapped him on the shoulder.

A nightmare, that was all.

Angus nodded his thanks and turned to leave. But a quailing enquiry from within stopped him in his tracks.

"Nella, is someone there?"

Nella spoke over her shoulder. "Only your son, my lady."

The cry of joy was unmistakable. "Lucan, my boy, have you come back to me?"

There it was. The name he dreaded hearing from his mother's lips.

Angus turned and followed Nella's footsteps into his mother's bedchamber. Lady Violetta de Neville had half-risen out of bed, though her frail legs were still entwined in a slew of rugs and she was precipitously close to falling.

"Easy, Mother, it is I, Angus," he declared, putting a strong arm around her shoulders and righting her. Clad in a nightrail trimmed with lace, his mother's jutting collarbones were all too visible. Violetta had never been a large woman, but she had eschewed nearly all foodstuffs since the recent tragedy.

"Angus, oh, Angus," the old woman murmured, reaching up to place a small, cold hand over his. "Of course, it is you." Her long white hair billowed around her; hair that had once been the colour of burnished gold. Angus had inherited his thick fair hair and piercing blue eyes from his mother.

"Pray take more care," he scolded her gently as he pulled a heavy rug over the slender figure. "These late summer nights carry a chill."

"Stay near me, son, for I had a terrible dream," Violetta begged, allowing him to lay her back onto her pillows. "I saw your brother, Lucan, tossed from a horse and killed." She paused, gazing up at him desperately as her fingers closed around his. "Will you fetch him for me? I long to touch his living face and banish the ghosts of that dreadful vision."

Angus froze in his tasks, half-closing his eyes as his mother's words settled within him. At the other side of the bed, he saw Nella clasp her hands together as if in prayer. He took a deep breath, exhaling through his nose as he wondered what to say in reply. The hour was late. Should he mutter bland words of comfort and let an old lady sleep?

Would that be cowardly? Or merely compassionate?

Angus took another ragged breath, wishing that at least his mother's chamber was kept in darkness so that Nella would not bear witness to the despair and indecision washing over him.

Appearance was everything. And as Earl of Wolvesley, he must appear to be calmly in control, even if the situation threatened to overwhelm him.

Alas, although Violetta's vision was failing, she held a deep dislike of shadows and insisted that her chamber be kept brightly lit, even in the darkest hours of the night. Oil lamps flickered in numerous sconces along the white-washed walls and a bright candelabra blazed from the ceiling.

"Rest for a moment, Mother," he said quietly, pleased when her eyelids fluttered closed. "Let me think on your request."

Still searching for inspiration, he glanced at the lowered face of his mother's faithful maid. Nella had pulled the folds of her shawl together for warmth, but was swaying where she stood with tiredness.

"You may retire for the night, Nella," he told her. "I will stay with my mother."

Nella bit down on her lip, her anxieties all too evident. "Lady Violetta does not like to be alone," she said, her voice catching. "For these last few nights I have slept here, in her chamber." She nodded towards a narrow cot pulled beside the foot of the bed.

Angus cleared his throat. The words that neither of them dared give voice to hovered in the candle-lit chamber.

"All the more reason for you to rest now, while I am here." He smiled again, projecting an air of calm reassurance despite his inner turmoil.

Nella tightened her lips and he could see that she remained uneasy. "Sometimes my lady wakes and says strange things." She hesitated, clenching her pale hands together. "I am sure she does not mean them. But mayhap, if she were to be overheard, people could get the wrong idea."

Her steely courage took his breath clean away. Most servants would have scurried from the chamber, hardly daring to meet his gaze. But Nella had served Lady Violetta since she came to Wolvesley as a young bride and her loyalty to the dowager countess was unswerving.

Angus folded his hands over his robe. His hands were large, his fingers long, his nails square-cut and buffed. They were the hands of a man in control.

"I understand what you are telling me."

Her gasp of surprise was audible. Angus lifted his gaze and met hers steadily.

"You know?" Her voice cracked.

He nodded once, pushing his reluctance aside. "I have known

for many years. Although my mother has never come so close to public exposure as in these last months. Her grief makes the situation more perilous."

Nella looked as if she might faint clean away. She stumbled to one side and rested an arm on the finely-carved headboard to steady her. All of the resolve in her lined face melted to nothing and he was alarmed to see tears shining in her grey eyes. Her next question was so quiet he had to ask her to repeat it.

"What will you do?"

Angus frowned. "Do?"

"You are the King's judiciary." The statement was high-pitched and accusatory.

Angus frowned. "I am also my mother's son." But his rush of anger cooled as her ageing body sagged in relief. "Do not fear, Nella," he added gently. "But we cannot risk anyone else finding out. This must remain a secret between us." He straightened his back, imbuing his words with all the authority of his recently acquired rank. "You cannot allow Lady Violetta to become so vocally distressed." He raised an eyebrow.

She caught his meaning quickly. "I will be more vigilant, my lord, and will wake her at the first hint of distress from now on."

"I would like some time alone with my mother."

He had given her the reassurance she needed. Nella bobbed her head with no further prevarication.

"I will bring some warm milk from the kitchens."

She left quietly, closing the panel behind her. Angus reached down to smooth his mother's white hair away from her brow. It was as long and thick as it had been in Angus's childhood; only the colour had faded. Her eyes were closed now, her face smooth and serene; he fancied that the danger had passed.

Aye, danger. That was not too strong a word for it.

If the wrong people witnessed Violetta in the grip of one of her 'visions,' his mother might be branded a witch. As the King's judiciary, he would be expected to arrest her.

Weariness tugged at his bones. He could not stand here all

night, with a lowered head and stooped shoulders. He spied a small footstool nearby, pulled it closer to the bed and sank down onto it.

"Lucan, is that you?"

"Nay, Mother, is it I, Angus," he said firmly, dragging his gaze up to hers.

But Violetta was not peering in his direction. She was sitting bolt upright in bed, her unseeing eyes fixed on the far corner of the room, directly next to the brazier.

Unsettled, Angus followed her gaze, satisfying himself that the room was empty.

"Lucan is not here, Mother," he tried again.

If only he was.

Angus's only brother, the former Earl of Wolvesley, had been killed just days after hosting a lavish midsummer ball earlier in the year. Lucan had been a skilled warrior, fearlessly leading the mighty Wolvesley army in service of King Edward on the Scottish borderlands. But he did not meet his death in battle. Instead, the experienced knight breathed his last after a simple tumble from his horse inside his very own stable yard.

The raw injustice of Lucan's loss did not simply sting, it had burned a hole through daily life at Wolvesley Castle. Nearly three months on, his absence was still felt in every corner of the fortress. He had been a just and fair earl, respected by his men both on and off the battlefield.

Angus swallowed down his rising grief. His pain at losing a brother could not compete with his mother's utter anguish at losing her eldest son. Her dream had been not a nightmare, but a memory. And much more terrifying for it.

"You have come back to me," Violetta said. Her voice had lost its edge of panic and a smile danced around her lips. "Come closer, son, so that I might see you more clearly."

Angus swallowed hard, unable to prevent his gaze from swinging back to the brazier, half expecting to see a broad-shouldered warrior with tumbling locks of golden hair reaching half way down his back. If Lucan was here, his keen blue eyes would look straight into Angus's soul, one clear question on his mind.

How will you protect all that was mine?

Angus would give all the gold coins in the castle for the chance to have that conversation. He had grown up a scholar and gone on to be a law-maker. Some ten years his brother's junior, he had never anticipated taking on the mantle of earlship. How could he now lead the largest army in the north?

On the day he met his death, Lucan had been still young enough to produce a nursery full of heirs. Two years earlier, he had been plunged into long mourning when his young wife died in childbirth; but they had all expected he would re-marry one day.

But that day would never come. Angus was Lucan's only heir. And now the mighty de Neville line stopped with him.

Another problem that he must solve.

"Such worry etched across your brow," Violetta murmured, her hands out-stretched in greeting.

Angus could bear it no longer. He sprang to his feet and snatched up a long candle from the nightstand.

"There is no one here, Mother," he stated, with more conviction than he felt. He didn't want to consider if his mother really had 'the Sight.' His main concern had always been ensuring no one else suspected it. And that task had never been more challenging than since his brother's death. It seemed her grief had overwhelmed her capacity for rational thought.

Violetta's head twitched, as if she were only dimly aware that he had spoken.

"Lucan, tell me what troubles you," she whispered.

Angus swung the candle around in an arc. Light blazed from every corner and the familiar chamber held nothing to fear, save his mother's increasing delusions.

Her increasingly *vocal* delusions.

He settled the light back onto the nightstand and cupped his warm hands around Violetta's.

"Mother, look at me," he ordered firmly. "I am here, Angus. We both know that Lucan has passed on. It is a truth that grieves me every day, but we cannot deny it."

Violetta's failing eyes gazed past him, but he could see he had her attention now.

"He is fading," she gasped, her face turning to his in a pitiful entreaty. "Angus, you frightened him away."

He chuckled at that, settling himself back onto the footstool. "Think on, Mother," he said, softly. "When was Lucan ever afraid of anything I did? He was the warlord. I was the scholar."

Violetta sank back onto her pillows, her long fingers patting her son's hand. "Aye," she agreed. "He liked his sword, and you liked your books."

"That's right, Mother," he said, breathing deeply to quell a surge of sadness. "Try to rest now," he added, more in hope than expectation. But Violetta closed her eyes and gradually, her breathing became slow and regular.

Nella returned and Angus took his leave, but he found no comfort in sleep that night, despite the softness of his bed and the many challenges awaiting him in the morn. He had kept his mother's secret safe all these long years, but would her grief expose them all?

HE ROSE BEFORE the cock crow and splashed water on his face from an earthenware bowl, chasing the exhaustion of the unending night from his skin. He dressed carefully, in a richly embroidered dark tunic, and pulled a cherry-wood comb through his thick hair.

Angus kept his hair cut shorter than his brother had. It hung in soft waves just above his powerful shoulders. He was a strong, athletic man, despite his preference for pursuing the law rather than enemies in battle. He'd known from a young age the vital importance of public image. For the de Neville men, appearance was all.

This was why Angus did not leave his bedchamber until he was satisfied that the looking glass showed him a man in control.

He was on his way down the stone-flagged stairs when a servant came running from the entrance hall.

"My lord, your visitor has arrived."

Angus's face creased with genuine pleasure. "He is early," he exclaimed. "Have refreshments brought to my solar."

Minutes later, Otto Sarragnac, Earl of Darkmoor, strode into Angus's private oak-panelled room and pulled his friend into a strong, wordless embrace. The two men stood shoulder-to-shoulder, both of them tall and broad. But while Angus had about him a whipcord energy, Otto was a man bred for battle. His forearms were those of a warrior well-used to wielding a broadsword, and the silvery scar snaking across his left cheek confirmed he had seen action aplenty. Otto and Angus had trained together at the renowned Knights academy in Lindum; although Angus had later turned to more scholarly pursuits.

Pursuits which meant he could ensure the safety of those he loved at home; even while the Wolvesley army campaigned far and wide under Lucan's wise leadership.

"I am sorry for your loss, my friend," Otto said gravely. "I am sorrier still that I could not attend Lucan's funeral."

"You are here now, and I thank you for it," Angus replied, chasing down a swell of emotion. "How is Alfred?"

Otto's young son had been taken with a fever, which had kept his father rightly at home.

Otto smiled briefly. "Much better, thank you. With his mother's careful nursing, he will see full health within days."

Angus gripped his arm. "It gladdens my heart to hear it," he said sincerely. "But I'm gladder still to have you here."

"I will help in whatever way I can." Otto's eyes ran quickly over the comfortable room, furnished with stuffed armchairs and a gleaming mahogany desk. "Although I admit, I am at a loss as to how I can be of assistance to the mighty Earl of Wolvesley."

Angus let out a short bark of laughter. "That is a title I am not yet used to inhabiting. But let us sit and talk for a while, before business claims us." He pointed to a patterned chair pulled up beside the fireplace. "Will you take a cup of small ale? Or would you prefer wine?"

"Ale at this hour." Otto smiled. "I must keep a clear head for whatever is to be asked of me."

Angus waved away his concerns as a slim serving wench backed into the room carrying a heavy tray filled with a pitcher of ale, freshly-baked bread, soft cheese and ripe figs. Otto sniffed hungrily, rubbing his hands in anticipation. The servant placed the tray on a low wooden table, nodded her auburn head and departed.

"Eat and drink, my friend," Angus urged, taking a small hunk of bread for himself. "You have had a long journey."

"And then will you tell me why you summoned me here?" Otto raised a dark eyebrow as he speared a hunk of cheese. "You do know that Darkmoor is but a poor estate compared to Wolvesley?"

"Hush, man," Angus said, with mock frustration. "Darkmoor suits you very well, Otto, and I will not feel sympathy for a man who boasts a loving wife and son."

"And another child on the way," Otto interrupted him, his joy evident in his wide smile.

"Wonderful news indeed." Angus inclined his head, ignoring the tiny knot of jealousy beginning to form in his stomach. "You must send my blessings to Ariana."

"I will." Otto chewed and swallowed. "And what of your own betrothed, Lady Emelia Foxton?"

Angus put aside his bread, unable to summon an appetite. "Emelia is still in Cheltenham." He forced a smile. "But I have no doubt I will hear from her soon." He flicked a glance at Otto. "Mayhap even today."

"You are in regular contact?" Otto was watching him closely, unable to hide his curiosity. "I was not sure if your betrothal still held?"

"Aye, it does." Angus swallowed the words *for now*. He leaned forward and pointed to a finely-detailed tapestry hanging on the panelled wall over the fireplace. It depicted Wolvesley Castle, from the two fortified towers to the high fountain in the courtyard. "This is Emelia's work."

"Lady Emelia stitched this for you?" Otto exclaimed, standing up to better examine the tapestry. "Why, the detail is exquisite."

Angus folded his arms. "We challenge one another. It is our long tradition."

Otto swivelled around. "How so?"

"You know she fostered here as a child?" Angus glanced up to see his friend nodding. "We were close in age and all but grew up together." He paused. "Lady Emelia has a strong competitive streak."

"As do you," Otto interrupted.

Angus nodded. "We competed over everything." It was, mayhap, the one thing that bonded them. He raised his palms upwards. "When Lucan and Lord Foxton arranged our match, she wrote immediately to tell me she could not countenance marrying me until I demonstrated some proficiency in the arts."

"What did the lady mean?"

"She challenged me to learn to play the lute." Angus raised an eyebrow and nodded towards the small wooden instrument which still resided on the plush window-seat.

Otto choked a little on his bread, surprise etched all over his chiselled face. "And did you?"

"Aye, I did." Angus repressed his smile. "It all but cost me my sanity, but I mastered the damn thing. And in turn, I wrote back to say I could not countenance marrying her until she demonstrated some proficiency in the more feminine arts."

Otto was grinning widely now. "Hence the tapestry?" he guessed.

Angus nodded, drumming his long fingers against the polished arm of his chair. "And so, I await her next challenge."

He had told Otto the facts of the matter; although he had not revealed the quiet secrets of his heart. When first they started, he had been happy for these childish challenges to provide a delay to their nuptials.

Emelia was an intelligent, beautiful woman. The perfect match for him, in the eyes of many. Angus, however, could not bring himself to see her in that light. There was no shared blood between them, but he still thought of her with the irritable affection of an older brother.

In truth, he did not wish to marry her. The older he grew, the more convinced of this he became.

Furthermore, he had long suspected that his reluctance was reciprocated. Why else would Emelia prevaricate so? But as yet, neither one of them had been courageous enough to admit their true feelings.

"An entertaining tale." Otto brushed crumbs of bread from his emerald green tunic. "When did you last see Emelia?"

"I have not laid eyes on her for more than ten years," Angus stated baldly. "We were but children when she left Wolvesley. And truth be told, now that I am earl, I have no time for these games. You know yourself the responsibilities that come with my position. Our old enemies in Powys are already re-grouping, bolstered into action by Lucan's death. And King Edward is an old man now. Who knows what the future holds for us all?" His frustration was beginning to show in his voice. Angus bade himself be quiet and took a restorative sip of ale.

"You already have a strong army, but you need an heir," Otto stated quietly, cutting straight to the heart of the matter.

That was the truth of it. Angus needed an heir.

"I need an heir. I also need a commander for my army. And god-willing, I need the grace of time to accomplish these things before our enemies strike." He sighed. "A wife is the first step."

A headache threatened at his temples. Aye, it was time for

him to do his duty.

Otto cocked his head to one side, his dark eyes fixed on his friend. "Does love play no part in this?"

Angus smiled at his whimsy. "Love is for stories, and mayhap those lucky few like you and Ariana. I have no time to look for it. An heir is what I need for Wolvesley." He picked up his cup of ale and raised it in a silent toast.

"And that is why you have brought me here?" Otto's eyebrows all but disappeared into his dark thatch of hair.

Despite his frustrations, Angus felt the laughter welling up inside him. "Nay. I do not look to you for advice on that. I know well enough what to do." He broke off with a smile. "It is your skills as a warlord that I seek."

Otto made an expansive gesture. "Pray, enlighten me."

"I must appoint a new leader for our army. There are many good candidates, all loyal knights who have long served under the Wolvesley standard."

"You will not lead them yourself?" Otto interrupted, frowning into a shaft of morning sunlight which slanted through the window behind them.

"Nay." Angus didn't want to explain how precarious his situation was. If he vacated his position as judiciary, another man must be found in his stead. He could not allow that, for his mother's sake. "I know where my strengths lay," he said, avoiding the real reason behind his decision.

Otto pursed his lips. "I am honoured, of course. But I also remember your prowess at Lindum. I believe you are a man of many strengths, Angus."

"Lucan was the warrior in this family." Angus would brook no further discussion on this point. "He trained his men well. And inspired loyalty which will hold true for many summers yet. I ask only for your opinion on which of them has the greatest propensity to lead. After all, it is some years since I last rode into battle, whereas you, my friend, were putting down skirmishes as we feasted for Beltane."

Otto lowered his head, his eyes humble. "I will help you in any way I can."

"Excellent." Angus jumped to his feet, eager for action and to dispel the slight awkwardness which had descended upon them. "The men train each day. We will go down to the grounds as soon as you have finished your meal."

But his plans were interrupted by a knock on the door.

"Come," Angus said.

It was the grey-haired, slightly stooped Seneschal who came hesitantly into the solar.

"Milords." He bowed first to Angus and then to Otto. "Forgive my interruption." He shifted on his feet uncomfortably. "We have a delivery for you in the stable yard."

"In the stable yard?" Angus repeated, his eyes flicking between the Seneschal and Otto. His friend shrugged good-naturedly. "Well, bring it in, man."

"I am afraid that will not be possible." The Seneschal developed a deep interest in the rushes on the floor.

"What manner of a delivery is this?" Angus leaned back against the edge of his mahogany desk, drumming his fingers on the wood.

The Seneschal's cheeks flushed red. "It is a horse, milord."

A beat passed. Angus scratched the back of his neck, his mind racing. "And was there a message with this horse?"

"Yes, milord."

The Seneschal held out a roll of parchment which Angus took and unfurled. His eyebrows rose higher as he read the elegantly penned note.

Dearest Angus,

I trust you liked the tapestry? I dare to own it was one of my finest achievements, even though the endless stitches made my fingers bleed and my back ache. But I could not allow your triumph on the lute to eclipse me.

And so, I have upped the stakes. Here is a horse which no

one can ride.

If you tame the horse, dear Angus, we will finally name the date for our wedding.

Yours in expectation,
Emelia

He read it twice, anger taking root in his gut and making his fingers tremble.

God's Bones. Emelia had gone too far this time.

He paced across the floor and sat down heavily in his recently vacated chair. Otto hovered over him, his face concerned.

"What is it?"

Wordlessly, Angus handed him the parchment.

"I see." Otto's expression was grave as he rolled it carefully back up and placed it on the desk. "This is too soon."

Angus nodded, grateful his friend had divined the reason for his distress without him having to explain.

"Could it be that news of Lucan's death has not reached as far as Cheltenham?" Otto bounced a little on his heels.

Angus took a steadying breath as some of his red mist cleared. "Nay, it is all over the country. Although the exact circumstances of his passing may not be known," he allowed.

"I am sure Lady Foxton would not be so insensitive…," Otto trailed off.

Angus dragged a weary hand over his eyes. "Our horses are the best in the land." He held up a hand. "And I make no apology for the claim. Not even before you, Otto."

"No apology required."

"My stablemaster served my father before he served Lucan. The man made one mistake, when he failed to check the girth on Lucan's saddle. It is a mistake he will never forgive himself for, although I have oft repeated that an experienced knight should know well enough to check the fastenings of his own girth." Weariness and grief were settling around him once again. "None of this is Emelia's fault. But I cannot countenance an unsafe horse in my yard at such a time."

"That is understandable." Otto put a hesitant hand on his shoulder.

"I will have the horse returned. Emelia needs to know that the time for games is over."

"Your situation has changed, certainly." Otto moved away to stand near the window, giving Angus the space to think.

"I need a wife and I need an heir," Angus repeated. It had become like a mantra to him.

"You do," Otto agreed quietly.

"I have no further time for this childish competition." He brought his heavy brows together and glared across the room at the tapestry. But this time, Otto did not agree. Angus looked over at his friend to find he had stilled in his position, his face unreadable as he gazed out at the castle lawns. "What is it?"

"Exactly that." Otto nodded towards the roll of parchment. "You need a wife. Quickly. And Lady Emelia herself has promised to name a date for your wedding once this horse is tamed."

"Another game." Angus shook his head dismissively. The familiar solar was beginning to feel close and oppressive.

"Ah, but one which you do not need to play." Otto tapped a finger against his cheek as he thought it through. "Keep the horse here and find someone else to train it."

Angus looked up at his friend, his head a jumble of conflicting thoughts. "But I cannot know that Emelia is telling the truth." He remembered a feisty, pink-cheeked girl with long flaxen plaits who took great delight in toying with him. She had never before broken her word over something so important. But nor had she ever raised the stakes so high.

Does she want me to fail?

"You have her promise in writing," Otto pointed out. "All you need to do is secure a horse breaker."

Angus winced at the phrase which he had never liked, before switching his gaze to the uneasy Seneschal. "Have you seen this horse?"

"Aye, milord."

"And what think you of it?"

The man coughed discretely. "A great, big brute, if I may speak freely, milord."

"I think you already have," Angus commented mildly, ignoring Otto's hastily disguised bark of laughter. "Would you say the horse is unrideable?"

"That's not for me to say, milord. Although Jacob the stablemaster was keepin' 'is distance."

"It's worth a try." Otto opened his arms. "What's the worst that can happen?"

Angus tapped his fingers on the arms of his chair. The worst that could happen was he would fail Emelia's challenge. Just three months ago, such a prospect would have filled him with dread. But he'd changed much since then. There was more at stake here than just his pride. Wolvesley needed an heir, and by playing one final game with Emelia, he may just be able to make that happen.

"I hear you, Otto," he said slowly, scratching at his beard. He addressed the Seneschal. "Send word to all four corners of the estate. I want a horse trainer brought here. Man, woman, old or young, I haven't the slightest care. Just so long as they can tame this horse."

Chapter Two

THE COCK CROW woke Morwenna from a deep, untroubled sleep. She was laying on her pallet in the far corner of her wooden hut, beneath a shaft of golden sunlight which had filtered through the myriad gaps in the roof. Dazzled by light and unaccustomed warmth, she lay there blinking for a good minute, before reality took hold of her shoulders and gave her a firm shake.

She mustn't lay here idly. She had far too much to do.

The cool morning air wrapped around her as she shrugged off her thin woollen blankets and pulled her aching limbs into a more upright position. Already, the demands of the day ahead were beginning to race through her mind. From the position of the sun, she could tell she had slept late. Mayhap too late. There was no time to lose.

Morwenna put a hand to her throbbing head as she lowered her bare feet to the earth floor. She had sat up overly long last night, counting out her remaining coin by the sputtering light of a single tallow candle and fretting about what was to come. That she had slept so well on the heels of so much upset, was nothing short of a miracle. It was as if her beloved grandmother had been here again, stroking her hair with a calloused hand and soothing her sorrows with wise, calming words.

All will be well, sweet Morwenna. You'll see that I'm right.

That feeling of safety, of being cared for, was still somehow present in the draughty hut. Even though her grandmother had been dead for almost a year now.

It must have been a dream, Morwenna realised. In the depths of her distress, her troubled mind had conjured a vision of the person she missed most of all.

If her grandmother were here now, she'd tell Morwenna that there was nothing to be gained by fretting. Hot tears and regrets wouldn't bring back her good name in the village. She could only look to hard work to answer her problems.

I'm not afraid of hard work, grandmother, she whispered silently.

Moving quickly against the morning chill, Morwenna crossed the cold floor to a small wooden chest upon which stood a roughly carved bowl. She splashed water onto her cheeks, chasing away the last vestiges of sleep, and then pulled on her cleanest kirtle. Starting from today, she had resolved to take no chances. She must make a good impression on the people of this village.

Left to her own devices, she would choose to leave her long blonde hair loose and flowing down her back. She liked to feel it move in the wind. But she also knew that a young woman of twenty summers should not appear so dishevelled – especially when rumours were already circulating. This morning she hastily combed it with her fingers and tied it into a long plait. Morwenna cared little for her appearance; but if she could have changed one thing, it would have been her height. How she longed to stand tall. Tall enough to tower over the sniggering folk of Escafeld. As it was, her short stature and slender frame lent her a girlish vulnerability.

It was hard to stand up to bullies when she had to crane her neck to look them in the eye.

She took a deep breath and lifted up the long wooden plank which had been effectively bolting her ramshackle door all through the night. As she shouldered open the door, she braced herself for a shock. Mayhap a poor dead bird, maybe runes drawn in the dirt outside, anything to ward off the evil eye of a witch.

For that was what her neighbours openly accused her of, now

that her grandmother had passed on.

The irony was not lost on Morwenna, for if either one of them had the gift of sorcery, it had been her grandmother. And mayhap the villagers had suspected as much, for while her grandmother lived, their days had gone by peaceably enough. Esme's healing salves had been highly sought after in times of sickness. People approached her with respect, tinged with just the faintest edge of fear. By contrast, Morwenna was an oddity who was viewed with far more suspicion: a girl who preferred the company of animals to people. She was treated with more derision than trepidation. Too different to be accepted, but not powerful enough to be feared.

But the only thing to greet her was a balmy warm breeze carrying the heady scent of honeysuckle and dried grass from the meadow. Morwenna clasped her hands together to hide their trembling and stepped out of the hut, carefully closing the door behind her. She must walk down the hill to the well and draw water before the villagers were up and about. Ever since the incident, she'd learned to accept their jeers and pointed fingers with a degree of dignity, but avoidance was better yet.

But a low wicker from the wattle-and-daub barn next to the hut made Morwenna pause. She turned to see two pricked brown ears and warm intelligent eyes looking at her from the half stable door.

"Good morning, Galahad," she greeted the horse.

He whickered at her once again, no doubt wanting treats or to be allowed out of the confines of the barn to run free on the meadow.

"Soon," she promised, crossing over to the barn and running a hand down the white blaze which carved a path through the centre of his intelligent face. "I promise, I'll be back soon." Galahad nudged at her pockets and she wished she had an apple for him. But her own fruit stores had near enough run dry. "Farmer Jerome is bringing supplies over for you today," she whispered to the horse. "I told him I'd fix your nerves in return for the cost of your keep. No charge on this occasion. That's because you're such a lovely boy."

It was only half true. Morwenna had always admired Farmer Jerome's steady bay cob and she hated to see him so traumatised. A sennight before Lammas, louts from Berneshay, the village over the border, had come to Escafeld with pitchforks and knives, plundering homes and shops and setting half the village on fire. Poor Galahad had been hitched to a wooden cart carrying produce for Farmer Jerome to sell at market when the first raiders struck. The cart had also caught ablaze, and now the horse reared in horror whenever he was shown to a harness.

But the real reason Morwenna had promised to cure Galahad for no charge, was because she was desperate for the work. If Farmer Jerome, who was well respected in Escafeld, could put in a good word for her, then mayhap many of her problems would be over. No one would dare tell the wealthiest man in the village – a man who gave work to many and whose crops fed almost all – that he was consorting with a witch. The refrain, which was gaining such a foothold in certain circles, would start to die down.

Galahad's arrival in her barn had been an unanticipated gift, for which she could never thank Farmer Jerome enough.

Galahad flicked his brown ears forwards, wanting her to stay.

"I'll be back soon," she whispered, giving his nose one last pat and turning to leave.

If only the Berneshay louts had passed the village of Escafeld by. If her former friends and neighbours had not lost their food stores, coin and other treasures, they would not be looking so hard for a scapegoat to blame for their troubles.

There were times when Morwenna even found herself wishing the Berneshay raiders had not spared her modest home. She would rather have lost what remained of her grandmother's careful savings than become an object of suspicion.

Morwenna sniffed back her tears, dragging a chilled hand over her face and straightening her shoulders. What was done was done. And in truth, it was her own actions that had brought about this recent slander. Her own carelessness, anyway. She'd forgotten, for a crucial moment, about the need to always be vigilant. To always check that there was no one watching. Lessons her grandmother had taught her from the cradle. *Protect our small secrets at all costs.*

It was not a mistake she would make a second time.

Morwenna's hut stood atop a high meadow which led down to the small village of Escafeld. She'd always enjoyed the peace and views, until these recent weeks when her solitude lent weight to the air of mistrust against her. Now she picked up her pail and set off down the winding rabbit path, trying to find solace in the soaring beauty of the blackbird's morning song. The well stood on the edge of the gently sloping village green. Thankfully no one was about to see Morwenna fill her pail and she crept back up the hill like a common thief.

It wasn't until she was all but home, that she realised something was wrong. The creak of the barn door gave it away, but the hairs on the back of Morwenna's neck had begun to lift long before then. She carefully placed her pail of water by the front door and flattened herself to the wooden wall, peering around the corner. What she saw made her heart plummet.

"Farmer Jerome," she gasped, walking forwards with her arms outstretched entreatingly. "Where are you taking him?"

Farmer Jerome was a bluff, middle-aged man, used to hard work and hearty meals. He had put a halter onto Galahad and was in the process of leading him out of the barn. He coughed into his hand and looked anywhere but at Morwenna as he answered her. "Home, I'm afraid, lass. I've no choice in the matter."

Morwenna took a deep breath and tried to steady her voice. "I understand you need him to pull the cart. Otherwise you can't take your produce to market." She stepped forwards and patted Galahad's shining neck. "But if he's scared of the harness, you won't get very far."

"It isn't that." Farmer Jerome looked at her frankly. "I've always liked you, Morwenna. I knew your grandmother well. She was a wise woman." He paused, noting the alarm in her eyes, and cleared his throat. "In the very best sense of the word," he added, softly. "And you've always kept yourself very respectable."

Morwenna felt a blush warming her cheeks. She knew where this was going. And she couldn't bear it.

"Please don't say you believe the rumours about me?" she forced out.

"Nay, not I." Farmer Jerome looked thoroughly embarrassed. He switched Galahad's halter rope from one hand to the other and shuffled his feet. "But folk around here are a superstitious lot. And my wife amongst them." He cleared his throat. "She's told me to fetch back the horse. I'm sorry, lass."

Morwenna's cheeks were stinging now. "But you must know I'm innocent?"

"I know that well enough," he said with sincerity. "But folk won't buy my crops if they think my horse has been bewitched." He screwed up his face to show his dislike for the notion as Galahad gazed at the distant hills.

"I would never bewitch Galahad," Morwenna said steadily. She put out a hand to the smooth stones of the barn, taking small comfort in their strength and solidity in a world seemingly gone mad.

He sighed heavily, making his nostrils flare. "Honestly, lass, if I were you, I'd look for work elsewhere. In time, the people of Escafeld will forget all about this. They'll move onto something else…"

"That's what I'm hoping," interjected Morwenna.

Farmer Jerome held up a warning hand. "But you might starve afore then," he said solemnly. He inclined his head to a shallow crate standing beside the barn. "I've brought you something to tide you over. And by way of an apology." His mouth tightened into a grimace. "I'd hoped we could help each other. I'm sorry." With a regretful shrug of his shoulders, he urged Galahad onwards and the two walked away from Morwenna, in the direction of his farm on the other side of the meadow. Galahad's brown ears flicked back towards her, as if wondering why she wasn't coming along. The horse's steady affection unleashed something inside her and she leaned back against the barn wall until the surge of grief passed.

Her last hope of restoring her good name in Escafeld had gone.

Tears blinded her eyes as she remembered the unfortunate events that had brought her so low.

Just days after the Berneshay raids, two families in the village succumbed to a dreadful flux, with those taken sick dying within hours of one another. The gentle cobbler and his kind wife were the first to go, leaving a son, Gerrault, newly orphaned with naught but a pillaged business, a half-burned home and a lame donkey to his name.

Minnie was the donkey's name. Gerrault had ridden her as a young boy and she'd become more a family pet than a beast of burden. At the end of a long, blustery day, Morwenna had come across a distraught Gerrault standing with Minnie in the centre of the village green. Minnie was laying down, four furry legs outstretched. Gerrault could not entreat her to stand.

"Is she dying?" he'd sobbingly asked Morwenna, who came to stand by his side. Tall and thin, he was almost a man, but not quite, and his boyish grief was the more affecting for it.

"Not dying," she reassured him, putting a placatory hand on his elbow and carefully observing the donkey. Minnie didn't appear injured or unwell, simply defeated. She didn't so much as flinch as a strong wind lifted her tail off the ground.

"Can you help me?" Gerrault had begged, reddish hair hanging over his eyes. "Please, Miss Morwenna."

"You don't have to call me Miss Morwenna, Gerrault, not anymore. You're the man of the house now," Morwenna told him. The donkey's eyes were rheumy with age. Her fetlocks were almost entirely white. "How old is Minnie?" she asked him.

Gerrault frowned as he worked it out. "Pa got her for me when I was a young'un. I'm near enough sixteen now, so Minnie can't be far behind. Is that old for a donkey?" He swallowed hard. "She's all I have left in this cursed place."

Morwenna tightened her lips. The setting sun was casting long shadows over the green and the buffeting breeze brought goose bumps out onto her arms. She guessed Minnie had been several years old when the cobbler first brought her home. But donkeys usually lived long lives, and even an ageing donkey deserved better than to end her days slumped on the village green.

She positioned herself in front of the donkey's head and squatted down next to her. Without thinking to check they were alone, she put her hands on either side of Minnie's soft head and stilled her mind.

After no more than a minute, her face stretched into a smile. "Why, Gerrault, I do believe she's thirsty."

"Thirsty?" The boy looked thoroughly confused. "But her water trough is full. I check it every day."

Morwenna slowly got to her feet, thinking hard. "When your parents first became sick, what water had they been drinking?"

"Water from our well at the south of the village," Gerrault began. He stopped abruptly as understanding dawned. "Is the water over there poisoned somehow?"

"The water source is fouled. No one is using the well." Alarmed, she glanced over at the boy to double check this was true, and he nodded his agreement.

"The apothecary told me to fetch water from here." He nodded towards the main well, a few feet away from them.

"Good." Morwenna heaved out a breath and drew her shawl closer around her shoulders. "Minnie's water trough is most likely fed by the same fouled stream as the well. She's a clever girl, Gerrault. She's not been drinking it."

"You mean, she might live?" His voice wobbled with hope.

Morwenna nodded. "But you mustn't think this village is

cursed, Gerrault. We've had a run of bad luck, that's all. You more than most."

His lips tightened and he looked away so she couldn't see the tears shining in his eyes. "I know it ain't the village," he said, sniffing loudly. "But life ain't got no joy in it without the people you love."

His words struck a chord deep inside her. In his stumbling eloquence, Gerrault had hit upon a truth.

Life had held no joy for Morwenna since the passing of her grandmother.

"Well, there's every chance you still have Minnie," she said briskly.

He gazed at her with wide, grey eyes. "I should have guessed about the water," he whispered. The boy looked in sore need of a good meal and Morwenna wished she had the means to offer him one.

"There's no reason you should," she said kindly.

But Gerrault was still wretched. "You worked it out so quickly."

She threw him a smile. "Only because Minnie told me."

He put a hand to his chest, over his ragged tunic, considering her words. As the seconds stretched on, Morwenna felt the first pinprick of worry, a harbinger of what was to come. But then Gerrault smiled back. "I'm that glad. You mean, I can fetch her water from here and she'll be okay?"

"That's what I think." Morwenna nodded once, warm with relief. "Why don't we give it a try?"

It had all happened as Morwenna foretold. The donkey perked up after Gerrault offered her careful drinks of clean water. She eventually walked gamely away, led by a highly relieved Gerrault, who shortly afterwards left the village in search of a brighter future elsewhere. Minnie was now in the capable hands of Farmer Jerome. Morwenna would have given the whole thing no further thought, were it not for the vicious rumours that began circulating shortly afterwards.

"Morwenna talks to animals. Morwenna's a witch."

She knew that young Gerrault wasn't the source of such slander. He'd gifted her a new pair of boots as a thank you for her help with Minnie. No doubt using the last of his father's wares to do so. The boots were a shade too small and pinched her toes, but Morwenna appreciated them nonetheless.

Nay, it must have been someone nearby who had witnessed the scene and heard Morwenna's foolish proclamation. After all these years of care, to have spoken out so rashly about her inherited gifts was sheer idiocy. And now she was paying the price.

It wasn't even true. She couldn't talk to animals. But she could *communicate* with them, which was a whole different thing.

Horses were the easiest. And most horses she'd come across were a whole lot better at communicating than the feckless folk in Escafeld.

Angry now, Morwenna stooped down to pick up the crate left by Farmer Jerome. A crusty loaf wrapped in muslins sat beside a basket of apples and some cured ham. Gratitude washed away her ire, making her weak-kneed and tearful once again. What was she to do now?

Eat, she heard her grandmother's voice speaking in her mind. *No situation is ever resolved on an empty stomach.*

With a hard lump forming in her throat, Morwenna shouldered her way back into the shack and placed Farmer Jerome's offerings on her small wooden table. She walked back to close the door and, after a moment's thought, replaced the heavy bar to ensure no one could enter without her say so.

How awful to live in fear and mistrust of those I've known all my life.

She tore off a hunk of bread and pushed it into her mouth. If only she was a witch! She would certainly feel less vulnerable, up here all alone. And mayhap she could cast some kind of spell to fix the roof and replenish her plundered supplies.

Morwenna shook her head at the fancy. She, more than anyone, knew that the Sight was not a gift to be wielded at will. Despite her grandmother's meagre powers, the two of them had lived a modest life. They didn't have much, but they never went hungry either. And they'd always had the security of a small stash of coin, hidden away for emergencies.

Emergencies like a leaking roof, which she couldn't afford to repair since she had been obliged to dip into those same savings on a regular basis lately. The last of her grandmother's salves had been sold. Without work, Morwenna faced a harsh winter ahead.

It was no good. Morwenna abandoned all efforts to eat and simply put her elbows on the table and sobbed. Salty tears stung her eyes and coursed down her cheeks.

Farmer Jerome had suggested she leave Escafeld. But she didn't want to leave this hut; the only home she'd ever known, where precious memories of her grandmother were at their most vivid and sharp.

Besides, when all was said and done, she lacked the courage to make such a change. How could she have faith in her abilities to better her situation, when all she had done was worsen things since her grandmother's death?

She put a hand over the white leather cuff which she always wore on her left wrist. The cuff was a relic from another time and place. A thing of elegance and beauty, despite its simplicity. Her grandmother had passed it to her, just days before her death. The pattern engraved into the leather had faded over time, but it was so familiar to Morwenna that her fingers could trace it without any prompting.

Morwenna was so lost in her grief that she didn't hear the footsteps trampling to her door, nor the first rap against the wood. It wasn't until the rap turned into a hammering that she raised her head and bit down on her lip in fear.

"Open up, in the name of the Earl of Wolvesley," came the order, accompanied by more hammering.

Morwenna's heart beat quicker. The Earl of Wolvesley had never once come to Escafeld, and neither had anyone representing him. She pushed herself up from the table on trembling legs and advanced to the door, where her nerves failed her. She paused for a moment and listened quietly, clinging onto a naïve hope that whoever it was might simply go away.

"Open up, I say," came the voice again. It was a man's voice, deep and masterful. A voice accustomed to being obeyed.

Morwenna's hands shook as she removed the bar from the door and reluctantly pulled it open. A uniformed guard stood on her threshold, wearing the dark green and gold colours of Wolvesley. He was tall and broad-shouldered, with a gleaming sword at his hip.

Morwenna swallowed hard. "What do you want?"

The man looked her up and down, his expression giving nothing away. "Are you the woman called Morwenna?"

Her heart jumped inside her chest. "I am," she whispered. There was no use denying it.

"Then you must come with us." He stood back to allow her to pass and indicated a stately green and gold carriage waiting on the meadow. It was pulled by a pair of gleaming black horses, who pawed at the ground and snorted impatiently. Morwenna had never seen anything so grand.

She shook her head, fear burgeoning in her belly. "This is my home," she whispered. "I have no wish to leave it." Suddenly, the familiarity of Escafeld, despite her recent troubles, had never seemed more precious.

"By order of the earl," the man added, in a tone that would brook no argument.

Morwenna's legs all but failed her. She could think of only one reason why the Earl of Wolvesley would trouble himself with a poor woman from a humble village.

And it was a reason which struck terror into her very bones.

She opened her mouth to protest, but closed it again for what could she say? The man had a sword. Heart beating wildly, she nodded once in assent and edged herself out of the door, keeping as far away from the guard as she could. He allowed her time to fasten the door, then marched her towards the waiting carriage.

Morwenna didn't dare look right or left, fearful that she'd spy villagers come to bear witness to her shame. Mayhap the same villagers who had reported her to the earl for witchcraft? Once again, her legs buckled and the guard shot out a strong arm to save her from falling to the ground in a crumpled heap.

"Thank you," she managed, as he helped her up the carriage steps and closed the door firmly behind her.

At least she had been handled with courtesy.

Morwenna folded herself onto the narrow seat, hoping to blend in with the dark interior and hide from prying eyes. Of all things, she had never expected this.

Her neighbours had betrayed her in the worst possible way.

How would the earl deal with a woman accused of witchcraft?

Her grandmother had told her many stories about the Wolvesley witch hunts. Nay, not stories.

Warnings.

Because the punishment for witchcraft was *burning.*

Albeit, these were in the time of the old earl, when Esme had been a young woman.

Morwenna dug her nails into her palm, unable to think of a way this might possibly end well. At least he had asked for her in person, rather than sending his soldiers to dispatch her in her home. Mayhap that hinted at a fair-minded man, who might yet give her a fair trial?

But she was naught, and he was the wealthiest earl in the whole of England. They were creatures from different worlds. How could she expect him to believe her?

Nay, even to listen to me?

She knew nothing of the man himself. Wolvesley was but a fantasy to her. A mythical place of beauty and riches, where an all-powerful earl presided over all.

Morwenna's stomach churned and she feared she may be sick as the carriage jolted down endless narrow lanes. The seat, after the first few minutes, became hard and uncomfortable, with tight springs all but protruding through the soft surface. The blinds at the windows were half closed and she dare not open them for fear she might see streets lined with hard-faced villagers, ready to throw eggs or worse at a woman such as she. Her back ached and her eyes stung with tears. More than once she eyed the door, wondering if she could force it open and make a bid for freedom. But the two black horses were travelling at a clip and she had no knowledge of the lay of the land in these parts. She might tumble hard and break a bone, only to be picked up by the guard soon afterwards.

The journey was interminable, but by the time she heard the driver give the order for the horses to slow, she had gained some semblance of composure. Her tears had dried and she sat quietly with her hands folded in her lap, pleased that she had donned her cleanest kirtle this morning. At least she would not be appearing before the Earl of Wolvesley in dirty rags.

The carriage rumbled to a halt and immediately the sounds of activity outside reached her ears. Scuffling footsteps, shouted commands, a horse whinnying in recognition of its stablemate. Her breath caught in her throat once more, and she regretted not taking her chances with a blind leap for freedom. Surely anything would be better than standing trial for witchcraft in the mighty castle of Wolvesley?

The carriage door was pulled unceremoniously open and Morwenna blinked in the sudden burst of dazzling sunlight. It took a few seconds for her eyes to become accustomed to the glare, and she shuffled back in alarm at the huge figure of a giant standing in the doorway.

The giant blinked in the gloom of the carriage, and she made out piercing blue eyes and a sweep of golden hair. Not a giant, a man. A man clad in the most sumptuous cloak she had ever seen.

"Well now," he said, his voice rich and rolling. "I hear you can talk to horses?"

Chapter Three

ANGUS LOOKED INTO the dark interior of the carriage at the pale, slender figure tucked all the way into the corner, and the strangest feeling came over him.

As a child he had thrilled to dive into the lake on a hot summer's day, relishing that moment when the waters closed over his head and dulled all sights and sounds of the world above. That was what he felt when he ducked his shoulders to behold the mysterious woman from Escafeld. A dimming down of the bright afternoon and the clamour of the courtyard. A sharpened focus on the beating of his heart and the shallow breathing of the person facing him.

Once his eyes had adjusted to the gloom, he made out an anxious, heart-shaped face framed with silvery blonde hair tied neatly back into a long plait. Her frame was thin, too thin. Narrow shoulders. Long legs. Angular joints jutting through the worn woollen fabric of her grey gown. He'd expected some wise old woman of the hills, but she was younger than he by some years. Her wide green eyes gazed up at him like a wild animal caught in a trap.

Gradually he tuned back in to the world around him. They were in the outer courtyard at Wolvesley and several of his men had gathered around, all craning for a first look of the woman he had summoned here. It was late afternoon and the shadows were beginning to lengthen.

"Morwenna, is it?" he asked gruffly, stumbling back to his

senses.

She nodded once.

"And is it true? Can you talk to horses?"

She shrank back further into the recesses of the carriage, as if wishing the cushions could swallow her up. "I have a knack for communicating with them, that is all." Her voice was faint and whispering. He had to lean closer to make out the words.

His disappointment was sharp, for the stable boy from Escafeld had been outspoken in praise of her talents. But mayhap the girl was being modest.

"Welcome to Wolvesley," he said now, trying to recover his composure.

He shouldn't even be here; standing in the courtyard as a welcoming committee to a young peasant girl. All of a sudden, he was acutely aware of his misstep. Lucan would never have stooped so low. But ever since his conversation with Otto, and subsequent decision to engage in one final round of Emelia's games, Angus had been consumed with a desire to see the thing over and done with.

His own stablemaster declined to go near the horse. Two trainers had been brought from York, highly recommended, but they also failed to make progress. This was his final chance; a gamble to be sure. He wanted to look upon this promised horse-trainer with his own eyes. To ensure she knew the importance of her quest. As soon as his Seneschal came with news of the approaching carriage, Angus had rushed to the outer courtyard like a man possessed. When by rights, he should have stayed where he was and had the girl come to him.

Slowly, the girl emerged from the darkness, like some nervous woodland creature creeping across a bright meadow. She faltered on the steps and he shot out an arm to steady her, noting again the impossible narrowness of her waist. "Forgive my lack of introduction. I am the Earl of Wolvesley," he added, shaking off the unfamiliar twinge of self-awareness.

She looked down at his large hand on her elbow and shrank

back against the wall of the carriage. Then her sea-green eyes glanced up at his face and what she saw there must have offered some manner of reassurance, for her breathing steadied and her face lost some of its grey pallor. She opened her mouth and closed it again without making a sound.

"You are fatigued from your journey?" he suggested, as the men behind him began to shuffle impatiently.

She nodded, wordlessly.

Immediately he waved his hand to the gaggle of men behind them. "Have refreshments brought to the stablemaster's rooms," he ordered. "And see the lady is made comfortable there." He gave her the smallest of bows. "I will speak with you shortly."

He walked smartly from the cobbled stable yard back towards the castle, then stopped abruptly, turned on his heel and took a small path leading up to the fenced off paddocks on the hill. A gust of wind ruffled his hair and lifted his cloak from his shoulders. It had been another warm day, but now there were faint spots of rain in the air, heralding the approach of dusk.

Autumn was coming, he could sense it in the sharpness of the evening breeze. The birds had begun to sing a different song, mocking him by chirpily marking the passage of time since Lucan's death.

Three months had gone by. Three months in which Wolvesley was without an heir. If anything should happen to him, the lands of his forefathers would pass to distant relatives in Powys. Relatives who, since Angus's boyhood, had morphed into enemies through their relentless pursuit of land and wealth.

A headache threatened to take root in his temples as he surveyed his soldiers releasing their horses in the paddocks after a long day of training. At least the army was in good hands now. Otto had agreed with his choice of loyal knight, Sir Henry de Gaunt, to take command of the Wolvesley men-at-arms. Henry had seen more than forty summers, but his youthful energy belied his advancing age. He had ridden out with Angus's father in service of King Edward in battle at the Scottish borders. Then later, swearing his allegiance to Lucan.

Yes, Otto had confirmed after overseeing the knights at training, Sir Henry would make a great leader. Angus now breathed easier, knowing he could give his full attention to his role as judiciary. Wolvesley was in most part, a peaceful land. But he knew how quickly unrest could spread.

He had seen firsthand where a frenzy of fear might lead.

When he was but a boy, an old woman from the lower town stood accused of killing a neighbour's infant son. The stricken family, distraught with grief and desperate for someone to blame, claimed the old woman had been spotted slipping a poultice of herbs beneath the boy's blankets.

To heal his fever, she claimed.

To end his life, they countered.

Before anyone could intervene, the villagers had taken matters into their own hands, accused the woman of witchcraft and burned her at the stake.

The incident had left a deep impression on young Angus. As did the horrific stench of burning human flesh which hung around the town for days afterwards. His mother's closest friend had fled from Wolvesley in fear that either she or her daughter might be next.

Shaking away the memories, he walked further along the path which led to an isolated paddock circled by a strong wooden palisade more than six feet high. Behind this fence, a tall chestnut horse snorted and pranced, distrusting of all.

This was the unrideable horse sent by Emelia.

He was a beautiful, wild creature, with a flowing mane and a coat of gleaming copper. His legs were finely-boned but strong. A horse capable of carrying the most muscle-bound knight into battle.

If he were made to submit.

Angus ensured that Jacob kept him fed and watered, but none of the stable boys dared approach him. All except one, the young boy who had spoken up about the trainer from Escafeld. Angus had learned the boy's name was Gerrault. He was but a young-ster, with arms and legs too long for his skinny frame, but he was a hard worker. Just yesterday, Angus had recommended him to Henry. The knight would need a personal groom now he held a more responsible position in the Wolvesley army.

Gerrault had a fascination with the chestnut horse and most often volunteered to fill up his water troughs. He was duly respectful of its height and power, but showed no concern about its future.

"Morwenna will work her magic," he'd assured Angus, when questioned.

Angus had checked they were alone in the paddocks and contemplated telling the boy to take more care with his claims, but he reasoned it was just a turn of phrase. Gerrault was overly excited to be of service to his new master. Besides, Angus was so quick to quell any rumblings of witchcraft, they had all but dried up in Wolvesley.

A burst of evening sunlight haloed the chestnut horse in a blaze of mellow gold. Angus couldn't help admiring the creature. If tamed, it would make an impressive steed.

Still, it was an audacious act for Emelia to send him to Wolvesley. Even if she had done so whilst ignorant of precisely how Lucan met his end, their previously good-natured competi-tion had soured for Angus. So much so that he was minded to wash his hands of the whole affair and simply find himself another bride.

But even as the idea took hold, part of him baulked at the fuss and bother that would involve. Balls, introductions, negotiations. He was weary before the search had even begun. Nay, it would be far easier to see this final challenge through to the end.

Unless of course, a potential bride happened to present herself at Wolvesley before Emelia named a date for their wedding.

If that were the case, Angus fancied he might consider his options.

He smiled to himself at the thought, even whilst knowing

that such an occasion was unlikely to pass. If he was a gambling man, he would put his money on the horse being tamed first.

But he chewed on his lower lip as he pondered on Morwenna's surprising youth and apparent frailty. Notwithstanding the undeniable fact that *she was a woman*!

A woman whose head did not even reach his shoulders.

Come here to do a job no man in his employ dared to take on. A job that two trained professionals had failed at.

Was she really equal to it?

Angus believed himself to be a fair-minded man. His youthful competitions with Emelia had proved to him that girls could do many things well, including shooting arrows from a bow and racing horses across the moors. But this task was of a different order entirely.

He must talk to her and discover her credentials.

Buoyed with resolution, he turned from the paddocks and walked quickly to the stable yard, which had emptied out after the earlier excitement. The carriage had been put away, along with the pair of horses, and many of the young grooms had retired for the evening. The brisk evening wind whipped up straw and grit from the cobbles, making Angus's eyes water. Blinking rapidly, he walked through the grand arch into the main stable block, passed through an empty stall and ascended a rickety wooden ladder which led to the stablemaster's room. He ducked under a low beam and pushed open the door.

Morwenna was inside, bent low over a wooden table on which stood a pitcher of ale and a simple bowl of broth. Upon seeing him, she immediately pushed back her stool and stood up. The room was small, furnished only with the table and two stools. A grimy window looked onto the stable yard but the rough, white-washed walls held no further ornamentation. The scent of hay mingled with horse manure drifted up through the floorboards.

"Forgive me," said Angus, noticing her eyes widen with alarm. "I did not mean to surprise you."

She lowered her head awkwardly, but said nothing. After a pregnant pause, Angus indicated her bowl of stew. "You can finish your meal."

She stood frozen to the spot until Angus kicked a stool closer towards him and perched down upon it, realising a moment too late that the diminutive furniture had not been made with his large frame in mind. Bending his long legs at the knee and folding his large hands upon them, he again nodded towards her abandoned meal. "My mother always told me it was a sin to waste food," he commented mildly.

Morwenna's eyes opened even wider. "My grandmother said the same," she whispered, the words rasping from her throat as if she hadn't made conversation for some time.

"Well then," he said. And at last, she perched back down onto the stool and picked up her wooden spoon. Now their eyes were on a more similar level, allowing Angus to take in the finer details of her pale face. Her cheekbones were high, her eyelashes thick and blonde. As Angus watched, her lips closed around a spoonful of broth and, as if sensing his attention, her emerald-green gaze flew to his in fresh alarm. His pulse sped up as their eyes met over the scratched wooden table and a faint flush stained her cheeks.

What lunacy was this?

His mind had wandered off on an adventure all its own, bringing Angus to an uncomfortable place of stirring attraction for a young woman here at his bequest and under his protection.

God's bones, what was happening to him?

He cleared his throat, trying hard to stem the tide of inappropriate thoughts. "Morwenna, isn't it?" he tried again.

She nodded promptly, her wide-set eyes fixed on the bowl. "Yes, my lord."

She spoke well, he noticed.

"I owe you an explanation," he began, one hand reaching up to loosen his cloak. It was damned hot up here. "I have brought you to Wolvesley for an important reason." His next words died on his tongue as the spoon clattered down onto the table and

Morwenna pressed her trembling fingers to lips which had turned almost white. "What is it?" he demanded, rising to his feet and all but banging his head on the overhanging low beam.

She tightened her lips and shook her head, unable or unwilling to articulate her fears. "What is the reason?" she whispered.

Bewildered, he sat back down. What manner of reputation must he hold in Escafeld for her to be so afraid of him?

"A boy named Gerrault has told me that you can speak to horses," he began.

But Morwenna spoke up with a high, quailing voice, preventing him from going any further. "It isn't true, my lord. I promise." She clutched her hands together and dipped her head.

"Alas, then I owe you an apology." Impatience flared within him. What a waste of time this had been.

She lowered her hands, her eyes fixed on his as if trying to read his mind. Seconds passed before she spoke.

"An apology?" she repeated, biting down on her lower lip. "How so?"

"For bringing you here, far from all that you know." Angus pushed himself up from the stool and stood with his palms flat upon the table. He was unaccountably disappointed. "I had hoped you might make progress with a wild horse recently come to my yard."

She glanced up at him, as if testing the truth of his words. "Is that why I was brought here?"

He frowned. "Was that not explained to you?"

She slowly shook her head, her expression unreadable.

Angus could feel the heat of the small room wrapping around him, and wished he had divested himself of his cloak before coming up here. He reached out for the pitcher of ale, poured himself a small cup and raised it to his lips. It was sour and tasted old. He screwed up his face and put it to one side, before forcing himself back down onto the diminutive stool.

"A friend of mine has sent me a horse," he stated, wanting to stretch out his long legs but conscious of the lack of space. "A horse which, it is claimed, no one can ride." Now he had her interest. "I've been set a challenge," he added. "And it is very important that I succeed."

She picked up her discarded spoon and placed it neatly inside the bowl. "You have been challenged to ride the untameable horse?"

"That's exactly it."

"And you wish for me to help you with this?" Her voice wobbled slightly.

This was the moment of truth. He looked her straight in the eye. "Can you?"

She met his gaze unflinchingly. "I have never met a horse I could not tame."

His shoulders relaxed. It was exactly as the boy had foretold. "Then perchance I have work to offer you."

For a moment, nothing happened, but then Morwenna's lips tugged upwards into the smallest of smiles. The smile transformed her face, bringing light and purpose to her sea-green eyes.

"You are offering me work, here in Wolvesley Castle?"

The edge of fear had gone from her voice. Indeed, it had all but gone from her person. She looked back at him steadily, calm intelligence shining from her face.

It was suddenly imperative to him that she stayed. Mayhap she would be the one to make a difference.

Angus spoke up again. "Of course, I will pay you for your troubles."

She regarded him steadily. "In coin?"

"In coin," he confirmed.

She clamped her lips together and focused her gaze on the grimy window. "How much coin?" she asked.

This was more like it. Angus knew where he was with people keen to divest him of coin. "I shall pay upon seeing results," he stated firmly. "But have no fear, I will pay you generously." He paused. "This may take some time. The horse is… complicated. I'll have the stablemaster find you suitable accommodation. You will be safe," he emphasised. "And fed. You will take your meals with the other servants."

She nodded quickly, her pale hands fluttering to the table as she mulled over his words. "I should be pleased to assist you."

He fished in his pockets and brought out a gleaming mark. "Here, take this."

"But I have not yet started," she protested.

He shrugged his shoulders, once again feeling the oppressive heat of the room. "You have travelled far from home," he said softly. "And your word is good enough for me." He leaned forwards and took hold of her hand ready to press the coin inside it, but as his fingers closed around her palm, a searing heat travelled up his arm straight to his chest. It was a frisson, like the flicker of a flame from a tinder box.

He dropped the coin into her hand and pushed himself up from the table, nodding abruptly to take his leave. He was desperate to get out of the room, to breathe freely outside.

Morwenna from Escafeld may or may not be able to talk to horses, but one thing was for certain; the effect she had on him was profoundly unsettling.

Chapter Four

MORWENNA CLUTCHED THE warm coin in her hand and watched as the Earl of Wolvesley ducked beneath the low timber door frame. She stayed still and quiet, crouched on the stool in the small room, listening to the heavy tread of his leather boots descending the wooden ladder and ringing through the stables. When at last they went quiet, she breathed out in relief.

He was a big, giant of a man. A handsome giant of a man. Sitting here, beneath the piercing impenetrability of his blue gaze, she had felt her pulse pound as it never had before. Even back in the carriage, straight after that interminable journey, the earl's unexpected appearance had set her heart racing; and not because of her rational fears of the reception she was about to receive, but simply because that was the effect he had on her.

He left her breathless.

But at the same time, he somehow made her feel safe. And how could that make any sense at all?

No man in Escafeld had boasted anywhere near his height, nor the breadth of his shoulders. She'd seen his muscles rippling beneath his fancy tunic and fancied he would have the strength to fell a tree in just one blow. But somehow, she hadn't felt fear in his presence. Not of him, anyway. He was like a big, strong horse which everyone but her was afraid of. She could see beneath the surface to the true man inside.

But it didn't matter how drawn she was to the man's deep blue eyes. He was the Earl of Wolvesley; renowned throughout the country for his wealth and privilege. And she was just Morwenna. A humble girl from Escafeld who lived in a leaking hut.

She gripped her hands together until the nails dug into the flesh. Nay, that was just it, she wasn't simply a humble girl from Escafeld.

She was a suspected witch.

Gripped by a sudden need to see him once more, she rose from the table and crossed to the dirty window which filtered a grey, grimy light into the stablemaster's room. There he was, on the edge of the cobbled courtyard. His golden blond hair shone in the blazing light of a dozen recently lit wall torches. He had stopped to talk to a horse, a fact in itself which lifted her heart. His large, capable hands patted the horse's neck as the evening breeze whipped his fur cloak around his powerful body. He radiated energy, like a tightly coiled spring.

She swallowed hard and backed away from the window. What was happening to her? She wasn't one to feel the pull of attraction for a finely built man. She'd rolled her eyes in derision when girls she'd grown up with became giggly and simpering over the pimply youths in their village. Only once had she faltered from this path.

Robin; a wandering bard, had passed through Escafeld more than three summers since. Unlike the other village youths, he didn't think Morwenna was an unusual creature to be taunted. He didn't look askance at her and her grandmother in their hut high above the settlement. Instead, they laughed together. She had thrilled at this joy of connection. And once, just once, they had come together as men and women did. Afterwards, Robin had asked her to leave Escafeld and come south with him. But she could no more leave her grandmother than he could find a new way to live.

Since his departure, she had remained unmoved and disinterested in romance. Not that she didn't want to settle down and have a family one day; she just didn't see that pathway as being open to her. Especially given the turn of recent events. And this really wasn't the time to start going sweet on a man.

And not just any man…

She startled as a door banged somewhere beneath her. Footsteps were advancing nearer, but this wasn't the heavy, measured tread of the earl. These footsteps were lighter and quicker. A small man, in a hurry. Seconds later, a brief knock heralded the door creaking open and a greying head appeared.

"Miss Morwenna?" enquired an ageing man clad in an emerald green tunic bearing the Wolvesley standard.

She nodded, keeping her hands folded to stop them from shaking.

He looked her up and down with no hint of emotion on his bearded face. "The earl says I'm to show you to your quarters. Come with me now. You'll be quite safe. I'm stablemaster here and I don't tolerate misbehaviour in my yard."

"Thank you," she said, her voice coming out in a croak.

"Do you have bags or belongings with you?" He glanced around the room.

"I have nothing," she admitted, shamed by the fact. She looked down at her feet, remembering the hot flush of fear that had flooded her veins when she opened the door of her shack to find the uniformed guard waiting outside. She'd thought he had come to arrest her, had acquiesced without question.

The stablemaster scratched his beard thoughtfully. "I can send someone back to fetch your things?" he offered.

"Nay, there's no need," she said quickly. She couldn't risk any more of the earl's men travelling to Escafeld and hearing the rumours about her.

The man shifted awkwardly from one foot to another. "We have grooms' livery for you. But there is nothing made for a woman. Mayhap, come the morn, one of the serving girls can lend you a dress."

"Pray, do not trouble anyone." She tried to smile even as her cheeks flushed, for she knew this would be considered indecent.

But she was here to work with a horse. And the horse would not care how she was dressed.

Besides, clad in braccae and tunic, like a young apprentice groom, it was more likely she would blend in with her new surroundings. She might pass the days unnoticed.

Which was all she'd ever wanted.

⚜

SHE AWOKE TO a bewildering reality.

The straw mattress in her allocated chamber was much thicker than the one she slept on at home. She was warm, snuggled beneath a soft rug. She was safe, behind a sturdy locked door. And for the first time in many days, her stomach was not growling with hunger.

She would have been less surprised to be thrown into a dungeon.

Hardly daring to believe in her fortune, she stretched out her arms and legs, luxuriating in the familiar smell of sweet hay and horses which filtered up through the slatted wooden floor. Her chamber was small and narrow, lit with a square window which overlooked the yard. Morning light was already filtering past the oil cloth and patterning the bare wall behind her, but aside from occasional hoofbeats in the stables below, all was quiet.

She remembered the stablemaster's words last night.

"I've put you in the room above his lordship's horses," he said, clearly discomfited by the obligation to find lodgings for a woman. "Most of the boys sleep over the main stable block, so you're less likely to be disturbed." He stumbled a little over the final word. "Although none would dare disturb you. That I promise."

She had nodded in recognition of his consideration, sparing the details of how she had spent many nights in Escafeld listening out for footsteps and quaking with trepidation.

How my life has altered in just one day.

She got up from the comfortable mattress, stretching her arms above her head and rotating her shoulders. Yesterday's long carriage ride had left her stiff and aching, for she was more accustomed to physical activity than sitting still. Today, at least, she would be outside.

With the earl's challenging horse.

She'd wrapped her silver mark in a handkerchief and hidden it beneath the mattress, buoyed up by the possibility that this was her first step towards recovering her savings. Mayhap she would earn enough here to pay for repairs to her roof? Hope, unanticipated and even painful at first, lodged itself into her heart.

My luck is changing.

As her grandmother used to say, fortune's wheel never stops turning.

Morwenna gripped her leather cuff and vowed to make the best of things, while fortune was on her side.

In two strides she reached the small, narrow closet into which she'd placed the tunic and braccae given to her by the stablemaster. She reached in and pulled them out, gazing in apprehension at the unfamiliar fastenings.

Boys' clothing.

She would look ridiculous.

Morwenna immediately stamped down on the thought. Why should she care how she looked? It mattered only that she kept her head down and succeeded in her work.

She pulled on the braccae, wincing at first at the strange feeling of wool wrapped around her legs. They were far too long, of course, but she dealt with the extra fabric by rolling them up at the ankle. The tunic was loose around her waist, but tighter across her chest. Morwenna was glad of her slender frame; a more voluptuous woman could not have worn such an outfit.

Her hair was a problem. If only she had a cap to pin it beneath. But she had to be satisfied with tying it into a long plait, just as she had done the day before.

Finally, she could delay things no longer. It was time for her to emerge from her seclusion.

Her heart pounded against her ribs as she walked across the stable yard towards the clatter and conversation of the grooms' eating quarters. Jacob, the stablemaster, had pointed out the low-slung wattle-and-daub building to her yesterday.

"That's where you'll take your meals," he said, shifting awkwardly in the manner she had grown used to. "I eat with the household servants in the great hall, but I'll tell one of the lads to look out for you in the morn."

She hoped he had not forgotten.

Pausing in the arched doorway to take in the scene, she almost turned away and fled back to the safety of her chamber. There were too many men in here. Men of all ages and sizes, but all of them clad in the smart green and gold colours of Wolvesley. Colours which she now sported in the crest blazoned across her tunic. They shouted to each other good-naturedly as they feasted on freshly-baked bread and salted fish, all sat at two long trestle tables running the length of the room.

The smell of the bread had her stomach rumbling afresh. Could she snatch up a heel and beat a hasty retreat?

Her eyes flickered to a wicker basket in which two loaves still remained. Most grievously, the basket had been placed on a low wooden table at the far side of the hall. Beside it were two large earthenware jugs of watered-wine.

If she wanted to eat and drink, she must enter the room and walk between the trestle tables full of men.

"Miss Morwenna?"

She jumped at the enquiry, which was softly-spoken and polite. A young boy, no more than twelve years of age, was standing by her side. They were evenly matched for height, but his build was sturdy and his dark hair stuck out in untidy tufts.

"You are Miss Morwenna, aren't you?" The boy cocked his head to one side, watching her closely.

She nodded mutely and the boy grinned. "Gerrault told me to look out for you. He wanted to be here to greet you himself, but he's been summoned to see Sir Henry."

Gerrault!

Her knees went weak from a combination of fear and shock.

Gerrault, the cobbler's son, was here in Wolvesley Castle.

"He said you most likely wouldn't want to sit down with us," the boy continued, oblivious to her horror. "In truth, miss, nor did I on my first day. It's dreadful rowdy."

Mind still reeling, Morwenna nodded again. If she made a sound, she might lose her composure altogether.

"So I've got you this." He thrust forward a package, which Morwenna quickly took from him, barely aware of what she was doing.

"Thank you," she croaked.

"I'll tell Gerrault I saw you," he chirped on. "He's been talking about you non-stop."

Her heart dropped like a stone and she leaned against a wooden beam for support.

"What did he say?" she managed.

"That you're a wonder." The boy grinned and Morwenna felt some of her worries lift from her shoulders.

It was a curious feeling, to be admired. It caused her belly to flutter, but not with nerves. Pride in her abilities was not something she had known in many a year. The first pinpricks began to warm her through.

"Is that her, Isaac?" came an enquiry from the benches.

Isaac didn't turn around but shouted over his shoulder towards a cluster of the younger stable boys. "Aye, it's her. But don't come pestering her, Sam," he ordered. "Jacob says she's to be left alone to do her work."

There was a discontented mumbling at this and Morwenna fixed her gaze onto the dusty ground, keenly aware of a blush heating her cheeks.

"Work that none of us could face doing," Isaac added firmly, shooting a glare towards his young friends. He leaned forward with excited eyes. "Good luck, miss," he whispered. "And I reckon you'll need it. Sam over there thinks that horse has been cursed."

"Cursed?"

Morwenna reeled backwards, but Isaac merely shrugged. "He'd believe anything," he whispered confidingly. "But either way, miss, the horse is scared half to death."

She took that as her cue to leave. Muttering an embarrassed thank you to Isaac, she clutched at the items he'd given her and stumbled from the hall into the brightness of the morning.

Her heart rate steadied as she walked across the stable yard, not knowing where she was going but wanting to put some distance between herself and the curious grooms. With relief, she found a path towards the paddocks, where horses grazed contentedly and spared her little attention. It was a blessing to be out in the fresh air, feeling the warmth of the sun on her face and bare arms.

And a further blessing to be wearing braccae. She discovered she could lengthen her stride without fear of tripping over her skirts. She could skip over fallen logs and march past brambles, all without a care.

What liberty.

She must find a cap in which to hide her traitorous hair. Then she might pass unnoticed amongst the men.

When she was satisfied that she was far enough away from the eating quarters, she sank down onto a mound of long grass and looked more closely at what Isaac had presented her with. A flask of watered-wine and a wrapped loaf of bread. The loaf was crusty and still warm, and she wasted no time in tearing into it while she ruminated on what she had learned.

Gerrault was here.

Could he yet spoil everything?

He must have heard the rumours circulating about her before he left Escafeld. But no one here had approached her with fear or trepidation. On the contrary, Gerrault had clearly sung her praises, providing her with paid work and a second chance. No one in Escafeld would dare to speak slander about someone who had served the Earl of Wolvesley.

Mayhap I owe Gerrault my thanks.

She swallowed a mouthful of bread and washed it down with some watered-wine. She would owe Gerrault nothing if she did not make this work. She'd seen doubt in the earl's eyes yesterday. He wasn't sure she could do it.

She must prove him wrong. She must tame this so-called wild horse and leave Wolvesley Castle with her head held high.

And a bag filled with coin.

Gritting her teeth, she brushed the crumbs from her tunic and got to her feet.

The stablemaster told her she would find her charge set away from the paddocks. The earl's newest horse was kept apart from the others, a fact she didn't overly like. Horses were herd animals, happiest as part of a group. And the Earl of Wolvesley was not lacking in horses. She scanned her eye over the fenced enclosures, quickly losing count of them. There were others kept overnight in the stable yard itself.

Enough horses to seat an army of hundreds.

The horsemen here must have many years of experience. Yet Isaac had stated none of them could master the earl's latest horse. For the first time, Morwenna felt a flicker of apprehension that she may not be equal to the task. But what she said to the earl was true, she had never met a horse she could not tame.

Though she had never worn braccae until today.

And it was some years now since she had been faced with a new and difficult animal.

Morwenna's gifts had not become apparent until her thirteenth year; at least, not to other people. The ability to converse with horses, ponies and donkeys came as naturally to her as breathing, but the only time she wielded her abilities was when Farmer Jerome needed help from the village with bringing in the harvest. She would join the other able-bodied men, women and children in the fields, but her attention would soon wander to the horse pulling the wagon, or the ponies craning their hairy heads over a stable door. During that particular summer, Farmer Jerome had purchased a new horse for his daughter. Blackie, it was called. And the creature seemed doomed to the slaughter-house for she would not allow anyone to stay in the saddle for more than a minute.

Farmer Jerome's daughter, having twice been bucked off, had declared that she would not be trying again.

Morwenna was alerted to the poor creature's plight by Black-ie herself. Not thinking to hide her unusual abilities, Morwenna rushed to Farmer Jerome's side and explained, loudly, how the horse's saddle was causing her pain. Ignoring the scalding look from his wife, Farmer Jerome duly inspected the saddle and found a large thorn trapped on the underside of the pommel. Once removed, Blackie was the most docile creature anyone could hope to sit upon.

That day heralded a whole new chapter in Morwenna's life. She was invited to ride the farmer's horses and regularly called upon to help with difficult equine situations. Word of her talents began to spread, and soon folk were bringing horses from beyond Escafeld for Morwenna to tend to.

It was her grandmother who put a halt to it all.

"'Tis better we live a quiet life," the old woman insisted.

And so instead of being a wonder, Morwenna gradually became known as simply an oddity. And instead of transforming their meagre household economy, she helped her grandmother find locally grown herbs, she mixed and sold her healing salves, and she learned how to make a handful of coins stretch through a winter.

The blackbird was in full song as she followed the path past the paddocks and up a high hill. She was panting slightly as she rounded a bend taking her out of sight of the castle.

Good. She did not want prying eyes watching her work.

Watching me fail.

Nay. Morwenna gritted her teeth. She must not allow doubt

to take hold.

Her breath caught in her throat as she beheld a mighty wooden palisade, higher even than the earl himself. The wood was thick and strong, topped with spikes, such as villagers might erect to keep out marauding hordes.

The earl's horse was kept behind this.

Morwenna walked closer, unable to deny her growing apprehension. She had not gone more than three paces further when she heard hoofbeats pawing at the ground, coupled with a frenzied snorting.

The horse had sensed her.

And what a beautiful horse.

His coat was a fiery chestnut red; his mane and tail long and flowing. He moved with a fluid grace, side-stepping across the circular paddock like a dancer. But his eyes were wild and full of fear. Even as she watched, he flung his finely-boned head up and down in a warning for her to keep her distance.

She would heed his warning, *for now.*

She paused some way from the gate and feigned a deep interest in the view beyond the paddocks, where dense forests wound their way along a gushing river. From her position of height, she had a glorious view of the Wolvesley lands; rolling green fields dotted with sheep and stone-built farmsteads. The air was filled with birdsong and not a cloud marred the deep blue sky.

Sky as blue as the earl's piercing eyes.

Morwenna pursed her lips and chased away the memories of his ruggedly handsome face, deliberately emptying her mind. The horse must be her focus, not his master.

Although no one was this horse's master. It was a creature of freedom and fire. Wild and untamed, exactly as she'd been told. She breathed deeply, quelling the flicker of fear uncurling in her belly. Fear begot fear. The horse would never come to trust her if she allowed her anxieties to surface.

She closed her eyes, allowing the sweet birdsong to wash away her worries. A slight breeze lifted the hair from her face and she widened her stance, planting her feet firmly into the ground.

Breathe in. Breathe out.

As her body relaxed, her mind cleared. She took a measured step closer to the paddock and waited until the ensuing rumble of alarmed hoofbeats ceased. Then she repeated the process.

When Morwenna opened her eyes, she was standing within reach of the gate. The horse had bolted to the far side of the paddock and stood on high alert, ears pricked, watching her closely.

Breathe in. Breathe out.

The sun had risen higher in the cloudless sky, causing heat to prickle beneath her unfamiliar clothes. But she dared not break the spell she was weaving by pushing up the sleeves of her tunic or lifting her heavy plait away from her neck. She forced herself to ignore her discomfort, fixing her gaze deliberately on a singular oak tree stood to the left of the horse. From the corner of her eye, she could make out a ramshackle wooden shelter erected just outside the fence.

If she had spied the shelter earlier, she could have stood out of the way of the sun.

Minutes past. Minutes that felt like hours. From the corner of her eye, she noted the horse gradually beginning to calm. His head lowered and his ears flicked backwards and forwards as he contemplated this new visitor. By the time he took his first cautious step towards her, Morwenna's stomach had begun to growl all over again. The sun was directly above them, and perspiration had broken out down her back.

But she was making progress. The horse gave in to his own curiosity and walked closer, nostrils flaring.

She didn't allow herself to feel victorious. She concentrated entirely on projecting an air of calm. Her mind was a blank space, open to receiving the emotions of this highly-charged, highly-disturbed animal.

The horse came closer. If the mighty wooden palisade was not there, she would have been able to reach his side in three strides.

But she would not approach, for she could sense that things had already progressed far enough for one morning. There was no cause to rush. Slowly, Morwenna turned to leave.

"What progress," came the low voice behind her.

The horse's ears flattened back. Betrayed, he veered to one side and bucked twice, kicking his heels at the visitor he had so recently come to accept.

Morwenna's heart had nearly jumped out of her chest, so great was her surprise. As the horse thundered back to the far side of the paddock, he projected a swell of frustration which came at her like a heady wind. It was so strong, she staggered backwards under the force of it.

"Steady," came the voice again, and suddenly large hands were grasping her shoulders, righting her balance.

Morwenna felt as if she'd been woken from a deep sleep. She blinked slowly as the world came into focus, resisting her urge to reprimand the interloper who had spoiled all her morning's work.

For she already knew who it was.

"Thank you," she muttered, moving away from the beguiling warmth of his hands and holding onto the wooden fence for support.

"No one has been able to get so close, not in several days." The earl rubbed his hands together, clearly delighted.

"I was making some progress." She kept her words balanced, allowing herself a faint spark of gratitude at his praise.

"Wonderful progress," he enthused. "Though it was never in doubt."

Morwenna was still feeling her way back to reality. Her thoughts were muffled, her mind not quite her own.

"I do not believe that is true," she said.

Several seconds passed before she realised her transgression. The earl had put his hands on his hips and was looking at her in surprise. Despite the warmth of the day, he was attired formally in a long cloak which fanned around his muscular body. His thick fair hair glowed more golden than ever in the noon-day sunshine. She felt her pulse pick up speed.

"I am sorry, my lord," she tried.

He held up a hand to stop her. "I insist that you explain."

She took a deep breath, considered fleetingly the wisdom of further prevarication, and decided to speak the truth. "When we talked yesterday, I had the impression you may not consider me equal to the task, my lord." She clenched her hands together, her nails biting into the palm of her hands. It was bold of her to speak so, but it was no less than an honest answer to a direct question.

The horse snorted at some unseen enemy within the distant trees. His blonde tail flicked over his muscular quarters and he picked up his legs in a neat, diagonal dance.

The earl's piercing blue eyes remained fixed on Morwenna. When he smiled, she was weak-kneed with relief.

"I cannot deny it," he stated, suddenly looking less like an earl and more like a man. "But it was only because of your youth."

"And my sex?" she added, shocked at her own daring as soon as the words left her mouth.

The earl put his head to one side and frowned as if thinking hard. "I'm minded to deny that allegation, Morwenna from Escafeld. One of the most dauntless riders I've ever known is a woman."

That he gave her audacious comment any consideration at all was reason for her cheeks to flush a deeper shade of pink. She pushed away an instinctive urge to ask more about this dauntless woman.

"I'm pleased to hear that," she said quietly, folding her hands behind her back and catching a glimpse of her dark-coloured braccae.

She had forgotten all about her unusual clothing.

What must he think of me?

The earl gave her another small smile which seemed to light a fire in her insides. "Indeed, my mother was the one who first taught me to ride." He paused, as if weighing up his next words.

"She did so wearing braccae, just as you are now."

She had not imagined a titled lady would ever do such a thing.

"Your mother must be an unusual woman."

It was the wrong thing to say. His expression became shuttered. "She is an unusual woman, in many ways." He nodded sharply. "I will bid you good day."

She lowered her head, blonde plait swinging before her eyes. "Good day, my lord."

What a disaster.

She waited until his majestic figure had stridden over the brow of the hill before she allowed herself to fully exhale.

"I'm an idiot," she said in the direction of the chestnut horse.

She was exhausted, hungry and increasingly light-headed from being out in the midday sunshine. It was time to head back to her chamber, to pull the oilcloth down over the window and lay in the dark until she was calm enough to resume her work.

Morwenna had made it as far as the paddocks when she heard someone calling her name. The voice was young and full of excitement, but when she spun around, she failed to recognise the tall, smartly-dressed youth running towards her.

"It's me, Gerrault," he called.

"Gerrault," she gasped. The boy had grown at least an inch since leaving Escafeld. His face was no longer thin and drawn, and his Wolvesley uniform hung well over shoulders that were beginning to broaden.

"I'm so glad you came." He fell into step beside her, swinging a halter rope by his side.

She pursed her lips, thinking she hadn't been given a choice in the matter, but then remembered her decision to thank him. She stopped so she could look at him properly. There was so much she wanted to say.

Have you told anyone about the rumours?

Does anyone else from Escafeld know that I am here?

Most pressingly, *do you believe that I'm a witch?*

But these were questions that could never be voiced. Morwenna had to content herself with a smile and a nod.

"I owe you my thanks, Gerrault."

He raised his eyebrows until they all but disappeared into his thatch of red-brown hair. "Never, Miss Morwenna, it's I who should thank you. Ever since I told the earl I knew someone who could train his horse, things have gone better for me. Not that they were bad before," he added hastily.

"How so?" she asked. They were almost at the stable yard now. She couldn't decide if she was likely to attract more or less attention with Gerrault by her side.

His grin almost split his face in half. "I've been made personal groom to Sir Henry de Gaunt." He saw her puzzled face and explained. "One of his lordship's knights. His best knight, in fact." Gerrault's chest expanded with pride. "Sir Henry has just been made commander of the Wolvesley army."

The stable yard was filled with more people than horses. A dusty cart had recently arrived and was being rapidly unloaded. Shouts rang out across the cobbles and Morwenna felt herself shrinking away from the noise, wishing the cool stone buildings could swallow her up but knowing that polite conversation was the least she could do.

"Is his lordship not commander of the Wolvesley army?" she asked, distracted by a black colt straining to look over his half stable door.

"Lord Lucan was." Gerrault lowered his voice respectfully. "But the current earl is too busy with the judiciary."

Morwenna hadn't really been listening to Gerrault. She cared little who had command of the Wolvesley army. Her main concern was to reach her chamber without attracting comment or incident. However, the boy's closing words could not help but snag her attention.

She stopped short, so caught up in the moment that she reached out a hand to grab his arm. "What did you say?"

"That I'm to be personal groom to Sir Henry, commander of

the Wolvesley army," Gerrault repeated, anxious that she understand.

"Nay, not that." Morwenna closed her eyes, swaying with a combination of fear and frustration. "About the current earl?"

Gerrault looked at her with concern. "That he's the judiciary. The lawmaker. If anyone does wrong in the north of England, it's Lord Angus who deals out the punishment. Did you not know that?"

Aye, she should have known. And mayhap if she hadn't been buried under a mountain of grief for her grandmother, she would have realised it sooner. Esme had been quick with her warnings about Wolvesley, but Morwenna had never considered the role of the earl. Her heart rate slowed as the meaning of this revelation slowly sank in.

Morwenna was a suspected witch. And she had come straight to the home of the lawmaker.

Chapter Five

ANGUS WAS WORKING in his solar when Nella came to see him. In all her years of serving the Lady Violetta, the loyal maid had never, to Angus's knowledge, ventured into the earl's solar. It was a masculine place, meant for study, contemplation or quiet conversation. Even in her younger days, his mother had rarely entered. Why would she, when the ladies' solar was equipped with long windows and soft cushions so its occupants could sit comfortably while they played board games or worked on their embroidery?

Thus, Nella gazed at his hard, dark-wood furniture and shelves of ledgers with wide, curious eyes.

"How can I help you, Nella?" he asked courteously, after several seconds had passed.

She blinked, recovering her composure. "I am sorry to disturb you, milord. I'm afraid I bring difficult news." She bit down on her lower lip and clasped her hands together.

Angus half rose from his ornately carved desk chair. "Please sit." He indicated the stuffed chairs by the fireplace and joined her there after putting aside his quill.

Nella smoothed down her grey servant's gown and placed her gnarled hands on her knees. "It concerns the Lady Violetta."

He nodded. "I had guessed." He unconsciously rubbed at his beard before realising his long fingers were stained with ink. "What has happened?"

She hesitated, choosing her words. "My lady… sees things."

This was not new information, to either of them. What was new was the need to discuss it. Until Lucan's death, Violetta had always been discreet. But her grief threatened to bring this carefully guarded secret out into the open.

Despite the weight of his mantle, Angus shivered. "Go on."

"She talks to people… who aren't there."

His eyes swung to the door, ensuring it was securely closed. No sound could permeate these thick, panelled walls. This was not a conversation he wanted to have, but he could hardly send the servant away unheard.

"You mean, my brother?" he asked abruptly.

Nella's grey eyes flew to his for the smallest of seconds. She nodded, her lined face full of compassion. "Every day," she whispered.

It was worse than he had thought.

"She has been weak, since the incident," she continued, carefully. "But now she is recovering her strength."

He knew what she was trying to say. "Soon she will want to leave her chamber," he guessed.

Nella nodded, unable or unwilling to say more.

"Where there is a greater chance of her being overheard by another." He nodded towards Nella. "One less faithful to the de Nevilles."

She looked down, her expression obscured by the folds of her hood. "I am worried, my lord."

"You are right to bring your worries to me." He sighed, stretching out his long legs. His body ached, both from that morning's ride and an ingrained weariness brought about by months of troubled sleep. "I will see what I can do."

But what could he do, save locking his mother in her chamber? Lady Violetta was a well-loved figure. As soon as she made her first reappearance in the great hall, many would call upon her. And with her new, unsettling lack of caution, it wouldn't be long before she shared her delusions with the wrong person.

Angus found his fingers unconsciously drumming on the

arms of his chair as his mind raced for a solution.

Nella took a deep breath. "There is hope, my lord, that the problem will be short-lived. Once Lady Violetta fully recovers her strength and grows more accepting of Lord Lucan's death, I believe she may also recover her…"

"Prudence," he supplied.

Nella nodded. "I was thinking, mayhap, we could provide a distraction?"

He was at first surprised, but his quick mind readily embraced the idea. "I like it." He glanced towards the window, looking for inspiration. "Another ball?"

But Nella shook her head. "The memories of midsummer may be too painful." She swallowed, seemingly nervous of his reaction.

"Speak freely, Nella."

"My lady always enjoyed the jousting." She glanced up at him, then settled her gaze back down to the rushes covering the floor.

Angus raised his eyebrows as he considered it.

Held at the end of summer, the Wolvesley Joust had been a staple in the calendar since before he was a boy. Angus had seen only six summers when his father was taken by a terrible sickness, but he could still remember the nail-biting excitement of watching him ride into the ring to the accompanying cheers of a celebratory crowd. Lucan, ten years his senior, had been quick to follow in Lord Tristan's footsteps; as brave and dauntless as his father before him despite his relative youth. Competitors had come from far and wide, with musicians and jesters providing entertainment in the castle grounds and the air thick with anticipation.

"I had not thought to arrange it for this year," he said, his voice regretful as he remembered how his mother's face would light up with excitement for the joust. She had always taken a seat in the family's enclosure, clapping and cheering along with the loudest villagers, particularly enjoying those moments when her two sons emerged victorious.

Aye, the thrill of the joust would have been the perfect distraction.

Nella nodded, her disappointment clear in the slump of her shoulders. "She had a fondness for the troupe of acrobats who came to the last ball," she suggested, pressing her lips together as soon as she realised her mistake.

Angus inclined his head. "They were here at midsummer."

Three days before Lucan's death.

His mind returned to the joust. It would be the perfect distraction, but it was too late now to organise such a grand event before the winter nights started drawing in.

"We could hold a smaller jousting tournament," he said slowly, turning over the idea. "Our knights competing against one another?"

Nella's eyes glowed. "It would do my lady good to walk outside and see beyond the walls of the keep."

As one, their eyes flicked towards the tall window which looked out onto the castle gardens. Beyond the gardens stood the large jousting field, ringed with wooden stands. It was all but ready to welcome a crowd.

"And it would do our men good to kick back and have some fun, after the summer they have had." He paused, pushing away painful memories of Lucan's funeral and the slow procession of grieving soldiers. "We could extend the invitation to our nearest neighbours," Angus murmured, stroking his beard again. "It is short notice, but some of them may make the journey."

"Short notice?" Nella lowered her eyebrows.

He gestured toward the window. "Autumn is coming and darkness falls sooner every day. We must act quickly." Despite the scale of the challenge, he was pleased at the plan. "I will speak to the Seneschal and set things in motion," he confirmed. "Thank you again for bringing this matter to my attention."

Nella rose and curtsied. "And if my lady does not recover her prudence?"

Angus gave her a tight-lipped smile. "We must hope and pray that she will."

❦

JUST SIX DAYS later, the men of Wolvesley were training hard in preparation. Angus stood on the wall walk and watched as his best knights pitted themselves against each other in a makeshift arena. The atmosphere was convivial, with much back-slapping and hands readily extended to help the fallen, but there was no doubting the air of excitement.

The competition was on.

To the north of the castle, a team of carpenters were busy at the wooden stands, which had stood exposed to the elements since last year's joust. The sounds of sawing and hammering filtered through the courtyard, even penetrating the thick walls of the keep. In the stables, young pages polished boots and saddles, while horses, alert to the change of mood, snorted impatiently in their stalls. Angus checked in with his Seneschal twice a day to ensure everything was proceeding smoothly, but the answer was always yes.

Wolvesley was all but ready for the show.

Best of all was the excitement of Lady Violetta, who had emerged from her trance-like state of grieving to watch the preparations from her chamber in the western tower. Every day she stood at the window, commenting on the progress of the carpenters and the likely performance of the eager knights.

"Who will you ride against?" she'd asked Angus, eyes sparkling, as soon as he told her about the upcoming joust.

Her innocent question threw him into a spiral of doubt for as earl, he knew that no one could be trusted to compete with him in earnest.

He and Lucan had always ridden against each other in the first round, drawing screams of appreciation from the crowd. The brothers had been evenly matched in speed and strength, with the outcome impossible to foretell. Whoever won would be obliged to take on the likes of Otto Sarragnac, Earl of Darkmoor, or their distant kinsman, the Earl of Felsham.

But no one of equivalent rank was competing in this year's joust; the pool of entrants much smaller than usual. And Angus refused to endure a parade of warriors holding back in a show of good manners for the newly ordained Earl of Wolvesley.

But from the expression on his mother's face, it was evident she wanted her only son to participate.

He had taken her hand, squeezing it gently. "I am not going to compete," he told her simply. "However," he spoke quickly before she could protest, "once the winner is announced, I will ride out against him. It will be an exhibition joust, nothing more."

Lady Violetta was accepting of the idea. And Angus himself couldn't deny a twinge of excitement. He had always enjoyed the thrill of a challenge. He had a notion he'd be facing either Sir Henry, against whom his victory was all but assured as the loyal knight would not dare unseat him; or Maxton of Dunlore.

Maxton was a knight once sworn to the Earl of Rossfarne in the far north of England. Two years earlier, he had taken over his family estate on the fringes of Wolvesley. Angus had dined with him on several occasions, and found him to be a man entirely devoid of humour. However, his horsemanship was undeniable.

He hoped he would ride against Maxton. That would be a challenge worthy of the name.

Lost in thought, he didn't hear the footsteps of the messenger boy until he was directly behind him.

"Milord?" the young boy said, hesitantly.

"What is it?" Startled, Angus spun around, his cloak swirling about his thighs. The boy shrank back against the low wall and, for a heart-stopping moment, teetered with his shoulders over the edge, hovering some fifty feet above the well-tended gardens. Angus shot out an arm in alarm. "Steady there."

The boy righted himself and held a trembling hand towards

him. "I have a message for thee, milord."

"And you nearly lost your life to deliver it," Angus commented mildly, unfurling the parchment. "Your future years are more important than any message, boy. Take more care in the future."

"Yes, milord."

The boy's cheeks had become burning patches of red. Angus dismissed him with a wave and settled back against the bailey wall to read the message.

Dearest Angus,

How do you fare with my latest challenge? Have you given up? Or is my wild horse tamely eating out of your hand?

Either way, I will witness it for myself in due course, for we are preparing to leave Cheltenham as I write. We will call at Stratford on our journey north and so I cannot say when we will reach Wolvesley with any certainty. But before All Saints Day, I'll wager.

Yours in anticipation,
Emelia

His blond eyebrows shot upwards as he read the missive once more.

Emelia will be in Wolvesley within six weeks.

His first thought was one of panic, for her horse was still a wild thing, unrideable by any but a lunatic. But then he recalled how, days earlier, he had witnessed the wild horse mildly plodding at the girl, Morwenna's, side.

Miracles could happen within six weeks.

Once Emelia had named a date for their wedding; the future of the de Neville line would not hang so much in question. His restless relatives would be less likely to challenge his earlship.

He would have done his duty to his family.

He unclenched his shoulders and exhaled, returning his gaze to the knights' training ground. Beyond that, rolling green fields swept down to the peaceful forest. This was the Wolvesley he loved.

And his plan to protect it was all coming together.

Or is it?

His fingers gripped the rough granite stone as he admitted that he did not fully know.

After his last trip to the circular paddock, he had taken steps to ensure he did not come into contact with Morwenna again.

He bit down on his lip, unable to control the wave of shame that washed over him as the unbidden memories rose up. For just a moment, she had stumbled against him; her slim body supported by his hands. And he'd felt something.

Something entirely wrong.

It was the same stirring attraction he'd felt when first behold-ing her face in the carriage; the real world receding as if warm waters were closing over his head. But added to the mix was a hot spark of desire. Desire he'd experienced once before, when his fingers accidentally brushed against her wrist as he handed her a silver mark.

What strange powers did this guileless young woman from Escafeld have over him?

Nay, he was a man of the world. He knew the answer well enough. It was in the fall of her hair, the intensity of her green gaze, the slenderness of her calves, encased in those incongruous braccae.

Her body called to his. *Sang to his.* But she was most likely unaware of the effect she had on him.

And he knew well the dangers of falling for a member of the lower social classes. The tanner's pretty daughter had haunted his dreams for years after the event.

It was not a mistake he would make twice.

Angus gritted his teeth and turned for the steps that led down to the stable yard. He would walk over to the paddock now, and witness Morwenna's progress.

Nay. He paused, one leather boot extended forwards. He would find Jacob and instruct him to bring the girl to him in his solar.

His boot sank onto the lower step.

Not my solar. He didn't want to be alone with her in a small room, closed off from the rest of the keep.

Angus frowned, disliking the self-doubt and uncertainty swirling within him. He did not fear that he would ravish her. The passion within him was not so strong as to override his humanity. It was more that his wish to do so might override his capacity for structured conversation.

To the great hall then. It was quiet at this time of day; but there were always servants and men-at-arms milling around in there. Their conversation would not go unobserved and he would feel more comfortable for it.

He would remember who he was. Not just the Earl of Wolvesley, but a man long-betrothed to another.

And that betrothal could be on the cusp of advancing to marriage.

His heavy boots made a clomping sound as he strode over the cobbles; announcing his imminent arrival to all. A team of builders paused on their journey to the stadium and stood with their heads respectfully bowed as he passed by, while a stable boy with mahogany curls tugged manfully on the halter-rope of a stubborn pony to ensure they cleared his path.

But when he reached the stable yard, a great clamouring reached his ears. Clapping and yelling, accompanied by what sounded like a stick beating against an empty barrel.

He rounded the corner and halted, unable to make sense of what he saw.

A group of grooms had gathered together around the arched entrance to their eating quarters. One of them had hoisted another onto his shoulders; and the one held aloft was noisily hammering something into the stonework to a great chorus of approval.

"Good job."

"That will see us right."

Angus cleared his throat and as if a spell had been cast; the grooms fell silent.

Angus stepped forward and tipped back his head to see what they were doing. The angle of the sun meant that all he could see was the glint of metal.

"What is happening here?" he asked.

There was no answer, save the man held aloft jumping down from his high perch. As one, the grooms straightened their backs and lowered their heads.

"Have you all been struck dumb?" He cast his eyes down the line, more curious than concerned. He knew that men must occasionally let off steam.

At last, the man at the head of the line spoke up. "It is naught really, milord. Just something to ward off bad luck."

There was a low murmuring of agreement at this; but Angus felt like his face had been dashed with cold water.

"Bad luck?"

Another man nodded. "One of the horses cast a shoe this morn. So we've hung it up for protection."

Heart beating heavily, Angus took a deep breath to slow his rising temper. "You are telling me that you have hung a horseshoe above the doorway to ward away evil?"

Half of him still hoped for a denial, but the men nodded uncertainly.

He widened his stance, preventing his hands from curling into fists. "Why should you need to do such a thing?" His voice was calm and quiet. The men furthest away had to crane forwards to hear him.

And no one dared to answer him.

The silence in the yard was absolute.

Angus looked up and down the row of smartly-attired, strong and healthy grooms. Most had started working in Wolvesley Castle as tousle-haired youths, much like the boy with mahogany curls who had struggled to move the pony out of his path. The horses of Wolvesley were renowned for their speed and condition; these men worked hard.

But he was minded to demand they all left his land, immediately.

How could they have brought a symbol of superstition – or *witchcraft* – into his home?

When Angus spoke next, his voice was icy cold. "Take it down." The men shrank further into themselves, away from the anger in his words. He let a couple of beats fall before letting out a mighty roar. "Now."

The men jumped into action and he turned away, sickened. When he next looked up, it was to see Jacob, the stablemaster, hurrying towards him. He was still wearing a long leather apron, usually donned for cleaning harness, and had a smear of grease across his chin.

"I heard your voice, milord," he wheezed, "and came straight away to see what had happened."

Angus folded his arms across his chest and nodded to the activity across the cobbles. "I discovered your men in the act of hanging a horseshoe over the door of their eating quarters." He watched Jacob's face closely. "Apparently, it was to ward off evil."

Jacob visibly blanched, but much like the grooms, said nothing.

Angus cursed in frustration. "Will no one explain or apologise?"

Jacob rocked on his feet, his eyes cast down. Angus resisted the urge to cuff the man on the shoulder to make him speak.

"You served my brother and my father before me," he said instead. "You have known me since boyhood, Jacob, and you of all people know of my aversion to superstition." He flinched, remembering what acts of violence such superstitions could lead to, even here in Wolvesley. The long-forgotten face of his mother's old friend had been flickering at the edges of his memory for days now. A quiet woman who had done no harm; forced to flee her home in fear.

He shook the memories away. Since taking on the mantle of

the judiciary, Angus had stamped down on all expressions of sorcery and superstition. It was but a small step from believing in the power of a horseshoe, to believing a fellow human could harness the power of the devil.

Jacob nodded slowly. "I know it."

"Well then." Angus waited. A few feet away, the army of grooms had removed the horseshoe and were in the process of slinking away. He fixed a steely gaze onto Jacob. "I believe I am a reasonable employer," he stated mildly, ignoring the stablemaster's enthusiastic nodding. "But if I do not get an answer to my question this instant, I will dock these men a day's pay." He ensured his voice carried to all quarters of the yard, gratified to see the grooms begin to hesitate.

Jacob shuffled his feet, indecision racing across his weatherbeaten face. "May I send them away?"

Angus nodded.

Relieved, Jacob spun around to face his men. "Go about your work," he ordered. "I want you all gone from here afore I next turn back."

His words had the desired effect and within moments, Jacob and Angus were alone in the yard.

"Tell me what you know," Angus demanded.

Jacob still looked thoroughly uncomfortable. "We don't talk of evil or bad luck here. I don't allow it." His eyes flicked up to Angus before settling back down on the cobbles. "But I've not been able to tamp down the rumours this time."

The old man paused, mayhap waiting for some sounds of encouragement, but Angus was not inclined to provide them.

"It all started when the horse arrived," the old man said in a rush, his eyes pained.

Angus frowned. "The chestnut horse?"

"Aye, milord. One of the young lads said he'd come across a horse like that before. And that he'd been cursed by a witch."

Angus felt as if he had been punched in the stomach. But he stood tall and unmoving, waiting for more.

"It was a joke at first. But when no one could get near him, it started to take hold." Jacob dampened his lips with his tongue. "And then the girl arrived."

The anger and apprehension swirling in his gut were quickly joined by a sharp dose of fear. "What about the girl?" he asked sharply.

Jacob shook his head. "Only that ever since she came here, she's been ever so quiet and reserved. The same as the horse."

Angus clenched his hands into fists, his knuckles white with rage. "Send the girl to see me in the great hall."

Jacob nodded. "Right away, milord." He turned away but Angus called him back.

"Jacob?"

"Yes, milord."

Angus held up a finger in warning. "I'll have no talk of witchcraft here. Not even a whisper of it. Such talk stirs up evil and brings it to our door. The next person to spread these rumours will leave without pay. Is that clear?" Passion infected his words and his voice rang about the yard.

"It's clear, milord." Jacob bowed his head.

Angus turned on his heel and strode from the yard, still not free of the blanket of rage that had descended around his shoulders when he first beheld the men hammering the horseshoe into the wall.

How had this taken hold in his own castle? Under his own nose?

How can I keep my mother safe if such superstitions are already ripe within Wolvesley?

Lost in his worries, he didn't notice the slender, blonde-haired figure pulling herself back behind the barn door as he passed.

Morwenna had heard everything.

Chapter Six

MORWENNA LEANED BACK against the hard stone wall, her pulse pounding with fear as the earl's words echoed through her mind.

I'll have no talk of witchcraft here. Not even a whisper of it. Such talk stirs up evil and brings it to our door.

Worse than the words themselves was the anger which had rippled through his voice. The very idea of witchcraft made the man twisted with rage.

She had to leave.

Alone and unobserved, Morwenna stumbled into the darkness of the barn and allowed her grief to surface. Her face crumpled and tears leaked from the corners of her eyes, leaving a salty sting on her lips. Grandmother was right, fortune's wheel never stopped turning. But the good fortune that had found her honest employment and regular coin, together with a roof over her head and a way to restore her reputation, had morphed into luck of the very worst kind.

She was living in the home of a judiciary.

Not a fair-minded and balanced lawmaker, as she had once hoped the Earl of Wolvesley may be, but one fired up with hatred of witches and superstition. Not a doubt remained in Morwenna's mind that the earl would lock her up as soon as a whisper of suspicion about her reached his ears.

She should have left several days earlier, as soon as she realised his profession. The only things that kept her here were her growing bond with the chestnut horse; and the thought of her wages. The coin she so desperately needed to pay for repairs to her roof, would be hers in a matter of days.

Two days to be precise.

The grooms had rejoiced that this year's joust would fall on the very day that Jacob was due to hand out their wages. Over mealtimes, which she now took with the young stablehands, there was much talk of a trip to the tavern to celebrate their hard work. Gerrault was convinced he would be celebrating a win for his new master, Sir Henry. Morwenna had listened to it all, daring to feel safe amongst so much banter and distraction.

Mayhap she had been deluded, but the fact remained, she needed the coin.

Two more days.

She bit down on her lower lip until she could taste blood, turning the idea over and over in her mind.

Was it safe?

Nay, but it wasn't safe anywhere for a woman with no protector. She had learned this long ago.

She'd be as safe in the stable yard of Wolvesley Castle as anywhere else.

Morwenna pulled down her sleeve and used it to wipe her eyes, sniffing away her tears. She'd been working hard at blending in with the other grooms and stableboys; and had yet to see any of them sobbing.

Pull yourself together, she ordered silently, rubbing her arms to chase away the chill of the barn and then gripping her leather cuff.

As her emotions settled, she began to see her situation more clearly.

So the men thought the chestnut horse was cursed!

This was news to Morwenna. News she was quick to dismiss as ridiculous. The horse had been frightened half to death, but by men, not by witchcraft.

And Morwenna should know. She'd lived most of her life

with a woman who recited incantations to repel ill fortune and openly conversed with spirits from the other realm. Her grandmother had the Sight, and in the eyes of the law, that made her a witch.

And in the judgemental gaze of Escafeld, Morwenna was a witch too.

But now, the grooms of Wolvesley were worried that some witch's curse may be rubbing off onto *her*!

Despite her distress, Morwenna couldn't help a smile.

In little more than a sennight she'd gone from being a suspected witch to a suspected victim.

That was progress *of sorts*.

"Morwenna, is that you in there?"

Startled, she placed a hand over her fluttering heart and turned back towards the daylight.

"It is." She shielded her eyes against the slanting glare of the sun.

The man shifted his stance, folding his arms and gazing down at the floor. She would recognise that uncomfortable shuffle anywhere. It was Jacob, no doubt come to find her with a message to speak to his lordship. She must not give him reason to suspect she had overheard their private conversation.

He cleared his throat, still peering into the gloom of the barn. "You've been summoned to the earl," he told her bluntly. "Best to make yourself presentable and go right away to the great hall."

Still conscious of her flushed cheeks and red eyes, Morwenna hung back. "Have I done something wrong?" she asked quietly.

"Most likely he wants to ask you about the horse," Jacob answered. "Quick as you can now."

She waited until he had walked away before emerging back into the day. Glancing around the empty yard, she ran to the safety of her chamber, where she splashed water onto her cheeks and tidied her hair. Her pulse beat quickly at the thought of standing before the mighty earl, with his commanding presence, golden hair and piercing blue eyes.

With his hatred of witchcraft.

Two more days.

Then she could make her way back to Escafeld with enough coin to fix her roof and purchase supplies before the chill of winter set in.

Morwenna closed her mind to everything else. This was her goal. To go about her work until the day of the joust.

She straightened her tunic and used a rag to polish her boots, feeling her resolve strengthening as she went about the regular tasks. The joust would mayhap be a fine occasion to slip away unnoticed, as everyone else in Wolvesley would be caught up in the action.

Two more days.

The phrase became a mantra in her mind as she made her way up from the stables, passing beneath the high archway and entering the immaculate inner courtyard. She deliberately looked neither left nor right, knowing the display of grandeur would wither her resolve. But the musical splashing of the fountain was hard to ignore, as were the intricately carved stone lions guarding the sweeping steps to the keep.

Swallowing hard, she began to climb, conscious of the clump of her boots on the stonework and the focused activity all around her. Wolvesley Castle was busier than Escafeld on market day, especially in the run-up to the joust. Delivery men and liveried servants walked briskly by, while uniformed soldiers stood smartly at every corner. Her groom's attire meant no one spared her a second glance. She was anonymous amongst the crowd, as she had always wished to be.

But once she stepped inside the vast arched doorway, her courage faltered. She had never seen wealth such as this. The floor beneath her feet was marble; the roof so high above her head she had to crane her neck to see it. And this was just the entrance hall.

Despite her new-found determination, anxiety tapped her on the shoulder. *How could she hoodwink a man with so much power?*

She would have turned back, but for a kindly, young serving girl who noticed her discomfort.

"Are you lost?" the girl asked. Even wearing her servant's cap, she was a head shorter than Morwenna. But her cheeks were full and her smile was confident.

"I am trying to find the great hall." Her voice only trembled a little.

"That's easy." The girl grinned. "Follow the passageway." She pointed to Morwenna's left. "You can't miss it."

"Thank you."

With another bright smile, the girl slipped away. Morwenna forced herself to join the milieu of people heading down the marbled passageway. At either side of her, intricate carvings graced high walls alternately patterned with bright frescoes.

She had heard talk of the wealth of the Earl of Wolvesley. But never had she expected anything like this.

The great hall took her breath away. It was a vast space featuring not one, but two enormous stone fireplaces. The floor, again, was marble, interspersed with smooth stone pillars reaching up to a vaulted ceiling. In one corner, a troop of musicians played a lilting melody and a small table of squires, already well into their cups, sang along to the tune. Her gaze followed long lines of trestle tables to the raised dais at the far end of the hall. Her pulse quickened, for there sat the earl; his height and bearing making him instantly recognisable.

As if she had stood back and shouted his name, the earl's eyes lifted to hers. And even from that great distance, she felt the heat of his gaze. He wore his emerald green cloak over a plain dark tunic; and his hair shone gold in the light pouring in from a series of high, narrow windows set just behind the dais.

He was waiting for her.

But she could not force her feet to move forwards.

Morwenna realised that every time she had conversed with the earl, it had been in the relative safety of the stable yard or outside, where all men are equal under the trees and the sky. She had always known him to be a rich and powerful man, but this was the first time she had come face to face with the everyday reality of his wealth and status.

It dazzled her; daunted her. Robbed her of rational thought. She wanted nothing more than to turn around and run away.

Which would be as good as an admission of guilt. And she had nothing to feel guilty about, she reminded herself, bidding her legs not to tremble as she began the long walk towards the dais.

Members of the household seemed to melt away before her; mayhap because of the burning gaze of the earl, which never left her face. Her cheeks were hot from his scrutiny by the time she reached the low wooden steps. Here, she hesitated, one foot placed on the first step. Were the lower orders allowed onto the dais? She had no schooling in castle etiquette.

Before she could ponder this further, the earl took matters into his own hands by beckoning her forwards. She scrambled upwards and stood before him, hands clasped behind her back and head bowed low. All she could see was his emerald-green cloak pooled around the ornately carved legs of his throne-like chair.

"Morwenna." His voice was deep and rich. She couldn't resist looking up into his searing blue eyes, although she flinched backwards as their gazes clashed together.

She was standing before a judiciary with a deep-seated hatred of witchcraft. And she, a suspected witch. It was the stuff of nightmares, yet her heart rate did not quicken through fear. There was another emotion coursing through her veins, catching her breath and making her freshly aware of how her snug-fitting tunic clung to her body.

"You asked to see me, my lord."

He nodded slowly, still gazing at her like a hunter assessing his prey. She noticed the sharpness of his cheekbones and the rasp of stubble on his cheek, before quickly looking away. Behind them, the clamour of the singing squires lessened as the musicians began to pack away their instruments.

"How goes your work with my horse?"

Relief flooded through her. "It goes well, thank you." She paused, noting he still looked at her expectantly. "He is quite tame with me now. I look forward to the day I can get upon his back."

It was a bold claim, but one she was confident of.

Or will be, if I am not intending to abandon my work.

Morwenna silenced her thoughts before her face gave anything away.

The earl nodded thoughtfully. "I am pleased to hear it."

She wondered if she was now dismissed. "Is there anything else your lordship wishes to know?"

The earl stroked his beard, considering her closely. Morwenna had never been so well inspected. He put his head to one side as if making a decision. "Have you any worries about the horse?"

"Worries?"

She bit her lip, fearful of what he may say next. *Worries that the horse has been cursed by a witch,* mayhap.

But he merely nodded.

"Nay, my lord."

"He has not acted strangely?"

"I would not say so. He is merely distrusting." He had been beaten within an inch of his life, but Morwenna could not reveal that now.

"And you are happy, here in Wolvesley?"

The question was fast and unanticipated. Fixed as she was by his piercing gaze, she struggled with the lie. "I am happy enough," she managed.

The earl did not react, nor did he shift his gaze and she felt herself becoming faint with fear. Had she appeared ungrateful?

"Wolvesley is a beautiful place," she added with a stammer.

He replied soberly. "It is."

He did not need a girl from Escafeld to point this out.

The earl pursed his lips. "So you are happy enough in this beautiful place. And my horse is responding to your training?"

Wary of making another mistake, she merely nodded.

"Excellent." He waved his hand and she noticed the gleam of his square-shaped fingernails. "I had heard that the horse was somehow troubled. And that you yourself were unhappy. I am delighted to learn otherwise."

It was as if his blue eyes could see straight into her soul. Morwenna bit down on her bottom lip, unable to make another sound.

"But I always prefer to see such things for myself." The earl stood up so suddenly, Morwenna darted backwards and all but fell from the dais, saved in the nick of time by the earl's quick reactions. He caught her about the waist, supporting her weight with his large, capable hands. "Forgive me," he said, his face hovering inches over hers, his warm breath fanning her cheek. "I did not mean to startle you."

Startled.

Was that the name for the emotion surging within her? Morwenna didn't know how to describe it. All she knew was she must put some distance between them. She must step free of his arms. Because this unanticipated proximity was making her heart flutter and dance. His blue eyes had her hypnotised; as if all her worries – who she was and why she was here – faded into nothing. The rational part of her expected him to set her down; to feel nothing in return. But the earl made no move to do so, as if it was right and natural to hold her in his arms.

"Forgive me," he said again, thick eyelashes batting in surprise. He gently but firmly helped her upright before backing away. For the first time, he seemed unsure of what to do next. They both stood on the dais and looked at one another. An earl and a peasant.

A lawmaker and a suspected witch.

Morwenna was the first to come to her senses. She cleared her throat and prayed that her voice would not wobble. "Thank you for saving me from a fall." She nodded towards the edge of the dais.

In truth, such a fall was unlikely to do her much damage. Mayhap a twisted ankle, nothing more. But a twisted ankle would have thwarted her plans to leave Wolvesley in two days' time.

She must remember her plan.

He smiled; himself again as he scanned the room. "Without further ado, will you demonstrate your progress with the horse?" He returned his gaze to hers and she felt a traitorous heat rise up to her cheeks.

It was as if he were asking her to meet him in secret; not step out to the paddocks and show him how his horse would now walk to her side without fear. A job he was paying her to do.

And he had every right to inspect her progress.

But still. "He is not a trained circus animal, my lord."

He raised his eyebrows a little and she marvelled at her daring, but concern for Fauvel over-rode any concerns over social etiquette.

"Indeed. But you are training him, are you not?"

"I am." She nodded for emphasis. "I ask only that you make allowances for any hesitation on his part." She sent up thanks that her voice came out level and strong.

A smile flickered over his lips and Morwenna wondered how often the Earl of Wolvesley was challenged, even in such a tiny way as this.

"If I agree to your terms, may we go?"

Morwenna clutched her hands together. "I should be pleased to do so, my lord."

Cloak billowing behind him, the earl led the way back through the great hall and out into the courtyard. They strode past the fountain and down through the cobbled stable yard, Morwenna having to jog to keep up. He was a tall man with a long stride and a natural propensity to hurry. She was much shorter and still shaken from all that had passed. But she was pleased he did not slow his pace, for a more leisurely stroll would have necessitated conversation. And she did not feel equal to conversation.

In no time at all they reached the circular paddock, where Morwenna had spent so much of her time in Wolvesley. The horse was cropping at the lush grass, but he picked up his head and watched their arrival, a note of wariness showing in his widened eyes.

Morwenna slowed down as soon as they crested the hill; gratified that the earl followed her lead. Her status could never rival that of the Earl of Wolvesley, but out here in the fresh air, approaching the wild horse she had successfully befriended, she felt her shoulders naturally straightening. She had faith in her skills and would not cower.

The horse recognised her, but was unsure of her companion. Morwenna kept her pace steady, her body language exuding calm. Without her asking him, the earl paused beside a nearby tree, allowing her to proceed undisturbed.

She had not anticipated such implicit understanding.

Morwenna allowed herself a small glow of gratification, before chasing down her emotions and presenting an unruffled exterior to the nervous animal.

She and the horse had grown to trust one another. The trust had been hard-won, and was all the deeper for it. Breathing deeply, she unlatched the gate and stepped inside the paddock. The earl's gaze was like a beam of light shining on the back of her neck, but she ignored it and concentrated on the chestnut horse.

"Come, Fauvel," she said, her voice clear and calm.

The horse lifted his head higher, assessing the risk. She saw the questions racing across his liquid brown eyes and the tension in his finely boned forelegs.

The horse was ready to run. If the earl moved or made a sound, this demonstration of her success would take an entirely different turn.

"Come, Fauvel," she repeated. She had an apple in her pocket, but reaching for it would cause alarm.

Seconds ticked by, but just as Morwenna was resigning herself to defeat, Fauvel lowered his head and walked steadily towards her. He reached her side and sighed, as if releasing his worries, before nudging gently at her pockets.

"You're a good boy," she told him, carefully extracting the apple and holding it out on a flattened palm.

Fauvel crunched up the fruit, his attention fixed wholly upon her as if he had decided the earl posed no threat to his safety. Morwenna stroked his neck, running her hand over his withers and admiring the honey-coloured hue of his thick mane. His winter coat was just beginning to grow.

"A good boy and a beauty," she added.

In that moment, she allowed herself a rare acknowledgement of happiness. The warm sun shone down like a caress; Fauvel was trusting and content; the earl himself had borne witness to her success. It was as if the perils of the world had receded. From the corner of her eye, she noted the earl stepping out from behind the tree and walking hesitantly towards them. So long as he made no hurried movements, she suspected Fauvel would allow it.

"You have him under your spell," he declared.

His voice was low and quiet so as not to scare the horse, but his words pierced her hard-won composure.

Was this an accusation?

"Not a spell, just the build-up of trust," she corrected, keeping her gaze fixed on the horse.

"I have only ever known the will of a horse to be broken by force."

She risked a glance in his direction, but the earl was entirely focused on the horse.

"I do not work that way."

He laughed quietly. "As I said, you have him under your spell."

Her cheeks burned, but she kept her voice level. "There is no sorcery here, my lord."

"Of course not." He looked surprised at the denial. "I was not suggesting..." He trailed off. "But how have you bent such a powerful creature to your will?"

Now she had done it.

How should she answer that? The question was dangerously close to Gerrault's innocent query back in Escafeld. A query which had propelled her along the road to ruin.

Morwenna's hands trembled and the horse's ears flicked backwards as he picked up on her distress.

Breathe, she told herself. *Stay calm.*

She had convinced Fauvel to trust her. She must do the same with his owner.

"My methods are not entirely conventional."

The earl leaned over the high paddock gate, linking his long fingers together.

"Tell me more."

She had piqued his interest. *The last thing she should have done.*

Morwenna's mind churned. How could she give a satisfactory answer and dispel his curiosity at the same time? Not with the truth, certainly.

She had always been able to read animals. In the same way that some people could enter a room and sense the mood of anyone in it, Morwenna could hear a horse's story through the way it stood and moved. Sometimes, if she kept her mind blank like a slate, pictures would appear upon it. Horses had always been able to communicate with her, and deep down inside she suspected this was a skill that most people probably could have had, with some practice. They'd just never learned to listen for it.

But she couldn't explain all of that to the earl. Not if she expected to keep her freedom. Still, she would not be cowed into a bashful silence.

"I talk to him, my lord."

She lifted her chin and met his gaze defiantly, even though a chill of apprehension chased down her spine at the disbelief showing in his face.

"You talk to him?"

She nodded, patting the horse's neck and pretending to be unfazed by this line of questioning.

"But what is your method? Whose learning do you follow?"

She frowned. "I do not follow anyone's learning. None but my own."

He folded his arms, watching her closely as if she had begun speaking a foreign language. "Perchance I have not explained myself." He cleared his throat. "Most often, those with a profession, or a trade." He waved his hands towards her. "They follow a prescribed system of learning. Tested and refined by those that have gone before them."

His words ignited a flicker of self-doubt, but Morwenna would not allow the flames to take hold.

Not when the doubt concerned her work.

"You explained yourself perfectly well, my lord. It is simply that in this particular area, I have confidence in my own abilities. They have never failed me yet." She bravely met his eye as he nodded slowly, considering her words.

"You mean, you use your instincts?"

Exactly that.

She put a hand to Fauvel's neck. "That is one way to explain it."

"And you adapt your methods for each particular horse?" He looked genuinely interested in her answer.

"Of course." His blue gaze was profoundly unsettling. "Each horse is an individual, with its own history, its own reasons for being troubled."

"Remarkable." He shook his head, a smile spreading across his lips. "Where most men use whips and force, you simply use your voice?"

"That is correct." She folded her hands together to stop them from trembling and giving her away.

"And your method works, clearly." He nodded towards the horse who was still standing calmly by her side.

Morwenna found a genuine smile tugging at the corners of

her mouth. It was a long time since her abilities had been recognised and praised.

"He had been cruelly treated." Her faint glow of pride receded as she recalled the awful visions Fauvel had shown her. Large men with horsewhips; a stone floor slippery with blood. Humans who used any means possible to dominate and subdue something stronger than themselves. "He needed to learn that not all people are bad."

"You have done well."

Four words which warmed her heart.

"How long before you put a saddle on him?"

"Tis difficult to put a time against these things," she hedged.

"A rough guess, then?"

"Mayhap one more week," she lied without hesitation, although her heart beat painfully at the realisation that this milestone would never come to pass if she left Wolvesley.

"Remarkable," the earl repeated, sunlight glinting off his golden hair. "You have given this horse a second chance."

But she would soon abandon him.

"Fauvel," she interrupted desperately. "His name is Fauvel."

"You have named him?" His eyebrows shot up his tanned forehead.

"It was forward of me, I'm sorry for it." She lowered her gaze.

The earl regarded the horse. "It suits him. Fauvel may yet make me a fine charger, what do you think?" He placed the tip of a boot on the bottom rung of the gate and leaned closer, his body relaxed and easy.

Despair washed over her. Fauvel would make no one a fine charger when the only person he trusted disappeared from Wolvesley.

"He is a handsome animal," she said tremulously.

"'Tis a pity he will not be ready before the joust," he mused, switching his attention from the horse to Morwenna. "There is no chance of it?"

"None," she answered firmly, glad to be finally speaking the truth even as she wilted under his blue gaze.

He thought for a moment, rubbing his blonde beard. "Before All Saints Day, will your work be completed?"

"Aye," she nodded, giving the question little consideration. She would be gone by then. Fauvel would… She closed her mind to what would happen to Fauvel.

"Excellent." He rubbed his hands together, before banging them on the gate for emphasis. "Then I will win my challenge."

She had forgotten about the challenge that brought her to Wolvesley.

"And what will you win?" she asked politely.

His face changed, like a shadow passing over the sun. All at once, the air between them became thick and charged.

"I will win security for my family. My mother has never needed it more." He spoke so quietly she wondered if she had misheard. It was a big departure from the earl's usual larger-than-life countenance. And an expression of weakness, from one of the most powerful men in the land. It left her puzzled and frowning.

The earl frowned too, as if she had reminded him of something he would much rather forget.

Security. It was all she wanted as well.

But she lived in a hut with a damaged roof, not an imposing fortress guarded by hundreds of trained soldiers.

A cold, leaking hut which she must soon return to; chased away from the comfort of Wolvesley through fear of rumour and gossip.

"I should not have thought you lacked security," she said shortly, before common sense had a chance to intervene.

If he was displeased by her outburst, his face bore no sign of it. He sought out her gaze, his face showing a rare glimpse of vulnerability.

"Sometimes appearances can be deceptive."

"That I know," she said with feeling.

"I lost my brother recently. My older brother," he emphasised. "It was unexpected."

"Lord Lucan?" she said tentatively.

He nodded, his eyes still locked with hers. Morwenna felt her certainties deserting her once again, just as they had on the dais of the great hall. Her pulse began to pick up speed as a brisk breeze flattened his tunic against his muscular chest.

He was a handsome man. A *beautiful* man.

A man who spoke to her as an equal, even though he was anything but.

A man she instinctively felt safe with, *even though she was anything but.*

She turned away, flooded with confusion.

Fauvel pressed his nose against her back, hoping for more treats. He also clearly felt safe around the earl.

And she had always found horses to be excellent judges of character.

"He was my friend as well as my brother," he said, surprising her. "'Tis difficult to follow in the footsteps of such a man."

Morwenna knew what it was to lose a loved one. In that moment, she forgot the differences in their station and wanted only to offer consolation. "The men in the yard speak well of him."

"He was well loved by all," he said emphatically. "My mother especially has taken his loss very hard." He leaned against the gate, looking down at the flattened grass beneath them.

"I am sure you are a comfort to her."

She must have said something amiss, for he pursed his lips and shook his head. "My mother only finds comfort in her memories of Lucan."

She frowned. It was natural for a grieving mother to reach for memories of happier times, but Angus seemed to hint at something much darker.

"Everyone must find their own pathway through grief," she said, softly.

Recognition flickered in his eyes. "You are right." He paused.

"Will you come and watch the joust?"

The question took her entirely by surprise. She turned back to him, her green eyes opening wide.

"I did not realise the servants were invited."

"Everyone is invited." He hesitated. "But I should especially like you to be there."

His words made no sense to her at first. Then came a rush of pleasure closely followed by embarrassment.

"How so?" she asked simply, feigning an interest in Fauvel's tangled forelock.

He pursed his lips and looked away at the distant woodland. "I have enjoyed our conversation."

So have I. Although she could barely admit it to herself, let alone out loud.

"But we shall not have opportunity to converse at the joust."

"True enough. I will be watching from the stands for the joust itself and then ride out once against the victor." He smiled as if newly entertained. "I have never found myself justifying such a request before."

A deep flush of humiliation washed over her. "Forgive me, my lord."

"There is nothing to forgive." He drummed his fingers on the gate, making Fauvel startle. "Now it is my turn to apologise." He nodded towards the horse's flickering ears. "In truth, Morwenna, I find myself surrounded by flatterers. With my brother gone, I cannot even compete properly in the joust for fear of my opponents yielding to my position. But you, I feel, will not flatter me." He inclined his head until she reluctantly nodded her agreement. "Mayhap you will bring me luck."

Her insides twisted with uncertainty. Was it advisable to be held in such regard by the king's judiciary?

And a man who makes my pulse pound.

Nevertheless, once the joust was over, she would be gone. The Earl of Wolvesley would be a memory.

She would like to be able to remember him on horseback.

"I will be there," she promised.

Chapter Seven

"LUCAN IS SO looking forward to tomorrow's joust."

His mother's words reached him as if through a fog. Angus fought the desire to sink his head into his hands and close his eyes; but he was on full view in the great hall and he could not risk attracting more attention from the men at arms seated below him. It was dinner time and excited chatter filled the air, together with delicious aromas from heaving platters of food. In the far corner, a trio of musicians played a lively jig, much to the displeasure of the dogs stretched out by the hearth.

Beside him, Lady Violetta settled herself more comfortably on her padded seat and indicated that Nella should pour her wine. "He tells me your victory is all but assured; so long as you watch for the starting flag." She giggled, looking for a moment like the vivacious young woman she once had been. "Apparently you have a tendency to be distracted by pretty faces in the crowd." She sipped her wine and arched a tapered eyebrow. "Lucan's words, dearest, not mine."

Angus lifted his gaze to Nella, who was studiously ignoring the conversation while she filled his mother's trencher. The table was spread with all manner of fine foods; roasted guinea fowl and smoked salmon paired with honeyed carrots and seasoned beets. Bowls of figs and sugared plums glistened temptingly nearby. Angus stretched out a hand towards them and then thought better of it. The sweetened fruit was usually his favourite, but his appetite had all but disappeared.

"When did Lucan say this to you, Mother?" Angus asked, trusting in the background noise of the musicians to drown out his words.

"Why, just this morn." Violetta speared a chunk of meat.

Angus felt his frustration go into battle with his instinctive sympathy. Part of him wanted to confront his mother; to make her admit that Lucan was dead and that this conversation had only taken place in her imagination. While another part acknowledged the comfort she must derive from her fancies.

And another small but insistent part of him wondered if his mother spoke the truth. She really *had* conversed with his dead brother this morning.

He forced a forkful of fish into his mouth, chewing to avoid having to speak. Deep down, he had always acknowledged this possibility. Even as a child, he'd noticed that his mother was somehow different to the other titled ladies that came to Wolvesley. It was something about her eyes and the deep wisdom they contained. He remembered walking into her chambers one day to find a small group of women standing in a circle, holding hands and chanting. A parlour game, his mother had laughingly explained. But the air in her chamber had been heavy with… something. Some intention. Some *magic*, mayhap. He'd long ago pushed these memories aside, not wanting to unpick them. Not wanting to examine what they meant. It didn't matter to him if his mother had what they called 'the Sight.' She was still his mother and he loved her.

Nay, what mattered was keeping her secret from the rest of the world. Though that task was harder now than it had ever been.

Nella lowered her head and prepared to move away to the servant's table, but he motioned for her to stop.

"Dine with us," he said, an order rather than an invitation.

He needed to know there was another witness to this conversation. That he wasn't imagining things himself.

"Oh yes, dine with us, Nella dear." Violetta nudged her chair sideways to make more room. "It is lonely with just two of us here on the dais."

Angus looked at her sideways, ignoring a childlike flicker of annoyance that his mother claimed to be lonely in his company. Must she make it so clear that Lucan had always been her favourite?

Violetta did not appear unwell. Indeed, the pall of grief and exhaustion that had hung around her in the aftermath of her oldest son's death had all but dissipated. Her eyes were sharp and bright; her movements deft and deliberate. Nella had pinned her long white hair into a neat chignon and hung bright jewels about her throat. Lady Violetta looked every inch the chatelaine of Wolvesley Castle, as she had been for most of her life. Lucan's young wife had never had the chance to take the helm; hampered by a difficult pregnancy and then dying in the throes of a futile labour. Violetta had not once flinched from her duty, until these past weeks, when she had taken to her chamber and refused to come out.

Mayhap it was during this time of isolation that her iron grip on reality had begun to loosen.

"I am happy to see you here in the great hall, Mother," he commented. "It felt lonely indeed, dining alone."

Her eyes clouded for the slightest of moments, but then she covered his large hand with her small one and squeezed gently. "You will not be alone for long, my boy," she said. "I foresee a wedding."

Across from his mother, Angus saw Nella's eyes widen with alarm. This was a new and unwelcome development.

"You foresee a wedding?" he repeated, testing out the words. "My wedding?"

"Oh yes." Violetta nodded happily. "It will be a wonderful day. Blue skies, and the most beautiful bride."

Angus reached for his own goblet of wine while his mind whirred. His mother must have known of the betrothal Lucan had brokered with Emelia's father. It was no secret; even if the apparent reluctance of the young people involved had invited frowns of disapproval.

But why would she speak of it now?

The wine turned to acid in his mouth as he pondered the possibilities.

Did this mean that Emelia would consent to their marriage once Morwenna had tamed the wild horse?

Was their dance of prevarication about to end?

He forced himself to swallow down the wine, despite the tang of vinegar.

This was too much. Too *dangerous*. He couldn't risk his mother talking like this and being overheard. As judiciary, he had been summoned to imprison people for less.

"Mother, please, do not speak of things that we cannot know for sure."

Her eyes flickered to his, like a sparrow looking for food. "But I do know it for sure," she contested gaily. "For I have seen it."

Enough.

He pushed back his chair, realising too late that the scraping sound would alert everyone in the hall to his actions. His rising temper cooled as dozens of people paused their conversations and swung their gaze towards him.

So Angus did the only thing he could do. He reached out a hand and picked up his goblet. "A toast," he declared. "To the bravery of the Wolvesley knights in tomorrow's joust," he paused. "And to the memory of my brother."

There came a resounding chorus of *ayes*, which echoed up to the vaulted ceiling as his men-at-arms and their families smashed their goblets together.

The moment of scrutiny had passed.

Angus lowered himself back into his chair, arms trembling.

"That was a lovely thought, dear." His mother turned to him, tears shimmering in the corner of her eye. "Lucan thanks you."

God's Bones.

What could he do? It was not safe for his mother to be out in public, but it was too late to cancel the joust now. Competitors had already begun to arrive.

Angus couldn't bring himself to acknowledge Violetta's latest proclamation.

If Lucan was somehow witnessing events at Wolvesley, he would be more likely to taunt his younger brother than thank him. Of that, Angus was sure. They had been friends as well as brothers and their good-natured rivalry had run deep. His mother's casual invoking of his brother's sentiments brought him a great deal of pain mixed in with the fear he felt for her sanity.

For her very future.

Responsibility had never sat so heavily upon his shoulders.

At long last, Lady Violetta rose elegantly from the table and said good night.

"Good night, Mother." He pressed a kiss to the back of her chilled hand.

"I will pray for her," whispered Nella, pausing by his chair, her face ashen with worry.

"Pray for us all," he told her. "We have never needed it more."

MORWENNA COULDN'T SLEEP. Usually she fell onto her narrow mattress with relief, minutes after eating the evening meal, and fell into her slumbers easily. But on this night, her thoughts refused to settle.

It had been a tumultuous day. There was small wonder that her mind—nay, her whole body—still hummed with the energy of it.

After what felt like hours of tossing and turning, she sat up, pleased to push away her rugs and feel the rush of air around her person. She was agitated, almost as if she had taken a fever. But she was not ill.

Silvery moonlight spilled through the narrow window. Morwenna made up her mind.

If she stayed in her chamber all night, sleep would never come. A moonlit walk would soothe the unending circle of her thoughts. She need not go far.

Moving quickly, she slipped on her usual tunic and braccae, covering them with a shawl for the night air would carry a chill. Outside, she blinked until her eyes grew accustomed to the darkness before padding down the wooden stairs, speaking soft words of reassurance to the palfrey in the stable below her chamber.

It was a clear night, filled with sparkling stars and illuminated by a large blood moon hanging over the distant woodland. She would have no need of a torch to light her way. Morwenna breathed it all in: the scent of horses and hay; the screech of an owl and an answering howl from far away. A whisper of wind tousled through her loose hair. Already she felt calmer.

She would walk in the paddocks, she decided. It would not be wise to venture far, nor upon unfamiliar paths. She half expected guards to rise up from the shadows and question her, but none came. They would likely be deployed within the keep itself, with others keeping watch on the outer walls. At least, that was what she hoped.

Not that I'm doing anything wrong.

Morwenna clutched the shawl across her chest and walked with purpose. Some of the tension in her shoulders eased away as she left the cluster of buildings behind her. The night air was cold, but not overly so. Her footsteps matched the drumbeat rhythm of the question in her mind.

What to do? What to do?

The answer had seemed abundantly clear when she hid in the barn earlier that day. But much had changed since then.

She paused beside a massive oak tree, steadying herself against its gnarled trunk.

Nay, that wasn't true. The only thing that had changed was the pattern of her thoughts. The knife edge of fear and distrust that had dogged near every waking moment of the last few months had relinquished some of its grip.

An old feeling of trust – in herself, in the future – had blossomed in its place.

It was mostly her success with Fauvel that had caused this renewal of faith. But it was also the admiration she had seen shining from the earl's eyes.

And the pull of attraction she felt in the pit of her stomach for the handsome man with the golden hair and towering strength. Being in the earl's company made her feel vital and alive. Reminded her of the good that remained in the world. Even as his very post of office reminded her of the bad.

What to do? What to do?

She walked on, noticing a group of horses stood resting in a hollow. She had no wish to disturb their peace. Morwenna turned away from Fauvel's circular paddock and instead headed for the long hawthorn hedge which marked the boundary of the usual paddocks, preventing the earl's livestock from wandering at will along the winding lane leading away from Wolvesley.

If she followed the inside of the hedge, there would be no chance of her getting lost.

The dense bushes were covered in red-gold foliage which glinted in the faint moonlight. Had she arrived in Wolvesley for May Day, she would have seen the same hedgerow bedecked in beautiful white flowers. She reminded herself that there was little chance of remaining here until next spring. Even if she stayed to finish her work with Fauvel, that would be completed long before winter was out.

The thought of leaving this place, of never seeing the earl again, caused a twinge of sadness.

Ridiculous. Especially as she still contemplated fleeing within a sennight.

Morwenna shook her head and huffed out a sigh, her warm breath floating on a cloud before her. There was nothing to be gained by pulling at the twisting threads of her own thoughts.

What she needed was a sign from above.

She lifted her eyes to the shimmering stars above, willing peace and certitude to settle within her.

What should I do? she begged silently.

As if in answer, she heard a rustle in the long grass behind her. Morwenna whirled around, peering into the darkness to try and discern what manner of creature approached.

At first, she could make nothing out. Then a small figure crept beyond the cover of the oak tree, making a beeline for the hedge where Morwenna herself now crouched.

Was it a child? It was small enough. But why would a child be creeping around the Wolvesley paddocks long after dark?

She shrank back towards the high hedge, unsure what to do next. Thankfully, it looked as if the child might pass her by without even seeing her.

But then the figure slipped and fell.

Without thinking twice, Morwenna emerged from her hiding place.

"Are you hurt?" She ran towards the child who looked up at her with wide, brown eyes.

"I lost my footing."

The voice was feminine, but it did not belong to a child. In fact, there was something familiar about it.

Morwenna extended a hand. "Let me help you up."

After a moment's hesitation, the person who was not a child took hold of Morwenna's palm and rose to her feet, limping only a little.

"Thank you," she said breathlessly.

Morwenna could make out little about her, only that the top of her head came lower than her own.

"Are you hurt?" she asked again.

"Nay. Only my ankle is a little sore. But it will pass."

She knew that voice, had heard it earlier today. "You are from the castle?" She wanted to be sure the girl was not left stranded.

"Aye." The girl squeezed her hands together, looking down.

"I am only out for a walk." The words burst from her.

"As am I." Morwenna paused. Overtures of friendship did not come easily to her these days, but she could not ignore the frisson of fear coming from her companion. "I think I spoke to you in the keep. You directed me towards the great hall."

The girl shook her head. Morwenna made out russet brown curls, glinting the same hue as the hawthorn hedge behind her.

"Forgive me, miss. I cannot recall it."

Morwenna found herself smiling in the darkness. 'Twas almost a relief to be so easily forgotten.

"You did not consider my outfit strange? I felt sure the sight of a young woman wearing braccae in the keep of Wolvesley Castle would be remembered."

This time there was a pause. Instead of issuing a hasty denial, the girl was considering her words.

Still, her next question came as a surprise.

"You are Miss Morwenna?"

"How do you know my name?"

She heard the girl swallow. "First, tell me please, is it true? You are the trainer come to work with the earl's new horse?"

Morwenna felt her pulse pick up speed, but she was more curious than alarmed. And still wanting to reassure the young woman before her, whose eyes shone wide with fear.

"I am Morwenna, yes. What is your name?"

The girl bit down on her lip. "I am Molly." She paused, anxiety coming off her in waves. "Older sister to Isaac."

Ah, that explained the air of familiarity. They had the same short stature and mahogany curls.

Morwenna had the same instinctive liking for them both.

"I know Isaac." Morwenna nodded, keen to reassure her. "Shall I take you to him?" It was a foolish offer, for she didn't even know where the boy slept, save that he and Gerrault shared the same loft.

But Molly was shaking her head vigorously. "He isn't there," she whispered.

A beat passed. "What do you mean?" Morwenna whispered too, even though they were alone in the paddocks.

Molly reached out and took her hand, the gesture so sudden and unexpected that Morwenna almost snatched her arm away. The girl's fingers were cold. She was wearing only a thin cloak over her servant's dress.

"Will you help me?" She bit down on her lip. "I mean, will you help Isaac?"

It was a long time since anyone had appealed to Morwenna for personal assistance.

She placed her free hand on top of Molly's. "Isaac is a kind young man. Of course, I will help if he is in trouble." Morwenna frowned. "Though I don't understand. What trouble can he be in?"

"'Tis better if you come and see."

Pushing further questions aside, Morwenna followed Molly along the line of the hedge until she came to an abrupt halt. They were far from the torchlit walls of the castle now. The only sound came from Molly's elevated breathing.

The girl flashed another quick glance at Morwenna before plunging into the hedge and emerging with part of it in her small hands.

Molly propped a wide branch against the hedge near Morwenna. "You won't tell no one, will you, miss?"

"About what?" She was genuinely perplexed.

"Isaac made this hole today. It's quite safe. He blocked it up with this branch, see?"

Morwenna nodded, still not following. "The hole is too small for the horses to get through anyway."

Molly gave her a strange look. "Most of them." She wrapped her arms about herself, shivering slightly. "If my suspicions are right, he's still not back."

"Back from where?"

Instead of answering her, Molly grasped her arm again. "Come with me, please. I can't help but worry he's come to some harm."

Morwenna ducked her head and followed Molly through the hole in the hedge. They emerged onto a farm track leading down a steep hill.

"This goes down to the village," the girl said softly. "Where my pa lives still."

"Is that where Isaac has gone?" Morwenna felt as if she were trying to piece together a puzzle.

Molly nodded wordlessly. "Isaac only went because pa has taken bad again. It's his chest, miss. It gets so he can hardly breathe. And then he can't work in the fields, which means there's no coin for food."

Morwenna digested this. "That is very grave."

"Pa has good days and bad days. He'll be up and about again soon." Molly's voice was brittle with determination.

"I'm sure he will." Morwenna was about to say more, but a high-pitched howling rippled through the stillness, making the hairs on the back of her neck stand on end.

"Wolves," whispered Molly, gripping Morwenna's hand tight enough to hurt. "God's blood, what shall we do?"

Morwenna reached for her courage, knowing that panic would not serve them well. "There are no wolves left in this part of England."

"So folk say." Fear made Molly's words run together. "But they were rampant once. It's what this place is named after."

"Hundreds of years ago." Morwenna spoke words of reassurance while her mind raced. The howl came again, no closer but more insistent. Morwenna relaxed slightly. "I do not think that is a wolf, Molly. 'Tis merely a hound."

Molly's breath still came in short bursts. "Are you certain?"

Morwenna licked her dry lips. She was not completely certain, but her instincts told her to relax. "Let us continue," she whispered.

They had not gone much further before a large shape loomed out of the darkness. Molly froze, but Morwenna smiled with relief.

"'Tis Isaac," she said.

Molly forgot all about the threat of distant wolves as she ran towards her brother. "Where have you been?" she demanded.

"Moll?"

"Aye. I was so worried." She gave her little brother a good-natured thump on the arm.

Isaac was standing by the side of a short, grey-coloured pony, the reins gathered in his hands. His voice wobbled with frustration. "'Tis Daisy you should blame. I don't know what ails her, but she won't take another step forwards." His eyes alighted on Morwenna. "Who have you brought with you?"

"'Tis Morwenna, the one you told me about," Molly answered quickly.

Is Isaac turning towards me with something like relief?

Morwenna walked quickly towards the pair of them. "Isaac," she greeted him, as if there was nothing untoward in their meeting like this.

"I am that glad to see you," the boy mumbled. "Although you shouldn't have told her," he shot as an aside to his sister.

"I didn't. Not on purpose, anyway." Molly's voice rose incredulously. "But now we may have to."

Morwenna's attention was mostly on the grey pony. If Molly had been frightened before, Daisy was all but paralysed with terror. She stepped closer, breathing deeply, conveying an air of patience and calm towards the little mare.

"We've only done it this once, Morwenna. And ne'er will again. My nerves aren't equal to it," Isaac declared.

Morwenna shifted her gaze to Isaac. His obvious nerves were certainly not helping the situation.

"What is it that you've done?" she asked quietly. "I can't imagine it is anything so terrible."

The siblings exchanged glances. Morwenna could almost hear their minds churning. Asking the inevitable question, *could we trust her?*

Molly spoke first. "When the old countess was up and about,

she would allow it. But now there's no one I can ask."

"Ask for food, she means," Isaac interjected. "Leftovers, from the castle kitchens." He nodded towards the saddle on the pony's back which was strung with saddlebags, now empty.

"To take to my pa." Molly's voice wobbled. "'Tis wrong for him to go hungry whilst we throw so much away."

Morwenna's eyebrows raised. "Wrong indeed," she declared.

"And it's not as if the earl would mind," Isaac blustered on, scuffing his boots on the dirt track. "If he knew. But no one can ask him a question like that. And there's no sign of a new countess coming any time soon."

Part of Morwenna's mind latched with interest to this throw-away comment, but this was not the time to ponder the Earl of Wolvesley's matrimonial prospects.

"I will say nothing of this, to anyone," she promised. "The important thing is for us all to return safely to the castle."

"But I can't make Daisy move since that dog started howl-ing," moaned Isaac. "And we can't abandon her here. I shouldn't have brought her, only I thought I'd be quicker on horseback."

"'Twas a foolish thing to do," Molly scolded him. "We've risked enough without having horse theft listed amongst our crimes."

Daisy's eyes bulged at the raised voices. Morwenna held out her hands in a silent request for calm.

"You two go on ahead," she urged them. "I will bring Daisy and turn her out in the paddocks."

"Nay." Isaac's curls bounced beneath his cap as he shook his head. "She stays in her stall overnight. The one next to the food store."

"Very well, then I will take her there."

"Will you be alright? I mean, can you manage her all by your-self?" Molly was visibly shivering with cold.

"Daisy and I will manage very well, I promise." Morwenna reached out for the reins, willing Isaac to hand them over without further protest.

They had problems enough with the pony standing stock still. If she turned and bolted, things would grow much worse.

Thankfully, Isaac and Molly agreed to her plan without further resistance. The two of them turned and retraced their steps back to the castle, the lilting flow of their sibling banter fading as they walked further away.

Morwenna and Daisy were left alone.

She turned to face the grey pony, pushing away spiky tendrils of worry over what would happen if she were to be discovered like this.

I have also risked enough, without having horse theft listed amongst my crimes.

But fretting would only increase the tension in the air, and what Daisy needed was calm reassurance that she had nothing to fear. Not from the howling. Not from Isaac's unfamiliar frenzy. Not from anything.

It took several minutes before the pony lowered her head and nudged at Morwenna's pockets, her worries abandoned in a quest for treats.

"I have nothing for you," Morwenna murmured. "But I shall find you a carrot, once we have returned."

Snorting gently, Daisy followed her back along the dusty lane, her hooves making scarcely a sound on the soft earth. Morwenna felt tiredness lapping at her and was pleased when they finally reached the hole in the hedge, which was only just big enough for the small pony to squeeze through. Looping the reins over her arm, she carefully repositioned the branch so the hole was hardly visible.

They made it back to the yard without further adventure. Morwenna returned Daisy to her stall, giving her a pat and a carrot in farewell.

But when she arrived at her chamber, she found someone waiting for her.

"Have no fear," came the whispered instruction when she reared backwards in alarm. "'Tis only Molly."

"Molly." Morwenna put a hand to her pounding heart. "Is all well?"

"Aye, thanks to you," the girl said, stepping closer so Morwenna could see her better in the faint glow of torchlight from the yard below them. "Isaac is safely back in his bed. But I thought to bring you this before I retired to mine."

She held out something long and flat, laid on the crook of her arm.

"'Tis a gift," she added, when Morwenna made no move to take it. Her smile shone brighter than the stars above them.

"For me?" Morwenna was touched by the gesture. "But Molly, you should not waste your coin on me."

"No coin was used, though it would not have been wasted," Molly spoke quietly but forcefully. "If it were not for your help, my brother might have been questioned o'er a missing horse come the morn." She shuddered at the notion. "Take it," she urged.

Morwenna stretched out her tired arms and took the item from her, gasping a little as the soft fabric unfolded.

"'Tis a dress," she said, surprised and a little bemused.

Molly nodded. "It was passed to me from the late countess's lady's maid when I first came to the castle. She didn't want it no more. But although the maid was only small, she still stood taller than I do. The dress pools on the floor about my feet and my stitches are not neat enough to make the necessary alternations." She closed her hands about Morwenna's. "It will be the perfect length for you."

"I cannot take it," Morwenna protested. "I will have no occasion to wear it."

Molly inclined her head. "You ne'er know these things. Mayhap the right occasion will come along soon enough."

Morwenna's lips inched into a smile. "Thank you. You don't know how much this means to me."

"Good night, Morwenna."

"Good night."

Morwenna stood and waited until Molly's light footsteps reached the bottom of the steps, then waved as the maid ran quietly across the yard. She was still smiling as she pushed open her chamber door and eyed her waiting bed with relief.

A tumultuous day had turned into a tumultuous evening. And tomorrow was the day of the joust.

Chapter Eight

THE NEXT MORNING brought mist and a fine drizzle to Wolvesley. Angus pursed his lips as he opened the shutters of his bedchamber and perused the expanse of grey. Was this an omen for the day ahead?

He shook his head at his own superstitious nonsense. The drizzle would clear; he could already see a gap in the grey clouds to the east. The joust would be a success; if he could only keep a lid on his worries.

All he needed to do was smile and convey the confidence and surety that everyone expected of the Earl of Wolvesley. His father had managed it; and Lucan had been a beacon of poise, even while consumed by grief for the death of his wife and unborn heir. If they could do it; so could he.

He dressed quickly in a plain tunic and riding breeches; saving his ceremonial attire for later in the day. He had just run a comb through his unruly thatch of hair when a knock came at the chamber door.

"Enter," he called.

It was the Seneschal. "Forgive the intrusion, my lord. Sir Maxton of Dunlore has arrived."

Angus felt his lips curling into a smile, which was more in anticipation of honest competition than from any fondness for the man. He had always found Sir Maxton a dour, cheerless soul. But praise where praise was due; he was a masterful opponent in the jousting ring. A fearless horseman all around, in truth.

"I shall come out and bid him welcome," he said, casting a final, appraising eye over his reflection in the looking glass. There were dark circles under his eyes which had become a permanent feature since Lucan's death. He must take care not to appear fatigued or jaded in the joust; who knew what spies may be lurking amongst the crowd, ready to report back to his enemies in Powys?

"Hail, Maxton, welcome to Wolvesley," he exclaimed minutes later, extending his hand in friendship to the tall, broad-shouldered knight waiting for him in the great hall.

"Hail, my Lord Wolvesley." Maxton clasped his hand and bowed his head. "Thank you for the invitation." His dark eyes showed a flicker of warmth. "I have not had cause to ride out against any knight worthy of the name since the last Wolvesley joust."

"Ah, we must give thanks for this short period of peace in our land," Angus said gravely. "And the opportunity for fun it bestows upon us." He nudged his companion jovially, but Maxton was not a man for smiling.

"I am pleased to see you looking so well, my lord." He folded his arms across his broad chest, the hilt of his sword glinting in the morning sun which filtered through the high windows.

"Never better," Angus assured him. His voice was too loud in the empty hall. His claim sounded dubious even to his own ears.

"And how fares your lady mother?"

Angus caught Maxton's eye. His gaze was steady, giving nothing away. "Very well, I thank you for asking."

"It is a terrible thing, to lose a son," Maxton added, quietly.

Angus bowed his head, remembering how he had all but held his mother upright during the awful hours of Lucan's funeral procession. Maxton had likely been among the armoured knights forming a guard of honour along the winding lane to the family chapel.

"Terrible," he agreed.

Maxton inclined his head. His once thick dark hair was now

thinning and flecked with grey. "But to brighter matters, I hear you have been provided with some distraction?"

Angus's first thought was *Morwenna*. The young horse trainer had proven a mighty distraction from all that was bad in the word. But so far as he knew, no one else had noticed her quiet beauty. She was a secret all of his own.

He raised his eyebrows questioningly.

Maxton cleared his throat. "Rumour has it, you've been gifted a new horse?"

"Ah yes." Angus exhaled with relief.

"You are disappointed that news has reached me?" Maxton suggested, misreading his expression. "You wanted to keep this horse all to yourself? I confess, Wolvesley, I'm intrigued."

"There is nothing to be intrigued about," Angus insisted, ignoring the tug of his conscience. "I will show you the horse now, if you wish?" he offered, expansive in his duties as host.

Maxton grunted his approval. "You know I have more interest in horseflesh than in fine wine and figs." He nodded disparagingly towards a table laden down with refreshments for incoming competitors.

"I must tell you though, this horse is not for sale." Angus led the way through the inner courtyard, boots crunching on the gravel as he nodded to acknowledge the liveried servants who scurried from his path. "At least, not yet anyway. Mayhap if things do not go to plan." He shrugged in a show of nonchalance. Deep down he had no fear that Morwenna would fail in her task.

"What plans are these?" Maxton paused briefly before the fountain, which looked especially beautiful in the autumn sunshine with the golden light captured in its sparkling depths. The cacophony of falling water was briefly loud enough to drown out all other thoughts and worries.

"The horse is currently unrideable," Angus explained, casting a sideways glance at his companion and wondering when the man had last allowed himself to smile. His sallow face appeared to be fixed in a permanent scowl of disapproval.

"An unrideable horse?" Maxton sniffed. "That is a challenge worth facing."

"Indeed." Angus forced a laugh and clapped Maxton about his muscular shoulders. "Those were mayhap my exact words."

"You have a system of training in place? Have you summoned a horse breaker?"

Angus suppressed an involuntary shudder at the term. "A horse trainer," he corrected, turning up the narrow path to the paddocks and wincing at a damp gust of wind; a harbinger of bad weather to come. Several feet away, a group of horses raised their heads to watch them over the wooden fence. "And she is yielding impressive results so far."

"She?" Maxon halted abruptly, hands on hips, his dark-coloured cloak trailing on the dewy grass. "You have entrusted this task to a woman?" His throaty voice rose with incredulity.

Angus smiled benignly. "I confess, I entertained doubts myself, at first. But her work speaks for itself."

Maxton only grunted. It was his favoured means of communication. "I'll wager I could have your horse backed and compliant within half the time of a woman."

Angus closed his ears to Maxton's chatter. They were about to crest the hill and suddenly he was assailed by doubt. What if Morwenna was at the circular paddock with the horse? She would not thank him for the interruption.

He frowned to himself, shaking the notion away. Was he forgetting that he was earl here? And she, Morwenna, merely someone in his employ?

He held out an arm to keep Maxton back as a young hare streamed out in front of them, bolting with impressive speed for the safety of the distant forest. His summing up of their relationship was factual enough, but it didn't speak of the innate connection he'd felt with the horse trainer just as soon as she arrived in the castle. It ignored the hum of chemistry between them; a spark which leaped into life whenever he brushed against her, however accidental the cause. Nor did it address the way they could converse, one to another, with an honesty he so rarely found. She challenged him, fascinated him. *Bewitched* him, almost. Just as he had jested that she had bewitched the horse.

He pushed the memories away, not willing to explore what these strange feelings meant.

"Angus?" Maxton's tone was insistent. "Did you not hear me? I said I'll wager I could have your horse broken within half the time of this woman you have found."

Angus blinked his way back to the present. The hare was long gone, its faint footsteps already fading on the trampled grass.

He inclined his head, neither agreeing nor disagreeing to the plan. "Come and see," was his reply. And the two men walked side by side over the hill.

His heart jumped in his chest as he beheld Morwenna standing with the horse. Nay, she was not just standing with the horse. She had managed to fix a halter rope to him, which was now tethered to the paddock gate. The horse stood calmly with his eyes half closed as she rhythmically groomed his chestnut coat. Fauvel, as Morwenna had named him, was an even more attractive proposition now that the tangles had been combed from his mane and the loose hairs brushed from his body.

"This is your wild horse?" Maxton demanded, one eyebrow raised mockingly.

At the sound of his voice, the horse's demeanour instantly changed. His head came up and his eyes bulged as he strained back on the halter rope.

"Steady there." Morwenna's voice floated over to them as she took a step away.

"Ah, I see how it goes." Maxton folded his arms across his chest, apparently enjoying the disruption he'd caused.

Angus bit back a shouted apology to Morwenna, realising that raising his voice would only alarm the horse more, but it was too late. The horse half reared and the gate strained on its hinges. Quick as a flash, Morwenna darted forward and pulled on the rope, releasing the knot. Immediately, the horse twisted around and bolted to the far side of the paddock, kicking his heels as the ground trembled beneath them.

"My apologies," Angus said, walking over to where Morwenna stood, one hand over her heart. She was wearing a long grey shawl against the weather with her long blonde braid tucked inside it.

She hardly seemed to notice him. "The halter rope is dangling." She frowned in concern. "If it becomes tangled in his legs…"

Angus grasped what she was trying to say. "What can we do?"

She turned her frown in his direction. "Once you have left, I will attend to him. My lord," she added, with the smallest of bows.

Angus opened his mouth to apologise again, but Maxton spoke over him.

"Your wild horse has an impressive turn of speed, Wolvesley."

"That he does."

"He will make a fine charger, if you can ever get a saddle on him."

Angus's attention was fixed on Morwenna. He'd seen her eyes flare with concern for the horse, and now they were as wide and distrustful as they'd ever been since she first arrived. What had alarmed her so?

"If I fail, you can have him," he told Maxton abruptly, his mind still on the beautiful horse trainer. He would like to put an arm across her shoulders and offer comfort; for the lass seemed sorely in need of it.

"That's a deal," Maxton seized upon his words.

"It's a deal that will never come to pass," Angus assured him, smiling brightly. "Morwenna here assures me the horse will be backed within days."

"We shall see." Maxton's covetous gaze flickered between the nervous horse and its agitated trainer. "First the joust, now this.

And to think, I considered passing up your weekend invitation."

"For my sake, I am pleased you did not."

Maxton grunted again in response and Angus felt a wave of disapproval emanate from Morwenna. He may be Earl of Wolvesley, but he was not wanted here. Nor was his companion. Smiling apologetically, he steered Maxton away from the paddocks and back towards the keep. Overhead, birds called from the treetops but he hardly heard them. The enigmatic horse trainer had gotten under his skin once again.

He clamped down on his spiralling thoughts, marshalling them in a more proper direction. God willing the girl would soon be finished with her work and gone from the castle.

Some hours later, Angus stood before the looking glass in the bedchamber holding himself still while his manservant fastened his armour in place. He hadn't worn his mail shirt in a long while and the weight of it had taken him by surprise. Now, with the addition of his gleaming chest plate, heavy boots and plush ceremonial mantle, he felt anchored to the wooden floor.

Good, he could do with some anchoring, whilst so many things floated upwards, apparently out of his control.

Why had he allowed that dour soul Maxton to talk him into selling his horse?

He knew the answer well enough. It was because he'd been distracted by Morwenna. Her physical presence had called to him; like a mythical siren from the rocks. Although the lass herself seemed completely unaware of the effect she had on him.

He'd been at first upset at how they had disturbed her work. Later, troubled by how alarmed she became. He'd wanted to take her to one side and ask what was wrong. To do whatever it took to bring a smile back to her face.

And he wanted to hold her in his arms, because that exquisite moment when he caught her from tumbling off the dais had stirred something deep inside him.

"My lord?" The manservant held out his silver helm and Angus took it from him, nodding his thanks. "Will there be anything else?"

"Can you check that my horse is ready? And that my mother is comfortable?" he added quickly.

The manservant bowed smartly and took his leave, leaving Angus alone to consider his reflection.

He had never considered himself to be a dishonest man. And these feelings for Morwenna made him exactly that. It didn't matter that he hadn't acted upon them. That he *would never* act upon them.

Aye, in the past his head had been turned once or twice by a pretty serving wench. He was a man made of flesh and blood, after all. But he had been brought up to know that appearance and propriety were everything. The Wolvesley men did not dally with the servants.

Angus certainly did not. After his youthful experience with the tanner's daughter, he steered well clear of romantic entanglements with anyone less than his social equal.

Those in his class married for coin all the time; but that at least was open and honest. There was no deception. A betrothal was little more than a business transaction.

Young Angus, however, had broken the rules, willing to abandon his position in society for the girl he loved. But when he bravely opened his heart, he was met with the cold slap of rejection. Johanna did not admire Angus the man; she admired his coin. Moreover, she did not want one without the other. So why was his mind so full of this mysterious horse trainer? She wasn't his class and she wasn't even his usual type. Angus liked his women buxom and curvaceous, but Morwenna was as slender as a willow branch. It was her calm intelligence that drew him in; her air of assurance. Her willingness to speak her mind, when others merely told him what he wanted to hear.

Or mayhap it was because his long-awaited marriage was finally drawing near?

He set down the helm and pulled at a snagged thread on his cloak, exploring this possibility. Was all this bewilderment nothing more than a perfectly natural urge to sew some wild oats while he still had the chance?

His mind returned to Maxton; a man who had sown plenty of oats, both before and after his marriage. If Angus did end up selling him the chestnut horse, it would be because he had failed Emelia's latest challenge.

Which would mean his impending nuptials would be once again delayed.

He snapped the thread free and re-arranged his cloak, noting how it swirled around his ankles. This cloak had last been fashioned for their father and last worn by Lucan. Angus remembered taking pleasure in teasing his brother about how it trailed on the floor behind him. Lucan had been a feared warrior, but was nonetheless half a head shorter than his little brother. He had removed the cloak and slung it towards him, laughing. "You wear it then, when you become earl."

Angus had not believed that day would ever come.

The man in the looking glass was tall and strong. Formidable even. Not a man to be toyed with. Yet with more than two years of games and challenges, Emelia was doing exactly that.

Angus sighed deeply, feeling the press of the mail shirt upon his shoulders. As Earl of Wolvesley, could he not insist upon marriage to his betrothed?

Yes.

Probably.

But he wouldn't.

Their betrothal had been brokered by two men who were now deceased. Emelia had long been in mourning for her father, but even without that burden, Angus would not place pressure upon her.

Because I don't really want to marry her.

He sighed deeply, letting the truth of it ripple through him. The situation had become more pressing with the knowledge that his betrothed would arrive in Wolvesley before All Saints' Day.

He had to face facts. The easiest way to secure the de Neville dynasty was by marrying Emelia Foxton. He owed it to his mother and to his people. With no clear line of succession, Wolvesley was open to attack.

Angus recovered his helm and tucked it under his arm, giving himself one final appraising glance.

"Very handsome, little brother."

He could imagine Lucan's gently mocking tones. In fact, he could imagine them so clearly it was as if his brother was sitting in the padded chair beside the looking glass, his long legs crossed over one another and his flowing blonde hair cascading over his powerful shoulders.

Angus chased down the wave of sorrow. He would never again enjoy brotherly banter with Lucan. Nor would he know that familiar life-long comfort in Lucan's all too obvious strength and fighting prowess.

The future of Wolvesley depended upon him alone.

He straightened his back, fixed his smile in place and made his way out through the castle towards the jousting arena. High on the bailey wall, the de Neville standard cracked in the brisk wind; the same wind that had chased away the morning's clouds. Now the mellow stone of the castle glowed in rosy sunlight. He heard the roar of the crowd, already seated and enjoying the pre-joust entertainment. He smelled leather mingled with horseflesh and sawdust. Ahead of him, smartly-attired knights led out their gleaming steeds.

Angus took a breath and lifted his gaze to the family enclosure where, as anticipated, Lady Violetta was already installed in the seat beside his. She was beautiful in emerald-green satin, topped with a fur-trimmed robe. Her eyes were bright and her smile even wider than his own.

Mayhap this distraction would work. His mother would recover her strength and return to castle life. His horse would be trained and Emelia would finally be crowned Countess of Wolvesley.

Appearance was everything.

Chapter Nine

MORWENNA FELT AS if she might be sick, even though she'd eaten nothing since breaking her fast soon after sunrise. Her stomach rolled and her head pounded in time with her feet as she paced back and forth across her narrow bedchamber.

She should have left at noon, straight after Jacob handed over her wages. She'd tucked the cloth bag of precious silver marks inside her belt, where it rubbed reassuringly against her hip bone. With everything in place, there was nothing now to stop her slipping away from Wolvesley into safe anonymity. She would go first to York, or even Lindum. Somewhere she could perchance find work until any efforts to locate her were abandoned. Within weeks, at most, she would be back home in Escafeld.

Her narrow face contorted into a grimace as she reflected that she didn't know who – or what – she was the most conflicted over.

This was the first time she'd held a position of respect; one which came with a roof over her head and regular coin. She was just beginning to feel at home in Wolvesley, relaxing in the presence of the grooms and confidently striding about the paddocks. The reality was, she didn't want to leave the castle for a leaking hut – no matter how many memories were held within its fragile walls. Nor did she wish to leave a job half done when so much trust had been placed in her abilities.

Trust. That was the crux of it.

No one trusted her in Escafeld, but here she was treated with respect; her judgement was valued. She was even beginning to trust herself more, to be less frightened of what the future may hold. Was even, mayhap, making friends. The pale blue hem of Molly's dress peeked out beneath her own neatly folded clothing. Morwenna couldn't decide whether it would be better manners to leave the dress here or take it with her. Either way seemed a betrayal of sorts.

She didn't want to betray anyone, least of all Fauvel, especially when she had so recently earned his trust. Abandoning him now was nothing short of cruel. Especially when she'd heard with her own ears the earl promising to gift him to Sir Maxton if his own efforts came to naught.

Maxton had reminded her of a wolf, with his greying pelt of hair and avaricious eyes. She didn't like him, and neither did Fauvel. Although, she reminded herself, one hand roaming to her belt to check the bag of coin was still in place, she didn't know Maxton. And Fauvel was afraid of almost everyone.

The truth was lurking in her gut, waiting for her to acknowledge it. *She didn't want to leave the earl.*

Morwenna clamped her hands over her mouth as if to keep the shocking words inside.

Had she lost her wits entirely?

This unfitting attraction was all the more reason for her to leave the castle with the greatest of haste. She shouldn't be craving the presence of the Earl of Wolvesley; like a drunkard staggering towards a tavern. She should be putting all possible distance between herself and a man with the power to imprison her.

But the weight of her alleged crimes would increase tenfold if she ran away. E'en more so if she were caught.

Morwenna was so deep in thought that she jumped in shock when a knock sounded at her door. In her confusion, she half-believed it was the earl himself come to arrest her. Or to hold her, like he had in the great hall. His muscular arms curling around her slight frame, holding her up as if she weighed almost nothing.

"Morwenna?" A familiar voice spoke through the wood.

It was Gerrault.

Unsure whether her relief outshone her disappointment, Morwenna opened the door.

"Gerrault." She summoned a smile.

He was all boyish enthusiasm, his face and neck scrubbed clean for the occasion. "We're going over there now." He nodded in the direction of the jousting arena. "Would you like to join us?" The tips of his ears glowed endearingly pink.

Morwenna looked at him properly, noticing his newly ac-quired height and bulk. The boy she'd known all her life was becoming a man.

"I'm not sure I'm going." She hoped it would not be obvious that she had so recently emptied out her chamber. She rubbed at her temples. "I have a headache."

Gerrault's face creased with understanding. "I know some of the lads can be noisy, but they all mean well, I promise."

"I know that." She nodded emphatically. "I've never felt otherwise."

"It's going to be a grand occasion." He folded his arms over a freshly laundered tunic. "I never thought the likes of me would get to sit and watch the Earl of Wolvesley in the jousting ring."

She felt her mouth dry up. "Me neither."

"It would be a proper shame to miss it." Gerrault politely offered her his arm and cocked his eyebrows expectantly.

She couldn't deny that she felt the same. Morwenna found herself taking Gerrault's arm and stepping out of her chamber, leaving her packed bundle of clothing sitting neatly at the foot of her bed.

Mayhap she could slip away under cover of darkness, she reasoned desperately as they walked together through the unusually quiet stable yard.

Mayhap that was a better plan after all?

It couldn't be that she had lost all her senses and would prefer to sit and admire a titled peer playing wargames than take action to save her own skin?

Though her wellbeing was hardly assured on an unknown road, all alone. Even less so were she to reach the *safety* of Escafeld.

Morwenna's stomach churned again. Her path forwards had never been more unclear.

As they passed under the arch, a gaggle of stable boys led by young Isaac swallowed them up and Morwenna found herself swept along in a tide of excitement and banter. It was hard to hold onto her bleak despair while surrounded by so much pink-cheeked enthusiasm, and some of the tension had left her shoulders by the time they reached the stands. Here, the smell of horse sweat and sawdust mingled with tastier aromas of hot meat pies and pastries, sold from a number of wooden carts which had been welcomed into the bailey for the afternoon. Throngs of villagers were walking arm-in-arm, all turned out in their Sunday best to watch the Wolvesley joust. The swell of conversation, together with shouts from the stall-holders, reverberated around her. After the peace of the paddocks, this was as foreign as another land.

Anticipation began to outweigh her nerves.

"Look out." Gerrault nudged her out of the way of a lumbering villager who had already consumed too much ale. He took in her wide green gaze. "We'll be better once we're sitting down." Taking her more firmly by the elbow, he steered her into the stands and she found herself squeezed between him and young Isaac, who gave her a wide, gap-toothed smile.

"Are you excited?" Isaac asked.

"Yes." Morwenna gave the simplest answer.

Isaac nodded. "His lordship would win easily, because he's the strongest and he has the fastest horse. But seeing as he's not competing, it will be Sir Henry." To Isaac, it was very simple.

Gerrault visibly swelled with pride. "I gave Sir Henry's horse extra oats this morning."

Morwenna thought to ask Isaac if Molly was here. Looking

about, she couldn't see her. Could see hardly any women, in fact, amidst the swelling tide of men. But when she turned towards him, Isaac was wrapped in conversation with an older groom sitting on the other side of him.

The thunder of hooves soon joined the cacophony of sound resounding through the bailey and encasing Morwenna as if in her own personal bubble. Everything was heightened, from the narrow hardness of her wooden bench, to the press of hot bodies and the appreciative roar of the crowd. Everyday reality faded away, she was aware of mahogany-curled Isaac abandoning his seat to jump up and down in excitement; of Gerrault on her other side, clasping his hands together in a frantic prayer as Sir Henry first rode into the ring.

He has found his place in Wolvesley, she thought.

If only it could be that easy for her.

But could it? a little voice whispered in her ear. Could she let go of her fears and allow herself to feel at home?

As Sir Henry lowered his visor and readied his lance, Morwenna's gaze shifted upwards and suddenly the tumult around her vanished.

There he was, the Earl of Wolvesley; clad in a rich ceremonial cloak of emerald green worn over gleaming plate armour. His golden hair shone brighter than the sun and his piercing blue gaze swept straight through the competitors to scan the crowded stands opposite his seat of honour.

Was he looking for her?

A spiky ball of excitement lodged in her stomach at the very idea.

It was a preposterous idea. One she should chase away and never again own.

But even as she shrank back on her narrow bench, willing Isaac's exuberant jumping to hide all traces of her, somehow she knew deep down that it was true.

His eyes were seeking hers, which meant she should look away, gaze at the ground, look anywhere but at him. But she didn't want to do that. Instead, Morwenna's eyes met the blue gaze of the earl across the busy jousting arena, and she was immediately transfixed. She couldn't have broken her gaze, not even if she were offered a whole sack full of gold coins. Tremors ran up and down her body, her lips parted voluntarily and her breath caught in her throat.

He was looking for me.

He was looking *at* her now. And just like Morwenna, the earl seemed unable to look away.

She grew hot and cold at the same time, as if infected by a fever. The width of a jousting ring separated them; yet it was as if the earl stood just feet away. As if there were just the two of them here.

And he was as aware of this as she was. He was feeling it too; she would wager her last mark upon it.

The tension rising inside her was almost unbearable, but then Gerrault grabbed her arm and broke the spell.

"He won," Gerrault cheered, jostling her elbow with his clumsy excitement.

"He did," she agreed breathlessly, although she'd paid no attention to the match.

"Didn't he look well? The horse, I mean."

"Aye." Morwenna nodded weakly.

Gerrault received a congratulatory punch on the shoulder from the groom on his other side and his attention left Morwenna. When she gathered her courage to look back towards the earl, he had gone.

Gone.

Her eyes raked over the enclosure, which was much grander and more spacious than the cramped stands on this side. There was no sign of the earl and her heart thudded with loss.

But she hadn't imagined it. She wasn't losing her wits.

Her gaze twitched back to the ornately carved chair on which he had been sitting just moments earlier. It had a high back, emblazoned with the golden lion of Wolvesley. The man was the personification of wealth and power; the very last person she should be making eyes at.

The earl's carved chair swum in and out of focus as her vision blurred. Memories of his anger in the courtyard over the simple matter of a horseshoe raced through her head. He had been enraged over nothing more than a foolish, ages-old superstition. What then would he say were he to hear of her recently tarnished reputation?

Her left hand clamped over the cuff on her wrist, twisting it around and settling her fingers into the familiar grooves.

Grandmother, she begged silently, *what should I do?*

As if hearing her prayer, the woman sitting to the right of the earl's chair suddenly got to her feet with her arms outstretched in welcome. She was white-haired and frail, but still stood with an air of grace. Morwenna watched as she tilted her face upwards, smiling happily.

Who could this woman see?

Immediately her pulse began to beat faster.

The woman was conversing with someone who wasn't there. Just as she had seen her grandmother do in her younger days. And this wasn't just any woman, Morwenna realised, one hand still clamped around her grandmother's cuff. She was clad in emerald green satin, with precious jewels sparkling at her neck.

Was this the earl's mother?

Morwenna must have made some exclamation of surprise, for Gerrault turned to her with his eyebrows raised questioningly.

"What did you say?"

"Nothing." She swallowed. "Who is that lady over there?" She nodded cautiously to the stand opposite, noting that the lady had once again sat down and was leaning forwards, her attention fixed on the ring below.

"Who? The one with the jewels?" Gerrault half laughed. "That's the Lady Violetta, of course. The dowager countess. Who else around here would own a tiara?"

Morwenna shrugged. "I have no idea."

"Usual rule, if they're covered in jewels, they're related to the Earl of Wolvesley." His gaze switched to the next competitors trotting into the ring. It was Sir Maxton against one of the knights of Wolvesley.

"His mother?" She wanted to be sure.

"The very same. The poor woman took the loss of Lord Lucan hard. They say she's not been out of her bedchamber in weeks."

Lord Lucan.

The earl's older brother.

In a flash, Morwenna glimpsed the outline of a muscular warrior seated in the earl's chair beside his mother. He was broad-chested and had long golden hair curling onto his shoulders. Despite his obvious physicality, the smile he bestowed upon Lady Violetta was gentle.

She blinked and he was gone. It could have been mere fancy on her part. Mayhap a trick of the light. She'd seen such flashes once or twice before, but she had never given them much credence. Still, Morwenna couldn't shake the conviction that Lady Violetta de Neville was talking to her deceased son.

Which meant the earl's mother had the *Sight*. Just as her own grandmother had.

Morwenna felt as if her world had tilted. *How can that possibly be?* She glanced around at the crowd, but everyone was focused intently upon the jousting. No one spared the grieving Violetta de Neville a second look.

A gasp reverberated around the stands, pulling Morwenna's attention back to the ring. Sir Maxton was lifting his lance in celebration as the horse beneath him gave a tremendous buck, all but unseating his rider. Sir Maxton, who had just ridden to victory, wobbled precariously, dropping his lance onto the turf and knotting his fist into the horse's mane in a desperate attempt to regain his balance.

"He's going to fall," exclaimed Isaac beside her, his brown eyes glued to the scene.

But Sir Maxton righted himself, plunging his spurs into his horse's sides and making the creature's eyes bulge with shock.

Morwenna dragged her eyes away from the red ribbon of blood spreading across the dapple-grey flanks.

"The earl looks none too pleased about this," Gerrault observed.

"It's because he doesn't want Maxton to face Sir Henry," Isaac opined.

Gerrault bristled. "Sir Henry will easily defeat him."

Morwenna's gaze wandered over to the side of the ring, where the two boys were gesturing. There stood the earl; imposingly tall even beside two prancing chargers. Gerrault was right, he looked mightily displeased, fearful almost. But as she followed his gaze, she realised he wasn't looking at Sir Maxton. He was looking at his mother.

Did he see what I did?

Morwenna felt her breath catch in her throat as she recalled how he had spoken of his mother in the past.

She was an unusual woman.

He needed to ensure her security.

She only found comfort in her memories of Lucan.

What if they weren't memories, but visions? That would explain the darkness that had crept into his tone.

With a growing sense of bewilderment, Morwenna understood that the Earl of Wolvesley knew that his mother had the Sight.

⚜

THE NEXT MINUTES passed in a blur. Morwenna sat silently on the narrow bench, oblivious to the unfolding spectacle of the joust; thinking only of what she had discovered.

The earl hated witchcraft. Did that mean he hated his own mother?

Nay, he had told her just days earlier that he wanted to secure his mother's future. And he had taken his seat beside her, in full public view, even though he was obviously aware of her powers.

None of it made sense.

She clasped her hands together, nails digging into the soft flesh of her palms. What should she do?

This changes nothing, she told herself angrily. She still had to leave Wolvesley at the first opportunity. She had no doubts about what she'd heard at the stable yard, and the expression on the earl's face just now had been thunderous.

She should never have allowed herself to become distracted by the joust. By foolish notions of... of what? *Of attraction?* Between herself and one of the wealthiest men in England?

Morwenna felt her cheeks sting at her own foolishness, even though no one else knew how her heart had raced at the mere sight of him.

She had to leave. *Now.* But she was hemmed in on all sides on the narrow wooden bench by the excited press of the crowd. A great roar took hold of the arena and she realised belatedly that the joust was over. Sir Henry's horse was being led away while the knight himself was helped up from the ground. Beside her, Gerrault was grey-faced with worry.

"He'll be grand in the morning," young Isaac sagely advised.

Sir Maxton swung his helm high above his head as he performed the expected lap of victory. His dark eyes gleamed with triumph.

"It's over," Morwenna stated, rising up from the uncomfortable bench "We can leave."

"Ach no." Isaac put a hand out to stop her. "The earl himself is about to enter the ring. 'Twould be more than your job's worth to leave now."

Sickened, she lowered herself back down. There was nothing she wanted to watch less than the Earl of Wolvesley pitching himself against Sir Maxton of Dunlore. But it didn't look as if she had any choice.

Morwenna kept her emotions at bay as the earl came into

view. His horse was a high-stepping bay, with bright eyes and a lustrous black tail. A resounding cheer erupted as he cantered into the ring; halting only to acknowledge the crowd and bow his head in a mark of respect to Lady Violetta.

His mother.

She didn't allow herself to ponder anything more. The man was a gentleman. Nay, he was more than that. He was a peer of the realm. Of course his manners were impeccable.

Her nails dug again into her palms as Sir Maxton joined him and the two men shook hands.

Let them get it over with, quickly, she willed.

She kept her eyes fixed straight ahead, focused on the point where the two warriors inevitably clashed in a great splintering of wood. But neither of them fell. The horses were spun around back to the starting point and the crowd hushed before the starting flag went up a second time.

The thunder of hooves seemed to come in slow motion. Morwenna saw the bay horse fly towards its target, like an arrow shot from a bow. The dapple-grey was tiring; his pace was slower. As the earl leaned forward to deliver his blow; his muscular arm braced for impact; his balance impeccable; she knew in her bones what would happen.

The crowd let out a collective gasp as Sir Maxton fell sideways, dangling dangerously from his stirrups for several seconds before his boots came free. He hit the ground with a discernible thump and a great swell of applause recognised the earl's victory.

Beside her, Gerrault and Isaac both leaped to their feet, as did the cheering villagers behind them. Galvanised into action, Morwenna slipped between the stableboys and the benches, gathering speed as she grew closer to the gate leading to freedom. Everyone was so focused on the jousting ring that no one questioned her bid to escape. Within seconds, she had pushed aside the wooden gate and was running as fast as she could back to her bedchamber.

She had a different plan.

A plan even crazier than before.

But there wasn't time to think it through. There wasn't time to do anything except act.

Breathing hard, Morwenna raced up the steps and kicked open her wooden door. There was her neatly packed bundle of clothing, waiting for her to scoop it up and go. Instead, she tore it apart, desperate to get her hands on the unassuming kirtle she'd worn on her last day in Escafeld.

There it was. The material felt thin and insubstantial beneath her fumbling fingers, but she couldn't dwell on that. As quickly as she could, Morwenna pulled off her well-fitting boots, her warm tunic and practical braccae, replacing them with a shapeless grey smock and her once favourite kirtle. It was several days she'd last worn women's clothes and she was immediately aware of how hampering and restrictive they were. She folded her groom's uniform as neatly as she could before pulling on the too-small leather boots Gerrault had gifted her all those weeks ago.

She winced as the leather pinched her toes. But too-small boots were far better than no boots at all. And she wasn't about to take anything else from the Earl of Wolvesley.

Stifling down a sob of dismay, she picked up the cloth bag of coin from where it had fallen on the floor. Her prized wages.

They would have to stay here as recompense, however small, for what she was about to do.

Morwenna placed the bag on top of her folded uniform and fled from the room, before she could change her mind.

She knew the path to the circular paddock well, even in the dimming light. An owl hooted overhead as she ran up the hill, past the regular paddocks full of curious horses who raised their heads to watch her progress. Her breath was coming in painful bursts now, but she couldn't slow her pace. There was too much still to do.

And too much at risk.

Morwenna's swirling clouds of indecision had narrowed to a single point of focus.

She couldn't allow cruel Sir Maxton to get his hands on Fauvel.

The plume of crusted blood on the flanks of his dapple-grey charger had been reason enough for her to come to this decision. The fury in Maxton's eyes as he fell to the ground was another. She knew, without waiting to bear witness to it, that the horse would be flogged as punishment for Maxton's defeat.

If the earl passed poor Fauvel onto him, the horse would be a broken mess within a sennight.

She couldn't let that happen.

What she was about to do was theft, pure and simple. And Morwenna had never stolen anything before, not even a heel of bread when hunger clawed at her stomach.

If she was caught stealing a horse, the consequences would be severe. Too severe for her to even contemplate.

But if she left Fauvel behind her in Wolvesley, he would not survive.

"Here, Fauvel," she called quietly as she reached the gate. Her eyes had grown accustomed to the dark and she could just about make out a tall horse-shaped shadow standing near the tree. But she was agitated and out-of-breath; she could hardly expect a horse famed for its nerves to obey her command.

She paused, centring herself in the moment. A cool breeze whipped around her legs and she flinched at the unaccustomed chill, before chasing such emotions from her mind. She breathed in the musty scent of early autumn, of dew forming on the long grass and leaves turning from green to gold. The world was closing in on itself, ready for the night. Darkness would be her friend.

Fauvel steadily walked over to her, breathing warm breath over her outstretched palms.

"Good boy," she told him.

Moving slowly so as not to alarm him, she unhooked the halter from the gatepost and hung the rope around his neck. Uncaring, Fauvel nosed at her pockets for apples and she cursed herself for forgetting to bring some from the store.

Apples could have fed both her and Fauvel, at least for a while.

Swallowing down her fears, Morwenna clucked her tongue encouragingly. "Walk on," she instructed.

Fauvel followed her, as obedient as a well-trained dog, and she knew a thrill of triumph.

She had gained his trust. That was the first hurdle passed, although many more remained. It was a shame they couldn't sneak through Isaac's hole in the hedge, but little Daisy had only just managed it. Morwenna's heart beat hard as they walked through the open gate. With any luck, they could slip through the paddocks and beyond the castle walls while everyone was still at the jousting arena.

But she had barely cleared the gate when a deep, male voice spoke through the failing light.

"May I ask where you are taking my horse?"

Chapter Ten

PURE BEWILDERMENT WAS his first reaction. Why was Morwenna leading his horse from the paddocks in the rapidly darkening evening?

Had the horse become ill, he wondered? Or was this all part of her unusual approach to horse training?

But his confusion was replaced by a cold feeling of betrayal when her anguished gaze clashed with his. Her lovely face was awash with guilt.

"Where are you taking my horse?" he repeated.

She flinched at the question, but held his gaze squarely. A chill wind had taken hold, blowing strands of silvery blonde hair across her sea-green eyes. She made no move to brush them away, nor to deny her intentions.

"I am taking him to a place of safety."

He took a step closer, not to indulge the magnetic pull of attraction which shimmered and snapped in the air between them, but to deter her from taking flight. She looked fearful, but beneath her nerves he saw a glowing defiance.

"Is he not safe here, in his own paddock?"

She pressed her pale lips together and shook her head. "Not when you promise to gift him to a cruel man."

He had opened his mouth to explain before he realised the scale of her impudence. It was a boldness that contrasted jarringly with the strong anxiety radiating from her. Angus stood silently amidst the long grass, letting the evening dew soak into his leather boots, unable to puzzle it out.

"God's Bones, woman," he said at last, hands on his hips. "He is my horse to do with what I please."

A gasp escaped her lips and her whole body trembled like a sapling tree in a storm. "He is a living creature who trusts me. I cannot see him harmed."

Angus folded his arms across his broad chest, conscious of the weight of his mail shirt pressing across his shoulders. Although he had been triumphant in the jousting ring, the evening had not passed easily. First, there was the incident with his poor mother, openly conversing with someone who was quite clearly not there. Bad enough in itself, but far worse in front of hundreds of witnesses. Then had come Sir Henry's heavy defeat, closely followed by Maxton's scarcely veiled anger. The man had made a show of himself.

Competitive by nature, Angus firmly believed one should be magnanimous both in victory and defeat. He had absented himself from the back-slapping throng, wanting only a moment of peace in which to calm his thoughts. But no sooner had he slipped from the arena, than he spied a slender woman in a shabby grey gown fleeing through the paddocks like one of the fairy folk. Her long, golden plait gave Morwenna away, and his feet had followed her here. His eyes, unable to comprehend what they were seeing.

"I am paying you to train my horse, not steal him away."

She broke her gaze and looked down at the damp ground, but her voice did not falter even as her limbs shook. "I have left all the coin you paid me back in my rooms. Together with my livery." She placed a quaking hand on the top of her dress. "My desire is not to steal from you, my lord."

Pity tapped him on the shoulder, but could not yet silence his anger. "You admit though, to the attempted theft of a valuable horse?" He didn't give her time to answer. "Do you truly imagine that your wages are equal to his worth?"

His harsh words seemed to burn away her fear and the face

she raised to him was newly set with purpose. "The horse will have no value at all once Sir Maxton has beaten the spirit out of him."

Morwenna cared for the horse; that much was apparent. And her passion moved him. No doubt she was right about the potential consequences of Maxton's cruelty. But Angus still couldn't fathom it.

"Why should he go to Sir Maxton?" His voice rose in bafflement. "You have sole charge of him. And as you say, he trusts you." He paused, clenching his jaw. "I also trusted you. Did you lie when you told me his training was in hand?"

"Nay," she whispered, her gaze dropping again.

Silence fell between them, broken only by the distant sound of a yapping fox. The horse breathed heavily before losing interest in the proceedings. He pulled at the rope until he could lower his head and crop at the grass. Morwenna let the rope run through her fingers, putting up no resistance.

The sun was slipping beyond the western hills, casting long shadows across the paddocks. Angus had removed his armour, but was still warm from his exertions in the jousting ring and the unaccustomed weight of his mail shirt. Morwenna, however, shivered before him in her poor grey gown.

"Have you nothing warmer to put on?" he demanded.

She started in surprise, hunching her shoulders so she appeared to shrink where she stood. "I am warm enough."

"You are no natural liar." He pulled off his own cloak and held it out to her, harrumphing in displeasure when she made no move to take it. "I will not see you stand and shiver," he declared, striding forward and wrapping it around her slender shoulders himself.

His heavy green cloak swamped her thin frame, pooling on the sodden grass and threatening to slip away entirely. At the last moment, Morwenna shot up a hand to grasp the fur-lined collar, her chilled fingers sinking into the soft material. He saw her eyes close in momentary relief.

He straightened his back and rotated his aching shoulders, clamping down on an unanticipated and wholly inappropriate wave of tenderness.

"Now that you are not about to freeze to death, I would like you to answer some questions."

A gust of wind snatched at his words but Morwenna showed she had heard with a barely perceptible nod. The horse, Fauvel, launched forwards in search of new grass, pulling his slight trainer after him.

Angus allowed himself to feel a flicker of admiration for her pluck. To stride into the night with a half-wild horse, leaving her earnings behind her, surely required equal courage to that of a warrior riding into battle?

Nonetheless, he had caught her in the act of thievery. As judiciary, he had locked men up for less.

"Did you come to Wolvesley intending to steal my horse?"

He was braced for the worst but she answered quickly. "I did not."

The first pricking of something like relief darted through him. "Did you tell me the truth about how well your training was going?"

She nodded soundlessly.

"Then why…" He paused, grasping for words and finding none. What he wanted to voice was a plaintive grievance, coming from some place deep in his heart.

I thought I could trust you.

Not because he was lord and master, but because of some honest, instinctive understanding he had believed existed between them. Because she felt right in his arms. Because she was different from everyone else. Because of a hundred reasons that had led him astray from his rightful senses.

It was not as an earl, but as a man that he asked. "Why, Morwenna?"

She gave a little sob, slumping forwards so all he could see was the top of her silvery-blonde head and the swamping folds of his cloak. The horse raised his head and nudged at her stomach, but Morwenna didn't react.

"I could arrest you. Mayhap I should arrest you." He ground his teeth, torn between frustration and that burgeoning tenderness which refused to yield.

Morwenna finally spoke up. "You could. I know right well that you could." She put a hand on Fauvel's nose and lifted her beautiful green eyes up to his. The expression on her face had changed from shamefaced fear to something harder and more resolute.

"You know that I am the King's judiciary?"

She drew herself up to her full height; still diminutive in her physicality, but larger in presence than he had ever seen her. Overhead, an owl took flight from the nearby tree, causing the horse to startle.

"It is one of the first things I learned about you." She shifted her stance, twisting the lead rope around her hand. "I have a question of my own, if I am permitted to ask it?"

Taken aback, he answered without pause. "Go on."

"As the King's judiciary, how is it that you don't arrest your own mother?"

Her words fell into the cold night air like a slap across his face. He felt winded, as if she had delivered a physical blow, but his deflection came with practised ease. "How can you ask such a thing?"

"Because I have nothing left to lose." He heard the break in her voice. "And because I believe the answer may be important."

He grasped for the gatepost to steady himself. *How much did she know?*

"Why should I arrest my own mother?"

He didn't look at her; couldn't look at her. An awful certainty swirled in his gut that Morwenna had witnessed his mother's actions during the joust.

This slender, slip of a girl from Escafeld had learned the secret he'd been guarding so carefully.

Morwenna inched closer, her green eyes full of compassion. "Because she has the Sight," she whispered.

Not an accusation but a simple statement of fact.

His heart plummeted. The horse paused from his grazing and pricked his ears as if conscious of his distress.

"You can't know that." Angus raised a trembling hand and pointed it towards her. "Not unless you also have the Sight." He was grasping at straws, still clinging onto hope that she may be thrown off the scent.

Morwenna shook her head steadily. "I do not have the Sight." She hesitated for a moment, weighing her words. "Not truly. But my grandmother did."

It was a confession not lightly made, for the girl was no fool. She would know that owning a grandmother with such gifts meant the finger of suspicion would also be pointed at her. Besides, she hadn't fully denied his own desperate accusation.

For a moment, time slowed down. They stood still and silent as the scent of woodsmoke drifted towards them from the castle.

Morwenna held his gaze, unflinching now. "I know the signs."

In amongst the sea of emotions crashing over his head, he recognised a faint glimmer of relief. Here was someone who understood.

He exhaled shakily, no longer intent on denial. The evening shadows had lengthened and Morwenna's eyes were the brightest points in the darkening paddocks.

"Why do you not arrest her?" she asked again, her voice level but insistent.

A nighttime insect zipped between them, but neither Angus nor Morwenna reacted. The horse lifted his head higher, following the small creature's progress towards the woods.

Angus yielded to the unlikely turn of the conversation, part of him grateful to speak truthfully about a matter that had grieved his heart for so long.

"She has done no harm."

Morwenna let out a short unladylike snort and folded her arms. "That is not always held to be important."

His eyebrows shot upwards. "Was your grandmother arrested?" he asked, following her lead for directness.

She shook her head. "Nay, she died peacefully, in her own bed."

"I'm glad to hear it." He found it was true.

Morwenna pulled his cloak closer around her. "So you do not believe that witchcraft in itself is a crime?"

Angus scratched at his beard. His beliefs had never been queried before. "I take a strong line on sorcery because I do not like to see peaceful people whipped into a frenzy of suspicion. But if someone's actions are quietly done and bring no harm, I see no need to intervene."

Morwenna inclined her head. She had grown in stature, from a guilty peasant to a lady of worth. "That is not a proper answer."

"It is all the answer I am going to give you." As his shock receded, Angus felt the first flicker of renewed frustration. "We are talking in circles. None of this is relevant to the fact that I caught you trying to steal my horse."

Her eyes met his and their gazes locked.

Morwenna was the first to look away. "You deserve an explanation."

"I am glad we agree on something." He rotated his shoulders, feeling again the weight of his mail shirt.

She ran a hand down the horse's neck, as if taking comfort from his warmth. "I never intended to steal Fauvel. Not before I saw how cruel Sir Maxton was."

Angus opened his mouth to point out that he would have no cause to give the horse to Sir Maxton if Morwenna trained him as agreed. But he closed it again. There had been riddles enough this night. She must tell the tale at her own pace.

"I had to leave Wolvesley," she continued, speaking so quietly he had to lean forwards to hear her. "Because I feared that you were going to arrest me."

"Arrest you?" He started backwards in surprise. "Why would I do that?"

She swallowed, leaning upon Fauvel's sturdy shoulders for support. "Because, back in Escafeld, some people believe me to be," she paused, licking her dry lips, "a witch."

For the second time that night, Angus was left speechless. A gust of wind stirred the heavy folds of his cloak and lifted Morwenna's silvery blonde hair around her pale face.

"Why?"

She looked down, but not before he had seen a tear gleaming in the corner of her eye. "I don't know. Nay, that's not true. It's because I made a stupid mistake. I healed a donkey and then I told Gerrault that I could talk to horses."

"Gerrault?" Angus felt as if the conversation was again spinning out of his control. "You mean the stableboy who works here?"

"Aye." She put a hand to her stomach as if she might be sick. "But all this happened just days after our village succumbed to the flux, and louts from Berneshay raided our homes. All that bad luck had to be pinned on someone."

"And they pinned it onto you," Angus finished for her, remembering the old woman who had been unfairly blamed for the infant's death in his youth. "Had you no one to speak for you?"

She shook her head, her eyes glassy with unshed tears. "None who dared."

This was a different woman to the horse trainer who had challenged his views on the fairer sex and warned him against seeing Fauvel as a circus animal. She was a creature of contradictions, both weak and strong. Though he felt instinctively that the weakness inside her was a product of circumstance.

Circumstance which he would like to change.

"Morwenna," he whispered, unable to quell the instinctive urge to offer her comfort. He stepped closer and opened his arms, pulling her towards him. As she stepped into the circle of his strong embrace, the burden of anxiety sitting on his shoulders seemed to lighten. She stood with her head pressed against his chest, his strong hands caressing her shoulders beneath the heavy fabric of his cloak. "You need not have worried," he said, his voice gruff with emotion.

She lifted a tear-stained face. "Nay?"

"You can trust me," he all but growled, his fierce eyes boring down into hers. Angus didn't know who he was most angry with; the ignorant mob who had instilled such fear into this pure-hearted woman, or himself for not detecting her fears earlier. Either way, he was determined to make sure she never felt that way again.

He could never explain what happened next. One moment, her lovely face hovered beneath his; the next, his mouth was pressed against hers. Their kiss was hot and urgent, as if all the emotion of their exchange had transmitted itself to their lips. His hands roamed over her back, pulling her closer to him so their bodies could meld themselves together. Morwenna rose onto her tiptoes, her cold fingers reaching up to his shoulders. The urge to span her waist and lift her against him was undeniable.

Almost.

Flustered with passion, Angus came to his senses. His hands cupped her face as he pulled away.

"I'm sorry," he breathed, his fingertips tracing the sharp line of her cheekbones. "Forgive me."

She shook her head, her breath coming in short bursts. "We should not have."

But God's Bones, it had felt good and right. For the first time in many months, Angus had been like a free man while he held her and kissed her. As if she alone could quiet the turmoil in his mind.

Still and all, she was a woman here in his employ. Under his protection.

And he was betrothed to another.

"We should not," he agreed. His voice was heavy with regret. "Morwenna, I do not understand what is happening between us.

'Tis as if you put me under a spell." She blanched and he cursed his idiocy. "'Tis as if something exists between us that I cannot deny." Her warm breath hit his cheeks and he was taken anew with the urge to press her to him; to lower his lips to hers and taste her sweetness. His voice shook with the effort of quelling all such instincts. "I am not in the habit of seducing my serving maids."

She showed a glimmer of a smile. "I am no serving maid."

"Nay, but you are in my employ. Under my protection." His hands were back on her shoulders, caressing them gently. He should let them go, but a force greater than his own reason kept them in place.

She whispered something that he did not catch.

"Say again." He ducked his head down to be closer to the words as they escaped her tremulous lips.

"I said that in this moment, I feel protected."

"But it cannot be, you and I." He growled, more to himself than her. "I cannot allow it."

"Just moments ago, I felt afraid. As if peril lurked all around me. But now, here in your arms, I feel safe." She moved imperceptibly closer, her soft curves pressing against his hard chest, through her poor shabby gown.

"But there is more than just this moment, Morwenna," he told her gently. "There is the morrow, and the next. I would not take your good name."

She put up a small hand and laid it against his stubbled cheek. He could do nothing but clasp it firmer with his own fingers, leaning into her quiet steadfastness.

"You will vouch for me?" She swallowed hard. "You protect your mother, because you see that she does no harm. Will you extend that to one such as me? Even though I am not of your blood and have neither name or status? I am just a girl with a knack for talking to horses." Her voice shook with daring. "Standing here, in your arms, I feel that you will."

"I will." The words were squeezed from his heart. "Morwenna, I give you my word, you are safe in Wolvesley."

It was so little to promise when he would readily offer her so much more.

She fixed him with her beautiful sea-green eyes. "Then I will kiss you again."

Chapter Eleven

ALL HER LIFE had been leading up to this moment. A life spent hiding in the shadows, flinching from the future, unsure of her rightful place. Now, standing in his arms, she felt free from the weight of worry. It was liberating, as if her belly was filled with warmth which bubbled up through the rest of her.

How could their bodies fit together so perfectly when he was a lord of the land and she just a nobody? When he was height and broad strength personified, and she scarcely came to his shoulders? It made no sense, but it was so. Like the sun rising in the east. With his hands on her body, she was whole.

She tilted up her face, daring to look directly into those piercing blue eyes which held command of England's greatest castle.

"I will kiss you again," she repeated.

His expression was open, as if she could dive straight through his eyes into his soul. Without allowing herself to consider it, Morwenna wound her small hands into his golden hair and brought his lips down towards hers. They met with gentleness, but that was not what she sought. Not now, when such passion flamed in her blood. Impatiently, she tugged his head closer, tingling with gratification when her urgency found a response. With an audible moan, he pressed his mouth upon hers, parting her lips with his tongue and sweeping her against him with strong arms which lifted her part-way off the grass. Her arms wrapped around his shoulders as if they had prior permission and he slotted her against him, just so.

Morwenna felt her limbs turn liquid, melting into him she was. His mighty forearms gripped her, steady and safe. The chill of the evening left her entirely, even though his cloak was slowly slipping from her body. With every probe of his tongue, she knew a jolt of warmth and excitement. And a delicious, twisting ache deep in her lower belly.

"Ah Morwenna," he said gruffly, breaking away. "You undo me with your words and your kisses." He set her down gently, though his large hands still cupped her cheeks.

Did his fingers tremble against her flesh?

She could not answer him for she had no words. Slowly, the world came back into focus. She heard Fauvel's heavy breathing as he grazed beside them. Woodsmoke from the castle fires drifted through the evening air.

She was standing in the embrace of the Earl of Wolvesley.

But when she opened her eyes and beheld his face, inches from hers, his status no longer defined him. He was a man, like any other. Nay, he was a good man. One who protected his mother and would extend the same to her.

"I do not even know you by your given name," she said.

Immediately she regretted her bold words. He was the Earl of Wolvesley; how could she address him as anything else?

But he only smiled, his thumb tracing the line of her cheek bone. "It is Angus."

Emboldened, she spoke what was in her heart. "May I call you Angus, when we are together?"

An unreadable expression passed over his eyes. "Aye, I should like that." He paused, heaving a regretful sigh. "But Morwenna, we cannot be together. I cannot take advantage of you."

He was pulling away, leaving her cold and exposed. But in truth, despite the world of difference between them, it was not Angus who had taken advantage of her that night. It was Morwenna, who had confronted him with a dangerous truth and been met with naught but integrity and compassion.

When he could so easily have refuted her claims, walked

away, cast her into the dungeons.

Drawing deep on an inner strength she didn't know she had, Morwenna laid a restraining hand on his arm.

"You said you would protect me."

"And I will. I have given you my word." Again, he was extracting himself from their close embrace. "You will be safe in Wolvesley." His lips creased upwards into a slight smile, the metal of his mail shirt glinting in the fading light. "Though if you kiss me like that, I cannot promise that you will be safe with me."

How could she be anything but? He was wealth and power intermixed with kindness. Strength and softness combined. He had intoxicated her.

"Mayhap I do not want to be safe with you." Her voice shook with her own audacity. "Not in the way I think you mean."

It was true. Those far-gone days with Robin aside, she had lived a virtuous and obedient life, but it had brought her no joy. No comfort.

She had been right to think her life in Wolvesley had come to an end. In a way it had. This was a new beginning. She had dared voice her truth and it had brought her more than she'd dreamed. Not only to a place of protection, but one where her limbs tingled with life.

He ducked his forehead until it touched with hers. "Do not tempt me further, lass." His hands went to her hips, holding her steady. "Do you know what you say?"

Aye, she did, in some way at least. Morwenna had grown up in the countryside, long understanding the so-called mysteries of creation. And she could not proclaim herself an innocent after what had passed between her and Robin back in Escafeld.

Nor did she need to. Innocence was for virtuous maidens seeking marriage. Not outcast village girls, wanting only a peaceful life.

Why should she not welcome a little adventure along the way? Some affection to counter her loneliness? Some joy to warm her heart?

Morwenna breathed him in. Whilst her mind raced with questions, her body wanted only one thing.

"I *do* know what I say," she whispered. She met the intensity of his gaze. "Does that shock you?"

If surprise flickered across his blue eyes, it was only for a moment. "I am not one to be easily shocked," he assured her.

It was as if she stood on the edge of a precipice. If she took a step forward, she would either fall to the depths or soar into the air. But she would never know unless she took that step.

Her hands travelled over his muscular shoulders and down his arms. His response was a sharp intake of breath as his eyelids fluttered closed. She had not been expecting to glimpse such vulnerability in him, even though it lasted for less than a heartbeat. It was a moment in which her own heart turned over, not with lust or anticipation, but with tenderness.

And in that brief second, a warning slid into her mind.

This is a man who could break my heart.

But not if she took steps to keep it safe.

"I fear you are right," she said hesitantly, into the still night air. "We cannot be together." To soften her words, she slid her hands down over his shirtsleeves until her fingers joined with his.

"I fear that too. But I do not want to walk away from here and think that I will never again look upon your face, or speak with you," he countered, urgency infecting his voice.

"Nor do I." She paused. She could hardly bear the idea of turning her back on such recently discovered joy. She groped for something, anything to offer. "I will continue to train your horse."

"'Tis not enough." He cupped her hands inside his, sending warmth all the way through her. "I desire your company. Not to merely watch you from afar."

Strength passed to her from the warmth of his palms. Untethered, Fauvel walked a few paces from the paddock gate, but Morwenna knew he would not run away.

And nor would she.

"If company is what you ask of me, I would be pleased to provide it." She paused, hesitant even now to use his familiar name. "Angus," she breathed out, finally.

He brought her fingertips to his lips and pressed on them gently. "Then I shall find a way."

GOD'S BONES IT had felt right to hold her in his arms. And her lips, so sweet and tentative, they had almost been his undoing.

Almost.

He had been right to break off that kiss, before the passion rising within him became impossible to deny. What was it about Morwenna that made him abandon his self-control? The girl could calm a wild horse, but in the same breath she inflamed his senses. His show of restraint had taken a mighty effort; one that left him trembling even now, hours later.

Angus had escorted Morwenna back to the stable yard and then walked swiftly, head down, back to the keep and his own bedchamber. He wanted neither wine nor entertainment this night. He wanted only to recapture every moment of that astonishing conversation and their wondrous kiss.

He was filled with a restless energy meaning he couldn't sit still. So he paced over the sumptuous rugs in his room, striding past his polished clothes chests and swivelling on his heel once he reached the window, only to begin the circuit again. Flickering candles cast a golden-hued light around the room and fresh rushes cast the scent of lavender into the air; but relaxation had never been further from his mind.

She was no traditional temptress, with painted lips and a low-cut gown. And yet she had enchanted him utterly, despite her modest demeanour. All he could think of were her beautiful eyes and silvery-blonde hair; of how he simultaneously wished to keep her safe from all harm, yet also to explore all of her body with all of his.

Desire, that was the size of it. He paused, one hand on his walnut bed frame, as the realisation sank in. He wanted her; like he had never wanted anyone before.

But if he bedded her, it would be an abuse of power.

God's Bones, he could not allow that to happen.

Seized with frustration, he lifted the earthenware pitcher of ale from a small side table and poured himself a beaker. But the ale tasted sour and unpleasant in his mouth.

Wine, that was what he needed. He had been wrong to dismiss it. He should ring for strong wine to chase these relentless thoughts from his mind and bring him peace.

But Lucan had withstood the heartbreak of losing his wife and child without resorting to liquor. Would Angus be undone where his brother had stood firm and strong?

Angus banged the beaker down with such force that foaming ale slopped over the sides and pooled on the table.

The physical irritations he could handle. They were naught that a gallop on horseback, or even a sword-fighting session with the knights wouldn't fix. The source of his pain was something different. He groped for the word, leaning against his plastered wall and gazing unseeingly at the darkened window opposite.

This pain, this frustration, this unceasing desire did not just live in his physical self. It seemed welded to his emotions. To the very essence of his being.

He desired Morwenna not simply because of her rosy lips and gentle curves, but because of her glowing inner strength and quiet courage. Because she did not flinch from the truth, however harsh. And because when her eyes met his, nothing else in the world seemed to matter.

He desired her with his very soul. And that wasn't something he could solve with strong wine or vigorous exercise.

It wasn't something he could deny, however much he might wish to deny it.

Angus sank down into a padded chair, crossing his long legs at the knee and propping his aching head onto his hands.

Fleetingly it crossed his mind that he could send the maid away. Out of sight, out of mind, however impossible it sounded.

But that could not be, for he had offered her the protection of Wolvesley.

And what of Emelia? His betrothed. The intended mother of his heir.

An heir that Wolvesley needed, as much now as ever before.

Angus gnashed his teeth together, swearing quietly. Most problems he could overcome, either with dedication or intellect. This challenge too would pass, in time. But here and now, he was a man almost brought to his knees with frustration.

He must spend time with Morwenna; yet for temptation to be held at bay, they should not be alone together. He dared not visit her in the circular paddock. And God's Bones; he could not ask her to come to his solar, however much the idea appealed.

He would deny himself her body, aye. But not her company.

He craved that as much as the other.

The endless night brought him no peace, only more heavy pacing of the floor, but by first light he had his answer.

The Vaulters of Volterfordas.

His Seneschal had brought word of the travelling troupe some days earlier, though at the time Angus had been too distracted to pay much heed. But before the morning fires were lit, a messenger was dispatched on horseback to York; the last known destination of fearless folk who performed daring gymnastics on horseback. The lad returned at luncheon, pink-cheeked with excitement, pleased to be bearing good news into the great hall.

"They are coming here directly," he piped, bowing low and holding out a scroll for Angus to take.

Standing before the fireplace, Angus unfurled it with a flourish, his keen eyes skimming the untidy scrawl.

"Excellent," he murmured, flipping the lad a coin for his troubles and nodding to the Seneschal who was waiting nearby. "See that preparations are made."

The Seneschal cleared his throat. "Will I send out the usual invitations, my lord?"

Angus made a show of deliberation, one hand tugging at his beard. "I think not on this occasion." He tapped his booted foot on the stone-flagged floor, as if the idea was coming fresh into his mind. "The workers here in Wolvesley have served us most faithfully during this difficult summer. I wish to reward them for their loyalty. Let us make this celebration one for the people to enjoy."

The Seneschal inclined his head, his expression inscrutable. "We will invite the servants?"

Angus waved his hand loftily. "The servants, the cooks, the carpenters, the grooms." He paused. "Most especially all who work with horses should be given the chance to witness these spectacular riders."

"Very good, my lord."

"I will even sit amongst them, so that I might better hear their opinions." Angus banged his hands together, brimming with entirely sincere enthusiasm for his plan.

He would sit beside Morwenna and watch the daring spectacle. He would breathe the scent of her hair and feel her excitement, all with due propriety, for dozens of others would be right there with them.

It wasn't much, but with his whole being burning for her company, it was a great deal better than nothing.

Chapter Twelve

THE LOW-SLUNG BUILDING where the grooms took their meals was full of chatter and conversation, even more so than usual. Small groups of ruddy-cheeked men and boys leaned close together over the scrubbed trestle tables, talking with great animation. Morwenna had taken a seat at her preferred small table in the corner, happy to munch her bread and observe the goings-on, too much absorbed in her own musings to much wonder at the gossip. But as soon as he spied her, Gerrault pulled up a small wooden stool and perched opposite.

"You'll never guess who's to come here on the morn," he declared, rocking the stool backwards on the soft earth floor. He was clad in a freshly laundered tunic with his brown hair neatly combed.

Reluctantly, she dragged herself from the rosy glow of reminiscence. The earl's hands around her waist; his lips upon hers. It was the stuff of dreams, only her dreams could never be so potent as to infuse her with this lightness of being; this heady rush of connection.

"I could not even try." She softened her words with a smile.

"The Vaulters of Volterfordas," he announced, beaming.

"The Vaulters of Volterfordas?" she repeated questioningly, her lip quirking at the undoubted excitement shining in young Gerrault's eyes. "I have ne'er heard of them."

"Oh, they are quite the thing, Miss Morwenna." In his eagerness, Gerrault slipped into their old mode of address. "And the best of it is, his lordship is putting on this show just for us servants."

Now it was Morwenna's turn to flush with excitement. Carefully, she put down her bread and folded her hands together, lest their trembling betray her.

"How so?"

Gerrault shrugged extravagantly. "That I don't know. But Isaac heard it from Jacob, who heard it directly from the Seneschal himself. These vaulters, they've even performed for the King." He lowered his voice reverently. "And now they're coming to Wolvesley, to perform for us."

Morwenna opened and closed her mouth, but no words came out. Her mind raced, piecing all of this together. "So we shall watch, alongside the earl and his family?" she guessed, affecting nonchalance.

Gerrault nodded. "Though it's my guess that only Jacob and the senior servants will sit with the likes of his lordship. The rest of us will be up in the stands. But that don't matter none." His gaze dropped. "I only wish my parents were still alive to see how far I've risen. Personal groom to Sir Henry, and now this."

In a rush of sympathy, Morwenna reached out and placed her own cool hands over Gerrault's. "They would be very proud."

He lifted his chin, meeting her gaze. "And your grandmother, she would be right proud of you too," he whispered, mayhap conscious of the hum of group conversation behind them. His eyes flickered over her wrist. "I see you still wear her cuff."

"Aye." Instinctively, Morwenna's left hand went to cover it, tracing the intricate engraving in the leather. "It is all I have left of her."

"She must have been a woman of means, once."

"Aye," Morwenna agreed again. Her grandmother had never liked to talk of her past, and even now she felt an ingrained reluctance to do so. Like it would be a betrayal.

"It's fine leather." Gerrault was peering closer at the cuff, oblivious of her hesitancy.

"I know it." On impulse she said, "I've always thought my grandmother fell upon hard times. The way she spoke, the way she acted. 'Twas as if she'd been born to more than a shack on a hill." Morwenna shrugged suddenly, not wanting to say more on the subject.

"Did you never know your parents?" His voice was sympathetic. "I can't remember them being in Escafeld."

"Nay. They died when I was very young. My grandmother was all I had. And I was all she had. And that was enough."

Gerrault squeezed her hand. "A lot has changed for us both."

Her breath caught in her throat. More had changed for her than Gerrault could ever know.

"Are you coming, Gerrault?" Isaac appeared behind him, his bright eyes widening when he saw their joined hands.

Blushing furiously, Gerrault shoved back his stool. "I'll be right there."

"Have you heard the news, Morwenna?" Isaac asked, raising his voice over a sudden hubbub by the ale pitcher.

For a moment her mind went blank. "About the vaulters?" she managed.

"Aye." Isaac tipped her a wink. "I'll wager you'll be sitting right beside the earl. He's that pleased with how you've tamed his wild horse."

Morwenna felt her own cheeks tinge with pink, but Isaac's suspicion may work to her advantage. "If that's so, then I'm happy to have done a good job," she said weakly.

"Come then, Gerrault." Isaac gripped the arm of his tunic and turned him towards the doorway. "We have work to be getting on with."

"Fare ye well, Miss Morwenna." Gerrault nodded his head.

"Fare ye well." She too rose to her feet, conscious of having taken a misstep somewhere in the conversation, but not sure where or why. And as she watched the grooms file out of the barn, ready to go about their day, she felt again the lightness in her heart, the reduction of the weight she had carried on her shoulders for so many years.

She was safe. She was protected. And upon the morn, she would be once again in the earl's company.

'Twas all she wanted and more.

THE NEXT MORN dawned bright with a brisk breeze chasing white-tipped clouds over the distant forest. The famed Vaulters of Volterfordas had arrived late in the evening; their horses clopping over the cobbles; the men making a poor job of blending quietly with the workings of the yard. Morwenna had heard them drinking and singing well into the night. When she went in to break her fast; the usually tidy eating quarters were littered with spilled pitchers of ale and snoring men.

Six of them there were. All small and muscular, with beady eyes and unsmiling mouths. Their hoses too were small and hardy. They were well fed, with long manes and tails that had been carefully combed, but Morwenna felt a nervous energy radiating from them, which she didn't like one bit.

The stable yard hummed with activity as everyone rushed to complete their day's work before the exhibition began. Morwenna was relieved to walk away from the hustle and bustle to the peace of the circular paddock, where Fauvel now whinnied in greeting as soon as he glimpsed her coming over the brow of the hill.

"You're a good boy," she told him, reaching up to rub his ears as he pushed at her tunic hoping for treats.

It was as if the night of the joust had changed everything. Not just her relationship with the earl; but with his horse too. Fauvel now seemed to trust her completely. She could run her hands over his withers and down to his hindquarters without him so much as flinching. He flicked his ears forward when she spoke to him; and showed no sign of skittishness, even when she bent to pick up his hooves. In her bones, Morwenna knew it was high time she put a saddle on his back. Her task was to make him rideable, not merely biddable. And accepting of people other than herself. But as soon as she had accomplished this; her work in Wolvesley would be done.

And what then?

But today, she didn't allow her thoughts to roam further than the exhibition. Would she really be seated directly by the earl, as Isaac had suggested? In a way, it seemed plausible, for the earl – Angus – had promised to find a way they could be together.

But it was also the most incredulous notion she had ever heard. How could the Earl of Wolvesley sit beside a stable-hand in public?

How could the Earl of Wolvesley have kissed her in private? How could he have entrusted her with family secrets and spoken to her with true feeling?

If her memories were not so sharp, she would have considered herself delusional.

Fortune's wheel never stops turning.

Her grandmother's voice seemed to whisper directly into her ear, as if the lady herself stood right beside her. Morwenna knew it was merely fancy, but there was no disputing that her fortunes had certainly changed since she left Escafeld.

Morwenna put her hands on the paddock gate and rested her head on her arms. Soon she would discover, one way or another, if the earl really had invited the Vaulters of Volterfordas to Wolvesley for the express purpose of spending time with her. And whatever the answer, she would remember her grandmother's lessons and behave with decorum. For if anyone were to see how his very presence affected her, her position here could soon grow untenable.

Morwenna stroked Fauvel's white nose and remembered another of her grandmother's wise sayings.

The more you have, the more you have to lose.

But she didn't want fear to dominate her thoughts, nor would she let it spoil the delicious anticipation rippling through her. The hours passed with interminable slowness. Morwenna put a halter onto Fauvel and led him around the perimeter of the paddock, making him by turns break into a fast trot and then slow to a steady walk. He followed her lead, behaving more like a gentleman than a wild horse. There was no denying that she must get upon his back within the sennight.

Then the earl would have won his strange challenge.

She would have kept her word and earned her coin. Enough of it to repair the roof of her hut.

Morwenna released Fauvel, watching him canter away and kick up his heels like a youngling. What she wouldn't give to be so carefree herself.

She made her way back to the stable yard, lost in thought and oblivious to the tumult around her. The vaulting exhibition would take place in the jousting arena; and many of the grooms were already turned out in their finest, ready to proceed beneath the stone archway and file into the stands. She saw that several of them had picked wildflowers from the meadow and tied them up into small posies, mayhap to present to serving girls from the castle. The air was thick with the pulsing excitement of Twelfth-tide. Good times were coming; and hard-working folk were determined to make the most of the revelry.

Morwenna alone had a strong dose of adrenaline laced with anxiety racing through her gut.

Adrenaline because she would see the earl again.

Anxiety because it was not proper for one such as she to desire the attentions of one such as he. Because she still didn't understand why he should have such an effect on her body and mind. And because part of her feared the magic that had sprung up between them in the paddock, may have been but a tempo-rary delusion.

But the drumbeat of fear that had dogged her footsteps for so long, had faded. Even if those moments in the paddocks were never to be repeated, she felt sure that she could trust in the earl's integrity.

She had admitted to him that her grandmother had the Sight.

And in turn, he had kissed her.

Her tumult of emotion forced her to sit on the edge of the bed.

She wrapped her fingers around her grandmother's cuff and closed her eyes, hoping to settle her racing heart and mind. A hesitant knock at the door almost had her falling off the bed and onto the bare floor.

"Come in."

Gerrault's smiling face appeared before her, then he opened the door more fully and stepped into the gap, his tall frame hardly fitting beneath the sloping roof.

"Miss Morwenna."

She shook her head at him; his steady presence helping to calm her thoughts. "I'm dressed exactly like a man, Gerrault, with mud beneath my fingernails and the smell of horseflesh all around me. 'Tis a wonder you can call me Miss Morwenna."

She hadn't meant to tease him, but he blushed at her words. "You will always be Miss Morwenna to my thinking." He took one hand from behind his back and thrust a posy of chicory flowers towards her. "For you."

Morwenna blinked in momentary confusion, before remembering her manners. "Why, they're lovely, thank you, Gerrault." It was her turn to blush as she rose from the bed to take the flowers from him. She inhaled their fresh scent, merely for something to do. "How kind," she said, her nose still pressed into the blue petals.

His long arms flapped by his legs until he folded his hands firmly together. "I will walk with you, to the joust, if it pleases you?"

What else could she say? "It will please me very much, thank you." She paused. "But you must give me a moment to make myself presentable."

His smile could have warmed the icehouse. "I will wait for

you down in the yard."

He bowed his head and was gone, leaving Morwenna more flustered than ever.

Was young Gerrault sweet on her?

Surely not. She was some years his senior. And whilst Gerrault had been a popular boy back in Escafeld, Morwenna had been treated as an oddity. But the boy she had once known was a young man now; with a respectable position in a wealthy yard. He would grow into a fine man, she had no doubt of it.

A fine man, who had set his cap at *her*.

Or had he? Morwenna placed the wildflowers in a basin of water, splashing a little onto her flushed cheeks. Mayhap Gerrault was only being polite. Or mayhap he didn't want to be the only groom without a girl on his arm.

She exhaled with relief, drying her hands on a rough cloth. That must be it. She was a friendly face to the lad; one he'd known since childhood. He wouldn't want to think of her sitting all alone.

The bare flesh of her arms tingled with fresh excitement, for there was a chance she wouldn't be sitting alone, but with the Earl of Wolvesley himself.

Should she change her groom's attire for the soft woollen dress Molly had given her?

Morwenna's cheeks burned afresh at the notion; for in doing so she'd be flaunting her femininity at the earl. At Angus. Why else would she swap her smart, warm clothes for a gown which the sharp wind would whistle through in an instant?

Was she hoping to draw his attention to her slender curves? She a peasant and he a man accustomed to having his pick of beautiful women?

Aye, mayhap she was.

Mayhap it was time to step out of the shadows and be noticed.

The pale-blue gown was comfortable and swirled gently around her ankles. As a further gesture towards the festivities, she untied her plait and allowed her long blonde hair to tumble freely about her shoulders. Without further prevarication, she strode out of her chamber and pulled the door shut behind her.

If it transpired that all of this had been arranged for her benefit, she would have serious words with Angus about not doing anything the like again. She had grown so nervous she thought she may well tumble into the water trough on her way down the steps.

"You look lovely, Miss Morwenna."

Gerrault greeted her with his customary smile and a courtly elbow.

Morwenna gave him a sharp look as she came down the steps. "Many more Miss Morwennas and I shall take to addressing you as Master Gerrault. How would you like that?"

His smile faltered. "I only…"

"Gerrault, you're the personal groom to Sir Henry and all but a man grown. I'm the last person you should be addressing formally." She stood beside him and took his arm, softening her expression to take the sting from her words. "I only wish to pass unnoticed through the world. You know that as well as anyone."

Although her decision to swap her braccae and tunic for a dress was drawing a lot of attention her way. Morwenna couldn't decide if she enjoyed the appreciative looks cast towards her from the grooms gathered around the yard. Her usual reaction would be to shrink her shoulders and try to make herself as small as possible. But somehow, today, she felt she could stand tall and withstand the attention without flinching.

Not for too long though.

She nudged him forwards and they began to proceed slowly over the cobbles towards the path that led to the jousting arena, tagging along behind the chattering groups already on their way. Ahead of them, Morwenna spied Molly waving excitedly in her direction. Morwenna waved back, but moments later, Isaac's sister had been swallowed by the crowd.

Gerrault was quiet. He stood a head taller than Morwenna,

meaning that without looking directly upwards, she couldn't discern his expression. She hoped she hadn't pushed away a good friend.

After a long while, he cleared his throat. "I mean no disrespect, Morwenna. I've always admired you, that's all."

She stopped in her tracks, tugging at his arm until his eyes met hers. "You mean, you've always admired my work, surely?" Her mind whirred. "I saved Minnie and helped Farmer Jerome's horses, when they needed it."

He nodded. "I admired that, for certain. You've a gift. Whatever it is."

"Right." She started walking again, anxious now to arrive at their destination before Gerrault said anything he might regret.

He pulled her back, his grip surprisingly strong. "But I admire you too, Morwenna."

This time, there was no mistaking the intent in his grey eyes.

"Gerrault, please," she began, conscious of a swell of people walking down the path towards them.

His lips tightened. "I admire the way you stand up tall, no matter what. And your kindness, it shines from you."

These were words she hadn't been expecting. Her mouth hung open but she could form no reply. Heavy footsteps came closer. At any moment, the approaching crowd would have reached them, and her hand still rested in Gerrault's.

"That's all I want to say. For now," he added. Then he sprang to one side and bowed smartly. "Your lordship," he said. "Sir Henry."

Morwenna's heart seemed to stop beating as she glanced sideways to see two tall, imposing figures bearing down upon them. With heavy cloaks swirling, and tunics glistening with gold thread, they scattered the chattering throng of servants. Morwenna's gaze reluctantly lifted and she beheld the lined face of Sir Henry, followed by a pair of blue eyes that brought a warm flush to her whole body.

"Well, whom do we have here?" demanded the Earl of

Wolvesley. "Henry, I do believe it is your boy, Gerrault." His piercing eyes rested on her face, looking directly into her soul. "Together with Morwenna."

Chapter Thirteen

*T*OGETHER WITH MY *girl, Morwenna.*

That was what he'd almost said, and he sent up thanks that he'd bitten back the words before they properly formed.

Morwenna wasn't his girl and nor could she ever be. But it had been such a shock to round the corner and come across the pair of them, hands and eyes joined, that Angus was still reeling from it.

And Morwenna in that dress. With her waterfall of hair cascading down her back. The beauty of her took his breath away.

Thankfully, Henry, with the instincts of a seasoned knight, took charge of the situation.

"Gerrault, just the man I was looking for," he boomed jovially, reaching out to clasp the boy's shoulder. "You must sit beside me for the exhibition. I look forward to hearing what you make of it all."

The boy blushed, clearly torn between a desire to please his master and a much stronger urge to sit beside a pretty girl. A battle played behind his grey eyes, but good manners prevailed.

He bowed stiffly to Henry, soft brown hair flopping over his face. "That is most kind, sir."

"The pleasure is mine." Henry's keen gaze switched to the petite young woman standing beside him. "Well now, we have never met, but this must be the horse trainer I've heard so much about." He clasped his hands behind his back and rocked on his heels. "A miracle worker, no less. I told Wolvesley here that his horse would never be ridden."

Angus knew Morwenna, and he could tell that Henry's praise made her uncomfortable. E'en more so than she already was. She lowered her eyes and bobbed her head.

"Your prediction may still prove correct, sir. I am yet to put a saddle on the horse's back."

At the sound of her sweet voice, all of Angus's petty jealousy faded away. He immediately spoke up in her defence.

"Your success is all but assured, Morwenna. I know it in my bones." He fixed his eyes upon her face, willing her to look up and meet his gaze; flushing with triumph when she did just that. He drank her in; unused to seeing her in anything but groom's livery. The hubbub of the jousting arena quietened in his ears and he grew oblivious to the press of the passing crowd. All that mattered was Morwenna.

A sharp nudge from Henry's elbow brought him back to his senses and he cleared his throat gruffly. "I echo the sentiment of my good friend. Pray, sit beside me, Morwenna. I am keen to discover your thoughts on these much-feted horse riders."

A pink blush stained her cheeks but her head stayed high and her voice was clear. "Whatever your lordship wishes."

"Excellent." He raised his arms, urging their small group onwards before he said what was in his heart.

That he wished for a good deal more than her opinion on the Vaulters of Volterfordas.

For the first time, the temptation to make Morwenna his mistress fluttered enticingly into his mind. Such things happened; many men greater than he enjoyed such arrangements, with the added benefit that no rival would dare stake a claim to the woman they desired. But he pushed the thought away. He was not a man who could marry one woman and bed another.

The smell of roasting meat wafted over from the wagon traders whom Angus had allowed to set up near the jousting arena. With half an eye, he noticed the castle servants all turned out in their best, jostling one another good-naturedly for the best places in the stands. Usually he would mingle little with the staff; arriving late and going directly to his seat in the family enclosure. Now he noticed that several of the young serving wenches carried hand-tied posies of late-summer wildflowers. He saw gangling house-boys with polished boots and freshly-scrubbed necks, smiling awkwardly by their sides. It seemed romance bloomed everywhere on this unexpected holiday. But his warm feelings evaporated as a new idea sliced into his mind.

Had Gerrault mayhap presented such a posy to Morwenna?

Frustration twisted in his gut. For he was Earl of Wolvesley, yet he could not present the girl he admired with a posy. Nor could he take a hold of her elbow and draw her close. Nor tell young Gerrault to get packing.

Morwenna's green eyes lifted to his, as if she could read his discomfort.

"'Tis a great occasion you have arranged for us, milord."

His frustration lifted a little, swirling up into the autumnal air along with the aromas of horses, woodsmoke and fried onions.

He smiled down at her, ignoring the press of bodies all around them as they proceeded through the wooden gate to the arena. For a long moment, he could not think of the right words to say. So accustomed was he to masking his emotions for the benefit of his public image that now, when it felt imperative to express himself sincerely, he did not know how to begin to articulate what was in his heart.

"'Tis all for you," he dared to whisper, after Henry and Gerrault had gone ahead.

Was it wise to say such words out loud? Mayhap not, when the risks were so great. But it was worth it to see the flare of recognition in her pretty face. She lowered her eyes and stepped to the side so he might take his seat first, with Henry on his left and a space for his mother between them. The very air seemed to crackle as she took her place beside him; her narrow frame all but swallowed up in the carved wooden chair. Angus was overly conscious of her feminine curves, enhanced by the flattering cut of her pale-blue gown. And how her hair cascaded over her shoulders, glinting in the late-afternoon sunlight.

"Will Lady Violetta be joining us?" asked Henry, leaning over towards him and breaking the spell.

Angus hesitated, guilt gnawing at him. In truth, he hadn't said anything to his mother about the occasion. He had e'en gone so far as to dine in his mother's chamber yesterday, in an effort to keep her from overhearing any excited chatter in the great hall. Memories of how she had behaved at the recent joust were still too sharp. She had stood, mere feet away from where he now sat, and openly conversed with the spirit of Lucan. In front of hundreds of people. It was nothing short of a miracle that no one had spotted her.

No one but Morwenna.

However, if Henry believed she was on her way, no doubt he would preserve the distance between them. Thus giving Angus greater opportunity to speak freely with Morwenna.

He cleared his throat. "Perchance she is delayed," he said evasively.

Henry nodded and withdrew, making some aside comment to Gerrault which made the lad chuckle. Angus shifted in his chair, stretching his long legs out in front of him to dispel the sudden air of awkwardness which had descended upon them.

"Have you seen the likes of these vaulters before?" he asked impulsively, his deep baritone rippling through the stands. Several heads turned in their direction and Morwenna squirmed.

He must speak quieter and draw less attention their way; though as earl, all eyes would instinctively turn towards him whatever he did or said. Angus was accustomed to living with such scrutiny, but Morwenna was not, and he did not wish to make her uncomfortable.

Her reply was steady. "I have not, milord." She hesitated, folding and unfolding her hands on her lap. He noticed her fingers were long and slender, even though the knuckles were reddened from physical work. "In truth, I am unsure I approve of such practices."

His eyebrows shot upwards. "How so?"

For a moment she didn't answer. "There are different ways of bending a horse to one's will." She inclined her head to one side. "Through kindness or through fear."

"And you believe the vaulters use the latter?" He nodded towards the ring, into which a line of high-stepping ponies was now entering.

"I will be happy to be proven wrong."

Angus harrumphed and sat taller in his chair; his hands rapping out a random tune on his breeches-clad knees as he pondered her words. His concern was most often with the surface of things; how they looked and how they might be perceived by society. For that was the root of his role as judiciary; keeping the peace and ensuring society ran smoothly. The idea that what ran beneath the surface might be equally important made him curiously perturbed, as if he had an itch that he could not reach to scratch.

The crowd let out a collective gasp of appreciation as the first rider somersaulted onto the back of a gleaming black pony. As if acting on a silent cue, the pony sprung into a fast gallop around the grassy arena. The rider crouched low over his neck, both feet planted firmly in the centre of the pony's narrow back. Then, once he had found his balance, he stood tall, arms outstretched to the side. A ripple of applause spread around the stands, but before it could properly take hold, a second rider joined the first. Side by side they galloped in endless circles; both standing tall in a daring defeat of gravity. But this trick paled into insignificance as a pony of brilliant white was led into the arena. This was the star turn of the Vaulters of Volterfordas. Angus felt his breath catch in his throat as the riders formed a pyramid atop his narrow back; one standing on the shoulders of the others.

Beside him, Morwenna let out a sound that might have been a whimper and looked away.

"What is it?" he asked, ducking his head down towards her.

For a long moment he had been so captivated by the daring display that he had forgotten the true purpose behind it all; that he might spend time publicly with Morwenna.

"His eyes," she whispered. Her own green eyes were wide with pain.

Angus was about to ask whose eyes, but when he glanced back at the arena the white pony was circling towards them; his dark eyes bulging with some strong emotion much like a battle charger plunging into the fray. All at once, the uncomfortable itchy feeling returned to him. He put out a warm hand and covered Morwenna's cold one; unthinking for once of what would happen if his actions were witnessed.

"I'm sorry," he murmured.

She looked up and gave him the ghost of a smile. "You are not responsible."

"But I brought them here." He tightened his grip on her fingers; thrilled when he felt an answering squeeze.

"For me?" she said, so quietly he wasn't sure if he had imagined it.

"For you," he confirmed.

She gave him a look that was humbling in its warmth. "You do not need to put on a show or spectacle to impress me, Angus." She hesitated over his name, articulating it slowly. "In truth, I prefer quieter pleasures."

Heat from their joined hands was travelling up his arm. He knew he should release his hold; that he was playing with fire and was likely to get burned. But it felt good and right to hold Morwenna's hand. She was a woman of truth and kindness. When she was near, it was as if the perils of the world could not touch him. And not because of any position or status she possessed – he alone knew how such things could not protect against death and despair – but because of who she was and what she had already survived.

He would not deny himself this. He *could not* deny himself any further.

"Quieter pleasures," he echoed, shifting in his chair so the folds of his cloak partially concealed their hands. "I'm afraid Wolvesley is a place of grandeur, where our safety is dependent upon a continual display of wealth and might. I am a man of excess and know little of quiet pleasures." He squeezed her fingers to take any sting from his words; schooling his face all the while into an expression of casual interest, his eyes gazing at but hardly seeing the riders in the ring. "What would you suggest?"

He squeezed her fingers and felt her jolt of surprise.

Will she pull away?

But after a long moment, she answered, albeit evasively. "I have always found horses to be the most constant of companions."

"Allow me to prove myself equally constant."

He fancied he could hear the hammering of her heart, or mayhap that was his own. His body grew first hot and then cold while he waited for her response.

"You are the Earl of Wolvesley. I will do whatever you wish."

God's Bones. That was not what he wanted.

"Angus is my name. And I am asking for your help." Instinctively, he knew he had hit upon the right way to persuade her.

Morwenna's nostrils flared at the surprise turn of their conversation. "My help?" Her voice was incredulous, but there was something else in her tone as well. Curiosity. And a deep-seated desire to provide succour to those in need.

Angus nodded decisively. "I should like to experience your quiet pleasures."

He was unable to prevent his gaze from drawing down to her green eyes, which were raised to his beseechingly. Eyes which would be his undoing.

"I don't know what you mean," she whispered. "I don't know how."

"Ah, Morwenna," he said her name like a caress. "You are allowing yourself to be afraid. Do not think of me at the Earl of Wolvesley. Think of me only as Angus. I am in your hands. You plan the occasion. An occasion of quiet pleasures, without show or spectacle."

He must look away from her finely-drawn face and wide sea-green eyes. He must fix his gaze back upon the Vaulters of Volterfordas, ready to cheer and celebrate with the crowd. But he could not.

Not until she agreed to his plan.

He saw indecision racing behind her eyes. Her lips moved but no words came out.

"How are we to manage it?" she said at last. "You will be seen."

Angus gave her slender fingers a final squeeze, before rising from his feet to applaud the riders who were now taking their bows. Around him, the stands erupted into cheers, with much stamping of feet and yelling for more.

Into the commotion, he said, "Allow me to worry about that aspect of the occasion."

"I will." A smile broke over her face, changing her expression entirely. "And I shall plan the rest."

"Tomorrow at noon," he confirmed, his mind-racing. "I will meet you in the paddocks."

She dipped her head, still smiling. "Tomorrow at noon."

Chapter Fourteen

MORWENNA WAS TRYING hard to control her nerves so that Fauvel wouldn't pick up on them, but it was hard work. Excitement had lodged inside her belly and was reaching spiky tendrils into every last bit of her. Thankfully, the horse had long since decided to trust her and he submitted gracefully to her fumbling fingers as she attempted to secure his halter.

Today was meant to be the day she finally put a saddle on Fauvel's back, but after the earl's request to meet her at noon for an afternoon of quiet pleasures, Morwenna knew it would not be sensible. Her heart threatened to jump out of her chest at the mere memory of that conversation, and she couldn't risk her jitters spoiling the occasion and mayhap putting the horse back several days. Not that she was in a rush to complete her work at Wolvesley Castle, but poor Fauvel should not be the one to pay.

"You've suffered enough," she told him, ducking beneath his head to comb a tangle out of his long chestnut mane. "I shall not do anything to make you doubt humans again."

Fauvel had been bred from a mighty destrier; likely intended for life as a warhorse himself. His early years had passed pleasurably amidst green pastures, with a kindly stablemaster seeing to his every need. Fauvel had been backed successfully, proving himself brave and fleet of foot. But then, disaster struck. He and two other chargers were stolen by unscrupulous horse dealers, with Fauvel briskly sold to a company of hackneymen who hired out palfreys along bustling Ermine Street that linked

York and London.

Fauvel was no steady palfrey, although he tried his best. Still young, the noises of the busy road unsettled him. As did the ungentle riders who hauled on his mouth and plunged sharp spurs into his side. When he threw a particularly cruel man off his back, to land perilously close to the wheels of a wagon, the hackneymen became keen to get him off their hands.

From here, Fauvel's life spiralled downwards as he was passed from one home to the next, each progressively worse. His trust in humans entirely disappeared as he was tied up, beaten and half starved. Only his height and breeding saved him. One particularly canny knight sold him as an untried charger and soon after, Fauvel arrived at Wolvesley.

All of this, Fauvel had shown Morwenna, with some details nearly too bloody for her to willingly receive. Not yet five years of age, he had seen the worst of humankind. Sometimes, Morwenna wanted to weep for him.

Now he stood in the paddock with his eyes half-closed and one hoof resting on its tip, entirely at ease with her ministrations. Part of her knew a glow of pride at all she had achieved, but another part couldn't help fretting that her work here was all but done. She had taught Fauvel to trust again. Everything else would come easily, relative to that first step.

Still, it was difficult to be downbeat on a day like today. The autumn sunshine was strong and bright, shining in a sky so blue it was reminiscent of midsummer. Morwenna had already abandoned her shawl and rolled the sleeves of her tunic up to her elbows. It was hard not to think of this unseasonal weather as a blessing on what she had planned. But she stamped down on such thinking with as much force as she could muster.

That way madness lay.

This late sunshine was a fluke. At best, an unanticipated gift; and one she would make good use of. Her eyes flickered over to two grey horses grazing steadily in the next paddock. Horses she had asked Jacob to move closer to Fauvel so that he might grow more used to their company.

True enough, but she had an ulterior motive as well. One that made her cheeks blush at her daring. She was playing with fire, there was no doubting it. Spending time with the earl gave her a rush of feeling, of life, of energy. It was almost an addiction. And why, she asked silently, should she deny herself this pleasure?

The earl was not married. Nor did it seem that he had any plans in that regard. Even young Isaac, who had worked at Wolvesley since his tenth summer, had stated that there was no sign of a new countess coming any time soon. Those, in fact, had been his exact words, that night in the lane.

She had memorized them.

The only reason to turn her back on this adventure was to protect her heart. She had so recently lowered her personal barricades and allowed herself to place a degree of trust in other people, in the future and herself. It made her vulnerable.

But nor could she countenance walking away from the one person who made her feel whole again.

"Am I a fool, Fauvel?" she asked the big chestnut horse, reaching up to stroke his silky soft ears.

He snorted gently, blowing hot air against the top of her head and disturbing a few strands which drifted across her face. Morwenna had tied her long hair into a neat plait, despite the fact she preferred it loose – and from the way he'd been looking at her yesterday, she suspected the earl did too. She'd also rejected the little voice in her head that told her to wear a dress today; to look dainty and feminine for this unanticipated event.

No, no and no again.

She must be true to herself and her position in the earl's household. She was no beguiling maid, nor fine lady, and she would stand for no pretence otherwise. The road she had found herself upon was tricky enough to navigate without entertaining false illusions.

And so she had dressed that morning in her usual groom's attire of braccae and tunic, emblazoned with the earl's coat of arms. A glaring reminder of the difference in their status.

Of the fact she would be a fool to lose her heart to such a man, even though the attraction she felt for him could not be denied.

"Oh, Fauvel."

She rested her forehead against his satiny shoulder and breathed in the familiar scent of horse and late-summer grass. Warmth from Fauvel's body stole over her, calming her thoughts and her increasingly erratic pulse.

A picnic, that was all she had planned. A picnic with a man who had so far proven himself trustworthy.

There would be nothing to fear, if only the very thought of him didn't make her weak at the knees.

"Where should I put these, miss?"

The hesitant enquiry broke through her thoughts. Morwenna pulled away from Fauvel, looking in confusion towards the man dressed in shabby servant's attire holding two pails of water. He was half turned away from her but could only have been directing the enquiry at her.

"Jacob sent me," he added. His voice was rough, the words tumbling together as if he had never learned to articulate.

Morwenna frowned. "I didn't ask for any water, but the trough is over there by the tree." She shrugged her shoulders. Mayhap the stablemaster had noted the dry conditions and was planning ahead.

It was only when the man began to walk away that she noticed his height and long, easy stride. He carried the heavy pails of water as if they weighed nothing. And as he tipped the water into the trough, the movement shifted his cloak and his hood fell away to reveal tumbling locks of golden hair.

It's the earl himself.

Morwenna's breath caught in her throat. For a moment, she simply observed him. His fluid movements, his muscular shoulders rippling beneath a thin shirt.

The second his eyes met hers across the paddock, he smiled.

And his smile released all of her pent-up anxieties. Suddenly, the day seemed full of shining possibilities.

And the lark of it. The Earl of Wolvesley dressed as a servant for the sole reason of spending time with *her*.

"Very good, miss," he called over to her. "I'll go and fetch the rest."

She took a few paces towards him, arms swinging by her side. "Is that really necessary?"

"I don't know, miss." He too closed the gap between them, coming so close she felt the hypnotic pull of his sparkling blue eyes. "I only follow orders."

Nerves fluttered in her stomach as she made a show of looking into the full trough.

"I think we have all we need."

"Shall I be off then?" He watched her closely, though his stance was casual. He placed one pail inside the other and pulled both towards his chest.

"I think I might find other work for you to do." Her voice wobbled with daring, but his gleaming eyes spurred her on. "In the shelter there." She motioned towards the simple wooden shelter standing beside the gate and at the earl's urging, preceded him over there. "See?" she declared, putting her hands on her hips and nodding into the gloomy interior.

The earl scratched his beard, peering into the darkness. "See what, miss?"

"There is a plank of wood coming loose. It needs a hammer and nails."

The earl broke into a broad grin. "Now you have me. The truth is, miss. I have never wielded hammer nor nails."

She tutted in surprise. "What manner of servant are you?"

"Not a very good one," he admitted sheepishly. "I did not imagine I would come undone so soon." He pulled off the shabby grey cloak and flung it over a wooden stool. "But I am glad my subterfuge is at an end. It is far too warm for such an outfit."

He stood before her in worn braccae and a faded shirt which

had two buttons missing. Just below his neck, Morwenna could glimpse the curves of his chest and a swirl of golden hairs. Swallowing hard, her eye unwittingly travelled down over his muscular thighs to a pair of shabby leather boots which barely encompassed his bulging calves.

Poor clothing could not disguise his power or strength. Nor dim his essential charismatic energy.

"And so, I am here at your bidding, Morwenna," he declared, his eyes glinting in the shadows. "What are you going to do with me?"

His words sent a thrill of adrenaline shooting through her, but she didn't let it show. Instead she lifted her head higher. "You asked for quiet pleasures, milord."

"Angus," he corrected her, placing his large hands on the rough edge of his torn shirt. "For today, at least. You must find it in you to call me Angus."

"Angus," she began again. "We are going on a picnic."

He put his golden head to one side in surprise. "Have the kitchens prepared something?"

Morwenna laughed. "Nay, milord. Angus. Nay. We have no show nor spectacle here, remember."

"No food either?" He frowned in confusion. "Morwenna, I am a man with an appetite."

Ignoring a new pulse of excitement which threatened to bring heat to her whole body, Morwenna gave him a little frown. "You are a man who must suppress his appetite in order to understand the quiet pleasures you seek."

For a moment, she held her breath. Had she pushed this joviality too far? But Angus was quick to dip into a bow, displaying the broad planes of his shoulders. "I am in your hands."

"You are here as my companion," she corrected, unable to withstand much more of his flirting. "Pray, fetch the saddlebag from the shelf."

Stumbling a little in the gloom, Angus located the partially filled leather saddlebag and slung it over his shoulder. "Anything else, miss?"

"Not for now," she answered primly. "Follow me."

It was something of a relief to leave the tempting confines of the shelter and stride out over open land. Morwenna went first to Fauvel, patting his neck and feeding him a small apple from her pocket.

"Be good," she told him, untying his halter to let him roam free for the afternoon.

"He is very easy with you now," observed Angus, watching from a safe distance.

"Aye," she agreed, evasively, watching the chestnut horse trot away to a patch of lush grass. Once there, he bent his front legs and laid down on the ground, kicking his white legs up into the air as he rolled.

Morwenna felt her face break into a smile. She risked a glance at Angus to see he was also smiling. Fauvel snorted and rolled again.

"He is carefree and happy," Angus said.

She nodded. "Like a young foal."

He chuckled. "Exactly that. As I said before, you have given him a second chance."

She pursed her lips. "Mayhap he has given himself a second chance by allowing himself to trust again."

His eyes met hers, approvingly. "Your words are wise indeed."

Morwenna did not confess that wisdom was not the guiding force behind her musings. Nor was it her experience with troubled horses. Nay, on this occasion, it was personal experience.

She was on the cusp of allowing herself to fully trust again. Perchance, on the cusp of her own second chance.

Warmed by their exchange, Morwenna walked through the gate and fastened it securely behind Angus. The two grey horses waited expectantly in the next paddock, ears pricked towards them.

"Are these to be our steeds?" Angus asked.

"You've guessed correctly."

Morwenna walked up to the horses, talking gently and allowing them to breathe over her outstretched palms.

Angus looked confused. "Where are the grooms with our saddles?"

She tutted again. "For one so intent on quiet pleasures, you are surprisingly determined to make a public show."

He considered her words while reaching over to pat both of the grey horses. "You're right," he said eventually. "Though I have ne'er considered it before." He pulled a face, seemingly addressing the horses as well as Morwenna. "My life is lived in full public view."

Despite herself, she knew a moment of sympathy. "Mayhap that is why the notion of quiet pleasures is so strange to you."

"Mayhap," he smiled again, turning so she experienced the full dazzling effect of his charms. "I am your willing apprentice."

Morwenna was already reaching for the horses' tack, which she had piled neatly by the gate.

His gaze went over the fence. "Which of these fine horses did you have in mind for me?"

She couldn't help a giggle as she slipped a bridle onto the nearest. "I shall let you choose. However, before we mount, we must first get them ready."

He frowned, but beneath his lowered brows, his eyes danced playfully. "Do you believe that I have never before saddled a horse?"

She put her hands on her hips and turned to face him. "When was the last time?"

He made a show of pretending to think. "In truth, I cannot remember. However, it is a skill I have not forgotten." He bent to retrieve a saddle and positioned it onto his horse's back with unquestionable proficiency. "See?" he asked pointedly. "Can you find fault with my work?"

"Not at the moment." She hid her smile. "How will you fare

without a mounting block?"

He paused in the process of fastening the girth. "Do I take it, Morwenna, that you doubt my ability to mount a horse without one?"

"Without a mounting block, without a groom, without a long line of servants anticipating your every move," she teased, patting her horse's strong neck.

"I tire of it all," Angus announced. "Mayhap from this day forward, I shall live my life on a simpler footing."

"I bid you not to speak too hastily, my lord. Not until you have tasted the food I brought with me."

"Wise words indeed." He ducked under the fence and looked consideringly at the waiting horses. "This one I think."

Before Morwenna could react, the earl placed one hand on the horse's withers and then jumped with surprising grace onto his back. The horse started a little, but soon dropped his head and stood comfortably, untroubled by the experience.

Angus threaded the reins through his hands and pursed his lips at Morwenna. "Are you not coming?"

"I was not expecting that," she admitted, unable to hide her smile.

"I like to believe I am a man full of surprises."

She could not respond for a swell of some unfamiliar emotion was rising inside her. It was happiness, she realised. The likes of which she had not known for many years.

She guided the second horse alongside the fence, which she climbed before mounting with slow dignity.

"Boring," Angus chided, wrapping his long legs around his horse's sides and urging him into a trot.

"Effective," she countered, reaching for the reins and patting her horse reassuringly. "It is not a race," she declared primly.

"And where's the fun in that?" He grinned wickedly over his shoulder.

"We're here for quiet pleasures," she reminded him. "Not competition and spectacle."

"You're right," he agreed, eyes still dancing as she drew up close. "And I have already acquiesced to the pleasures of a simpler life. But there's no simpler pleasure than galloping over a field, do you deny that, Morwenna?"

She couldn't deny it.

All of a sudden, she was surrounded by memories of childhood. Long, happy days spent outside and the pure adrenaline-fuelled joy of galloping one of Farmer Jerome's horses over the fields for the sheer thrill of it.

Mayhap she had grown too accustomed to turning her back on thrills.

"What are we waiting for?" she cried, pointing her horse towards the distant woodland and giving him a sharp squeeze with her heels.

With a whoop of delight, Angus was close behind her. The two horses broke into steady canters, extending their strides when urged on by their riders. At first Morwenna was conscious of the uneven ground and the unfamiliar mount, but then she decided to put her worries to one side and simply enjoy the moment.

From the thundering of hooves at her rear, she knew Angus was still seated and gunning for victory. But she was just ahead. Out of nowhere, Morwenna was seized with a desire to win this impromptu and most likely foolhardy race. She wanted to prove – to herself as well as the earl – that she was still young, still capable of having fun.

A copse of holly stood before the first line of trees denoting the woods. Morwenna fixed her eyes upon it, holding the horse steady with her thighs and her voice until they had barrelled past it. Then she straightened her back and gently pulled back on the reins.

"I won," she declared breathlessly, looking back to see Angus pulling up a little behind her.

"I let you." He winked, reaching down to clap a large hand on his horse's neck.

"You did not." She was indignant. But when Angus broke into a low chuckle, she realised he was merely jesting. "You did well," she allowed.

"Praise indeed." He rode up beside her, only slightly out of breath.

"For an earl," she added.

He raised his bushy eyebrows and clutched a hand to his heart. "Forsooth, Miss Morwenna, you wound me."

They rode companionably along a wide woodland path, weaving between majestic oak trees with leaves turning red and gold above their heads. Birds called melodiously from high branches and the horses ambled slowly, content to catch their breath after their burst of speed.

"This is nice," commented Angus.

She flushed with pleasure, glad of the distraction of a small stony slope so he wouldn't see how much his praise pleased her.

"There is a shady spot by the river where we can stop and eat."

"Good." He flashed her a grin. "I'm ravenous."

Morwenna's heart beat faster as the horses came side-by-side and Angus's lower legs pressed against her own. Heat from the horses drifted upwards so she felt suffused with a heavy, languid warmth. It intoxicated her, lending the scene an edge of unreality. Morwenna wondered if she might even be dreaming. Surely, she wasn't alone in the woods with the Earl of Wolvesley? The colours were too bright, the sun too strong, the woods seemingly waiting to welcome them. None of this could be real. And if it wasn't real, why should the usual rules apply?

"I'm curious," he continued, breaking the spell of her wandering thoughts. "What exactly do we have in the way of food?"

His mundane obsession made her chuckle. "Wait and see."

"You're a very hard taskmaster," he grumbled.

"We're here." She drew her horse to a halt and sprung off before unfastening the saddlebag.

Angus tutted. "You should have let me take that."

"Admit it." She held his eye. "You'd forgotten all about it, hadn't you?"

He held his hands up in an admission of guilt, swinging one leg over the horse's neck and jumping lightly to the ground. "I'm very much new to all of this. You'll have to allow me one or two mistakes."

"Well, that was the first." She looped the reins over some branches and picked up the saddlebag.

"Allow me?" He held out his hands and she passed it to him with a smile.

"That's better."

"Thank you." He gave a mock bow.

Giggling, she led the way down a natural staircase of long, flat stones to a grassy glade beside a small, gurgling stream. Buzzing insects darted for food and birds called from the golden-hued trees. It was the perfect spot for basking in rare autumn sunshine.

"Beautiful," said Angus.

Morwenna folded her arms, forcing herself to be still and enjoy the surroundings. "It is."

"Nay," he said quietly. "I meant you."

"Oh." Heat rushed to her cheeks all over again as she became newly aware of her masculine attire. "Don't embarrass me," she begged.

"I am only telling the truth."

In two strides he crossed the clearing and stood by her side. Tall and broad and warm. She breathed him in, knowing it would be the easiest thing in the world to reach out for him and tilt her face upwards for his kiss.

A kiss she would freely give. If only he would take it.

The Earl of Wolvesley had said he could not kiss her again. But by the rules of the game they were playing, this was not the Earl of Wolvesley.

"Are you still following orders?" she asked, her voice full and throaty.

He only hesitated for a second. "I am."

Her heart threatened to jump out of her chest. "Then kiss me," she whispered.

In no time at all, his warm hands were around her waist, drawing her closer. Then came his lips, soft and gentle. His kisses were like butterflies at the corner of her mouth. She breathed out heavily, stepping closer in the circle of his embrace, wanting more. Angus stroked a hand down her spine and rested it on the curve of her hip. With the other, he cupped her chin, holding her steady.

"Is this what you want?" he breathed.

Nay, it was not enough. Any hesitation burned away in the flames of their connection. Her reply was to stand on her tiptoes and claim his mouth with her own. She experienced a fierce rush of energy as the tip of his tongue touched hers, then all rational thought deserted her as she wrapped her fingers in his golden hair. Angus pulled her against him, more roughly now, then lifted her so her head came level with his. She opened her eyes to meet his blue gaze.

"Don't stop," she whispered, even though commonsense dictated they must.

But this moment would likely never be repeated. Morwenna would take what she could. The memories might have to last her a lifetime.

He burrowed his face into the softness of her neck, as if seeking to prolong a pleasure he knew must come to an end. Acting purely on instinct, Morwenna wrapped her legs around his waist, drawing her whole body closer to his. She gasped out loud as she encountered the muscular hardness of his chest, and the hardness of something else pressing below.

There it was. Proof he wanted her just as much as she wanted him.

"We must stop," he said raggedly.

"No." She was determined now. Her hands roamed his face down to his shoulders, slipping beneath the thin shirt.

"Morwenna." He spoke her name pleadingly.

Morwenna didn't hesitate to consider what he was pleading for. Her hands were on a journey of exploration over his warm skin and taut muscles. Another button pinged off his shirt and she dropped her lips to his bare shoulder. But no sooner had her lips met his golden flesh, and her nostrils inhaled his distinctive masculine aroma, then he was carrying her over to the shade of a towering oak tree, where he laid her gently in the soft grass.

"My turn," he said.

One of his hands stroked back her hair while the other danced across her tunic. Angus made short work of unlacing the front and she gasped as the rich fabric fell away. Desire such as she had never known pooled inside her as she wrapped her fingers in his hair and pulled him against her; her body writhing with passion as he gently kissed and suckled.

But it still wasn't enough. She tugged again at his thin shirt, delighted when it fell away and her hands could roam freely over his body. Angus groaned, the sound coming from deep inside him.

"I shall not be able to hold back," he said into her ear.

"I don't want you to hold back."

He leaned on one elbow and rose above her, tracing a hand over her jutting breasts. He bent his head for another kiss as his hand travelled lower, skimming beneath the waist of her braccae and increasing her desperate need for him.

"Angus," she said, her voice pleading now.

His breath was warm against her cheek. His hand moved delicately between her legs, first finding her curls and circling slowly, then, when she thought she might explode with wanting, sliding inside her.

She gasped and reared against him, pleasure coming over her in waves which made her hips lift and her mouth fall open. He kissed her softly, nibbling gently at her lips before returning to her breasts, all the while stroking her core with infinite gentleness. She felt herself opening up to receive him as the energy built inside her.

"Don't stop," she begged.

He didn't stop until long after her pleasure peaked and she bucked against him, crying out with her mouth pressed into his chest.

"Beautiful, beautiful," he murmured as her breathing finally slowed and her sharp waves of delight softened into a tingling warmth.

She opened her eyes, blinking as his handsome face came back into focus. He smiled softly, still dropping gentle kisses onto her cheeks.

"I don't know what to say."

She rolled onto her side and immediately he pulled her against him, soothing the first twinges of awkwardness with his warm hands and calm certitude.

"You don't have to say anything," he whispered.

That was good. Tension flowed away from her as she tuned into the regular rhythm of his breathing, his heart beating steadily just inches from her ear.

"But you could do something for me," he added after a long while.

Startled, she looked up into his eyes. "What?"

He grinned. "Tell me what we have to eat. Or better yet, allow me to fetch it."

Morwenna couldn't help breaking into a laugh. "You can fetch it. I left the saddlebag just over there."

She hastily made herself decent as Angus rose up in search of food, his long limbs moving as gracefully as an acrobat and his golden hair reflecting back the rays of the afternoon sun.

Morwenna tightened her lips, knowledge sliding into her like a blade.

Her tentative feelings for Angus were blossoming into something else entirely.

Which meant that the trouble she had been in when she first arrived in Wolvesley, was nothing to the trouble she was facing now.

She had played with fire and now she had lost her humble heart to one of the wealthiest men in England.

Chapter Fifteen

A NGUS FISHED INSIDE the cracked leather saddlebag and encountered several lumpy packages which he brought out and laid on the grass. Morwenna had re-tied her tunic, more was the pity, and a pinched look had come over her pretty features.

"Do you regret what we have done?" he asked her bluntly, never one to beat about the bush.

She smiled faintly. "Not in the way you might imagine." She folded her arms across her chest in a protective gesture.

"Then how?" He sank to the ground beside her and put a hand on her knee. He would offer her all the comfort in the world if he knew what ailed her.

She nibbled on her lower lip, not knowing how the gesture affected him. "There are moments when we are together that I forget you are an earl. Then the moment ends, and I remember."

He found himself staring at her open-mouthed. He had not expected that.

Morwenna shrugged and busied herself unwrapping the longest of the oilskin packages to reveal a rough hunk of bread. With capable hands, she tore it in half and held one half out to him. He sniffed cautiously, but his rumbling stomach would gladly accept anything.

Exhaling heavily, he bit into it. "Would you prefer that I was not an earl?" he asked, chewing ruminatively. The bread was surprisingly tasty.

She answered quickly. "Of course."

Of all that had passed between them, this was the most surprising. Angus swallowed hard and turned to look at her. "Is that the truth?"

"Aye." Her green eyes flashed in puzzlement. "Why should you doubt it?"

He put the bread down, no longer interested in food. His hands shook as if he had taken a fever. He cleared his throat, needing to be sure. "You would take me as I am now? In these poor rags, with nothing to offer?"

She nodded, her face still a picture of bewilderment. "Then we would be equals. We could build a life together." She also placed her uneaten bread down on the grass and grasped a white leather cuff worn around her left wrist. The fingers of her right hand traced the pattern engraved into the leather, as if they had done so a thousand times.

"A future?" He wanted to be sure of her meaning.

Her cheeks tinged with pink. "Aye, a future. Though 'tis bold of me to picture such a prospect."

"And you would like a future with me? Even one without the wealth of Wolvesley?"

Morwenna shook her head at him so her blonde plait fell over one narrow shoulder. "Look at me, Angus. Do I appear to you as a woman who needs wealth to make her happy? Nay," she answered her own question. "Coin enough for food and shelter. That is all a body needs." Her conviction flowed through her voice.

He took up the bread again and began breaking it into pieces, needing a distraction. "I do not believe that everyone thinks as you do."

She shrugged. "My grandmother used to say that people with great riches don't know the true value of them. But the folk working the fields, they do."

"Your grandmother with the Sight?" he queried, noting how her voice broke when she spoke of her.

She nodded. "The only family I ever really knew."

"I'm sorry."

They sat in silence for a while. Angus finished the bread and discovered two rosy-red apples in another package. The fruit was sweet and juicy, almost as good as a dish served in the great hall. Such a swirl of emotions fought inside him as he ate. Memories stirred from his youth and mingled with a dull longing for what could never be.

Here was honesty. A relationship of equals indeed, when it came to what was in their hearts and their minds. But not when either name or rank was considered. For this brief moment in time, he had taken the great risk of disguising himself so that he and Morwenna may spend a few stolen hours together. But this escapade could not be repeated. The risks were too great, for both of them.

"Ah, Morwenna," he sighed. "You don't know how much I too wish things were different." He meant it with every fibre of his body. He could so easily take this wondrous young woman again into his arms and profess feelings for her that were entirely honest and true. He would cherish her, protect her, worship her with his body.

And in so doing, risk her ruin.

It could not be.

He was an earl and must marry accordingly. Not only that; he was an earl who had long been betrothed to another.

Angus swallowed the last of his apple and flung the core into the stream. The mid-afternoon sun was hidden behind the tall trees and their golden-hued glade was now cast into shadow. He was conscious of a creeping chill; of the horses grazing nearby and the need to return to the castle before he was missed.

"But I can tell you this," he spoke up. "Your grandmother sounds like a wise woman, but not all poor people understand the true value of things as she did. I once knew a girl..." His voice broke off. He had not intended to share this memory, but when he was with Morwenna, somehow he found himself airing his proper feelings, however long he'd been keeping them under wraps.

But will she want to hear this?

She leaned over and touched his hand. "Go on."

He took a breath. "Johanna, she was called. Her father was the tanner in the village. We played together as children. I thought she was wonderful." His eyes flickered over to Morwenna and saw her watching intently. "Wild and wonderful. I was very young," he added, making sure she knew. "This was all a long time ago."

"What happened?" Morwenna bit into her apple and fixed her gaze on the stream.

"We planned to elope." His voice shook with the echo of laughter and the remembered daring of youth. "Lucan was earl by then and I knew he wouldn't approve. But I told Johanna that I didn't need my brother's blessing. That we could do well without his coin or his castle. I thought we could ride off together and start a new life somewhere." He fell silent.

"And?" she prompted, turning to face him.

"And it turned out that what Johanna in fact wanted was to be aligned to the Earl of Wolvesley, not to be the wife of a poor, disinherited labourer." Angus smiled at Morwenna's shocked face. "She was most probably right. After all, I would have a lot to learn as a labourer."

Morwenna let out a short laugh. "What became of Johanna?"

"She turned her sights elsewhere. I believe she is now married to a publican who runs an inn on the road to York. They make good business and mayhap enough coin to satisfy her." He pulled a face. "Mayhap we both had a lucky escape."

He saw the moment the gaiety left Morwenna's face. "I am not the same as Johanna."

"Not in any way," he agreed softly, reaching out to grasp her wrist. "And it is a great gift that you have given me."

Morwenna tossed what was left of her apple into the stream with a good, strong aim. "What gift?"

He fumbled for the words. "That you would choose to spend this time with Angus the man. Not Angus the earl."

Sighing, she interlinked their fingers. "You are one and the same."

"But if we were not?"

She tilted her face up towards him, a smile playing around her pink lips. "Then I fancy we might do this again."

The jolt of elation he felt upon hearing her words was instantly subdued by the knowledge they were both weaving a fantasy. Dreaming of a future that could never be theirs. He would insult neither Morwenna nor his future wife by taking a mistress. And he could not marry a horse trainer – however skilled or beautiful she may be.

But he didn't want to let go of her hands. He didn't want to ride back to the castle and return to reality.

"Cruel fate," he said.

"Fate brought us together."

"It did. And I will never forget this day." He pushed down a wave of sorrow, determined to commit every detail of the afternoon to his memory. The soft breeze playing with Morwenna's pale blonde hair; the sincerity in her green eyes; the slenderness of her wrist and the surprising intricacy of the engraving in her leather cuff. He looked more closely at the bracelet. "What is this?"

"It belonged to my grandmother."

Angus blinked, not sure if his eyes were playing tricks on him. Their meeting had been so charged with emotion; mayhap he was seeing things that were not there? But no, the pattern on the cuff was familiar to him.

"What was your grandmother's name?"

She startled at his abrupt tone. "It was Esme."

"Lady Esme of Ember Hall?" His voice sounded strangled, as if all the air was being pushed out of his lungs.

Morwenna let out a peal of laughter. "My grandmother was hardly a lady. I think I should have noticed that."

Angus felt his heart beating hollowly in his ribs. "But she had the Sight?" he whispered.

"Yes, I told you already." Morwenna tried to pull her hands away but he held them tight. "Angus, what's going on?"

"This is the Ember coat of arms."

She successfully wrestled free of his grasp and peered more closely at her wrist. "It's just a pretty pattern."

"Nay." Angus stood up, the muscles in his legs feeling tired and cramped. "I would recognise it anywhere." He held out a hand and pulled her upright, for now uncaring of the panic in her eyes. "Morwenna, we need to go and see my mother."

THEIR RIDE BACK to the castle was, if anything, faster than their ride away from it, but Morwenna was no longer the one in control. The earl led them both, needing no spurs to urge on his horse who instantly picked up on the urgency.

An urgency which left her head spinning with unanswered questions.

Angus had claimed the pattern on the cuff was a coat of arms, but Morwenna did not see how this could be true. Her grandmother had been no titled lady but she *had* been a woman of principle; she never would have taken anything that did not belong to her.

Perchance she had once been in service to this house that Angus spoke of, with the cuff presented to her as a gift. But Esme had never mentioned anything of the sort. And she had treated the cuff as if it was something personally precious, more than a token from an employer.

In truth, Morwenna couldn't think of any time when Esme had explained how she came to own such an exquisite item. Was that odd? Maybe she should have asked more questions.

But Esme had rivers of reserve running through her and Morwenna had learned from an early age that there were limits to how much she would share. She'd always assumed memories of the past caused her beloved grandmother too much pain.

She tightened her lips as the landscape whipped by. There was no mystery here.

The cuff had simply always been a part of her life. Her grandmother had worn it constantly; pressing it into Morwenna's hand only when her frail body no longer had the strength to get out of her narrow pallet bed.

And if Angus – *if anyone* – thought they could take it from her, they would soon learn otherwise.

Angus rode directly to the stable yard and dismounted on the cobbles, handing his reins to a young groom who had the misfortune to be present. Morwenna sent up thanks that they weren't greeted by Gerrault or Isaac, for she couldn't have withstood the scrutiny, nor the inevitable barrage of questions afterwards.

"Can I help you?" stammered the boy, mayhap unable to reconcile this newcomer's unkempt appearance with his regal bearing. His eyes then moved to Morwenna, who he recognised at once.

Morwenna held his eye and gave a slight shake of her head. The last thing any of them wanted was a scene.

Angus straightened his shoulders, looming over the boy, but instead of explaining he merely held out a hand towards Morwenna.

"Come," he said.

Not an invitation, *an order.*

She dismounted on legs that threatened to give way beneath her, but she managed to summon a smile as she held over the reins to the young groom. She had seen him once or twice in the eating hall and had no doubt he knew exactly who she was. Had he recognised the earl? She must hope not, else word of this would spread throughout the stable yard by the time she returned.

If she returned.

Her position at Wolvesley had withstood witchcraft and

attempted theft. Perchance all would be undone by her grand-mother's cuff.

Angus barely waited for her to reach his side before he set off, striding beneath the archway and into the immaculately-kept courtyard. Morwenna scurried after him, unable to spare a glance towards either the imposing stone lions nor the splashing fountain as his long stride ate up the ground.

"Angus, please," she gasped, as they hurried up the steps to the keep. "I don't understand what is happening."

He turned his deep blue eyes upon her. Those eyes had looked at her with kindness, connection and passion just hours earlier, but now that warmth had been replaced by a searing urgency.

"You have no reason to be concerned."

Small comfort indeed.

He set off again, his shabby clothing striking a discordant note amongst so much marbled grandeur. And yet, their presence was not challenged. Neither guard nor footman barred their path, nor even looked askance at them. It was because of the earl's commanding presence, Morwenna realised. The clothing of a peasant could do nothing to dim his natural air of authority.

When they reached the stairway, he stood aside to let her pass.

"After you," he said, curtly.

Was that his good manners? Or a desire to keep her where he could see her?

She preceded him up the stairs, one hand trailing on the pol-ished dark wood banister to keep her balance. Her sense of bewilderment increased with every step Additionally, she was conscious of damp and grass stains on her tunic, from where she had lain in the grass. And she had no idea if she had tied her laces correctly; not having recourse to any kind of looking glass.

This was not how she would choose to enter Wolvesley Castle.

High windows together with well-spaced wall torches lit the

upper storey of the keep. Angus urged her along a spacious gallery which overlooked the entrance hall, and then down a narrower passageway. The apprehension building inside her reached new heights as she realised they were heading towards a doorway at the end of this corridor.

She paused again, desperate to ask Angus again why it was so imperative they visit the dowager countess right away, but one look back at his grim-set face sent all her intentions into dust. He reached past her and knocked brusquely on the door, not waiting for an answer before he turned the handle.

Morwenna's first impression was of a blaze of light; so intense after the shadows of the passageway that she had to blink until her eyes adjusted. Ahead of her, Angus was talking, but Morwenna was so overwhelmed she couldn't tune into the words. She was both curious and terrified. Violetta de Neville was spoken of with warmth and respect by the men in the yard; but what on earth would the dowager Countess of Wolvesley make of her son's strange appearance and even stranger companion?

She leaned against the panelled door for support, trying to steady her breathing and summon the resilience required for this challenging turn of events.

"Angus?" she heard a high-pitched, cultured voice saying sternly. "Where are your manners? Pray do not leave this young woman standing alone in the doorway."

Morwenna opened her mouth to demur, but no sound came out. Her head spun and her stomach churned, but then she felt Angus's warm fingers wrap around her wrist.

"Come in, Morwenna," he said, impatience flickering across his face.

"My boots," she faltered, cringing at the notion of her muddy boots dirtying the finely embroidered rugs on the floor.

"To hell with your boots," Angus muttered.

"Angus!" His mother's voice was loud with admonishment.

"We have much to discuss, Mother."

"No doubt we have. But first, pour your companion a

draught of wine."

Wine was the last thing Morwenna wanted. It would muddle her thoughts which were already scattered and confused. But it would be rude to refuse. Perhaps she could merely sip at it. Angus ushered her towards a tapestried couch, and she sank to the edge of it, darting quick looks around her.

What she saw was less than reassuring. Violetta de Neville stood some feet away, regally attired in a rich green gown. Her long white hair was neatly pinned up. Her blue eyes as sharp and piercing as her son's. And those eyes were fixed on Morwenna's leather cuff.

"You see what I mean?" Angus asked, walking back towards the couch with a silver goblet of wine in one hand.

His mother silenced him with a slight shake of her head.

"No more until her cheeks have more colour in them. I have no wish to summon the physician. That man has already exhausted my patience once today."

Angus pulled up a short stool and perched beside the cot, holding out the wine to Morwenna who took it with trembling hands.

"Drink," he urged.

Morwenna lowered her lips to the goblet. She intended to take only the smallest of sips, but the wine was sweet and rich and she found herself taking a long, restorative mouthful.

"Good," said Angus, and she finally found a flicker of *something* in his voice. "What is this about the physician?" He turned to his mother.

"Tsk, the man is a tiresome pest. Drink this. Don't drink that. Full of orders, when I believe after all these years, I have finally earned the right to do as I please." The dowager countess drew herself up to her full height, which wasn't much. "I shall outlive him, I'm sure of it."

Angus pressed his lips together, but Morwenna could tell he was suppressing a smile. "Well, it's good to see you out of bed, Mother."

She prodded her son with a manicured finger, jewels glinting from her hand. "Nothing ails me, Angus. Nothing but grief and the passage of time."

A cloud passed over his eyes, but he rose to his feet to fetch a cushioned chair from the corner. "Here, Mother. Take a seat."

"Thank you. For now, I would prefer to stand." Her blue gaze switched again to Morwenna who felt herself shrink backwards under the scrutiny. "Aren't you going to introduce us?"

"Mother, this is Morwenna. She has been training one of my horses. Morwenna, this is my mother, Lady Violetta, Dowager Countess of Wolvesley."

"I am pleased to meet you," Morwenna murmured. The air of unreality she had experienced down by the river was still wrapped around her.

"You too, my dear," the countess replied kindly.

Violetta linked her fingers together and took a few regal steps towards the high arched window, seemingly deep in thought as she gazed out over the castle gardens.

Morwenna almost fell off the couch in shock as she felt Angus's hand close over hers. "Have you finished with the wine?"

Further startled, she realised she had drained the goblet. "I have." She sat up straighter. "Mayhap you can tell me why I am here?"

Violetta swivelled around at her words, a smile playing around her lips. "I hear Esme's determination in your voice, my dear. You have her courage, as well as her green eyes."

This was the last thing Morwenna had expected to hear.

"You knew my grandmother?" she forced out.

"I knew her very well." Violetta crossed the room with small elegant steps and lowered herself onto the couch next to Morwenna, eschewing the more comfortable chair Angus had fetched for her.

Morwenna bit down on her lower lip, her mind reeling. "How?"

Violetta pressed a gnarled hand down onto Morwenna's, making her startle again. "Our families were close neighbours. Esme and I grew up together. Her parents, Lord and Lady Howell, took me in while my father was away fighting. Much later, when I first came to Wolvesley as a bride, Esme came with me."

"As a maid?"

"As a friend."

Morwenna used her free hand to rub her aching forehead. None of this made any sense. "But my grandmother was not a grand lady."

Violetta surprised her further by letting out a tinkling laugh. "Believe me, my dear, nor was I. My father was a mere knight; not even a favourite of the King. The Howells of Ember Hall seemed very grand to me back then."

The old lady's grip on her hand was warm and comforting. Strength flowed through her touch. Gradually, Morwenna felt her bewilderment lessen and her interest grow.

"And you recognise her cuff?" She held her wrist towards the dowager countess, no longer anxious that anyone would try to take it from her.

"May I?"

Morwenna nodded and Violetta placed her jewelled fingers on the leather bracelet, smiling softly as she traced the pattern.

"I would recognise the standard of Ember Hall anywhere. I spent many happy days there."

"Nay," Morwenna whispered, unable to reconcile these pieces of information with the life she had known. "There must be a mistake."

"Many mistakes." Violetta sighed deeply. "But not on this occasion. You are the granddaughter of one of my oldest friends."

"I can't be." Morwenna resisted the urge to snatch her hand away. "We lived a modest life, my grandmother and I. Nothing like this." She looked around the beautiful chamber, at the carved oak furniture, the fur rugs covering the floor and the bright frescoes on the plastered wall. How could her grandmother have left this magnificent place to end her days in a draughty wood hut on the edge of a poor village?

"I am sorry to learn she fell on hard times." Violetta's eyes glistened with unshed tears. "She left us in such difficult circumstances and I tried to find her afterwards, I really did. But I should have tried harder."

Morwenna found herself moved by the dowager countess's emotion. Those tears were real; so was the break in her voice.

"My grandmother came from a place called Ember Hall?" The words sounded strange in her mind, but even stranger voiced out loud. "And she once lived here, in Wolvesley Castle?"

Violetta took a breath. "Together with your mother."

Her *mother*.

This was too much. Her voice was a mere croak. "What about my grandfather?"

Violetta winced, before casting a glance towards her son who was hovering at the other side of the couch. "Fetch us more wine, if you please, Angus."

Morwenna wanted to refuse. If she drank more wine, she would be intoxicated. Mayhap unable to walk out of this chamber. And right now, she was filled with the desire to do exactly that. Get up and leave this woman who was taking everything she thought she knew about herself and turning it inside out.

Angus poured wine into three goblets and passed them around. Morwenna took hers silently, but didn't drink. Angus, however, drained his goblet in one gulp.

"You must tell her about the land," he said in an aside to his mother.

Violetta flapped her hand. "All in good time. People are more important than property." She turned again to Morwenna. "Your mother, Giselle, was born right here in this very room."

Morwenna was beyond words now. She sat limply while Angus paced up and down the chamber and Violetta told her strange tale.

"When I met Tristan, he was not the Earl of Wolvesley. Nor did he expect to become so. He was merely a cousin to the old earl, second heir after the earl's own son. I was a country lady. We married for love." She shrugged at the surprised expression on Morwenna's face. "And I was less than thrilled when our plans for a simple life together turned to dust, the day he inherited this title." Her sharp gaze softened as she looked towards the window. "Though it is true, I have been happy here." She held up a hand towards Angus as he moved to interrupt her. "I know, this is not my story, it is Esme's."

"I shall ring for some refreshments," Angus declared. "Morwenna looks in need of them."

Violetta tutted. "It is more likely the case that you are in need of them yourself. You think of nothing but your belly."

"That is not true." He grinned boyishly, making Morwenna's stomach flip. "It is not *always* true," he corrected, pulling down on a blue cord hanging near the fireplace.

"Esme was with child," Violetta said unexpectedly. "She was unmarried and she was with child," she added, making her meaning clear.

Despite her best intentions, Morwenna took another mouthful of wine. "I had guessed as much, long ago."

Violetta nodded. "The obvious solution was to bring Esme to Wolvesley, where no one knew her story. We let it be known that her husband had died. Giselle was born, and never was there a more lovely baby girl."

Morwenna leaned forward to place her goblet down on a side table before she drank too much. "Did you ever know my grandfather?" she asked quietly.

"I knew him." Violetta compressed her lips. "Your grandmother was a wise woman, but even wise women sometimes make mistakes." She paused. "He was not an honourable man."

Morwenna clutched her hands together to prevent them from shaking. "Was she unhappy?"

"For a while. Her parents were good people, but they could not see past her indiscretion," Violetta admitted. "But once Giselle had arrived, we looked only to the future. My son Lucan was born a few years later and the two of them grew up as close as siblings." She smiled in memory. "They were happy days."

Morwenna looked up at Angus, who was now standing by the window and looking out "Did you know my mother?"

He shook his head briefly. "I have some memories of Esme's daughter, but I didn't know her properly. There were more than ten summers between Lucan and I. Giselle was a young woman by the time I was born."

"A young woman with gifts," Violetta interjected, meaning stamped all over her face.

"Mother…"

"I must tell the story as it happened."

"What kind of gifts?" asked Morwenna, although she already knew the answer.

"It will come as no surprise when I say that Esme had the Sight?" Violetta looked quickly to Morwenna for confirmation. "Both of us, in fact, had some small ability." She paused and shot a look of pure steel at her looming son who looked poised to interrupt. "You must let me tell this tale in my own words, Angus."

Angus scratched at his beard, looking for all the world as if he wished he had never brought Morwenna here. "You should be more careful in what you say," he insisted.

"Morwenna is Esme's granddaughter. She will not be easily shocked."

Morwenna tried to speak up, to acknowledge the truth of this, but Angus did not seem willing to hear her. In the small time since Violetta had started telling her tale, their roles had reversed. Morwenna was now strangely calm, whilst Angus quivered with agitation.

"Mayhap. But there are others who may hear." He nodded towards the closed door and, as if to prove his prediction true, a knock sounded at the other side of the wood. With a warning look at his mother, Angus crossed the room and paused before the panel. "Don't say another word," he whispered.

Morwenna exchanged a glance with Violetta before fixing her eyes upon Angus. Whatever was about to happen now?

Chapter Sixteen

A NGUS OPENED THE panel and looked out, overly relieved to find two liveried servants each holding a silver tray of refreshments.

Of course. He had ordered refreshments himself just minutes earlier.

He tugged at his beard again, briefly wondering why the servants were looking at him so askance, seemingly frozen into place in their obscure tableau.

"My lord," one of them said, his brow clearing. He bowed as low as he could, the task made difficult by his laden tray.

"My lord," the other echoed.

Angus caught a glimpse of his grey coloured, worn braccae and suddenly their behaviour made sense. He had completely forgotten that he was still dressed as a peasant. He stood aside to let them through, waving apologetically at his mother.

"'Tis only the refreshments," he declared over his shoulder.

"Enough to feed our army." His mother raised her eyebrows as the servants jostled for space on the low table.

"Let me help." Morwenna sprung to her feet and swept away the empty goblets of wine. Angus folded his hands, aware of a pinprick of remorse. He should have gone to their aid afore Morwenna.

How was she to stop thinking of herself as a servant if he allowed her to act the part of one?

He surveyed the latest offering from the kitchens. Sugared

plums, honeyed figs, fruit scones, a platter of cold meat – artfully arranged. Plus three different types of cheese and a glass bowl of strawberries. His stomach rumbled in anticipation, but then he remembered the bread and apples he had feasted upon down by the river with Morwenna, and he thought that nothing would ever again taste so sweet.

"Eat," he urged both of them.

His mother's expression was indulgent. "Unlike you, I cannot eat at all hours of the day. If I partake of this impromptu feast I shall have no appetite for our evening meal."

"Morwenna?" He beckoned her forwards. "You must be hungry," he said, seeing her hesitate.

They had both ridden hard across the fields; that was what he meant. But when he saw Morwenna's blush, he realised she was thinking of the other ways they had worked up an appetite that afternoon. He popped a berry into his mouth to hide his smile.

"Mayhap I will take something small," she acquiesced.

"Take a scone," his mother advised. "They are my favourite."

Some of the tension in Morwenna's body eased as she chewed the sweet pastry. For a moment, they were three people enjoying afternoon tea. But there were things that Morwenna needed to know.

"You should return to your story, Mother," he declared, brushing crumbs from his shirt.

Morwenna looked stricken. "I should return to my duties."

He held up his hand. "You must stay." He bit back what he was about to say, that Morwenna would have to give up her lowly position in the stables.

"But the light is already fading and I must attend to Fauvel."

He opened his mouth to argue but his mother spoke first.

"I shall be quick." She laid a reassuring hand on Morwenna's shoulder, making Angus wish that he too could touch her so freely.

"Very well." Morwenna perched on the edge of the couch, her pale face looking strained all over again. Angus longed to take her fears away. She had no idea how much had changed, for her and mayhap for the both of them. If only his mother would hurry with her tale.

Violetta settled herself on the cushioned chair, leaving Angus to lower himself onto a small stool.

"You were speaking of Giselle," he prompted.

"Ah yes, Giselle." His mother rested her chin on her hand. "Had she lived in the time of our forefathers, she could have been a powerful priestess. As it was, her gifts were a continual source of worry for Esme. And for me also."

"How so?" Morwenna's voice was tight with apprehension.

"The small gifts I yield are not constant. My Sight comes and goes. It does not define me. Esme was much the same. We were both normal women, able to lead normal lives." She tightened her lips and looked directly at Angus. "I understand, my boy, that my actions recently have not been conducive to leading a normal life. I can only hazard a guess that during these weeks of mourning I have received such strong visions as Giselle was wont to experience all the time. So vivid and so affecting that one cannot keep them under wraps." She blinked away the tears shining in her eyes, showing with a brief shake of her head that she did not require assistance or sympathy from him. She cleared her throat and continued. "Giselle had tremendous power, even as a small child. She could talk to spirits and predict the future, always with uncanny accuracy." His mother paused and an expression of pain washed over her. "Even when the future was not something one wanted to hear about."

Angus leaned forward, drawn into the tale. He had not anticipated such detail. Morwenna was listening closely too, her face rapt with attention.

"Giselle predicted your father's illness, but could do naught to avert it."

"I didn't know that." He was moved to lay a hand over his mother's. "It must have been a difficult time."

"A terrible time. But things were about to become so much

worse." His mother took a breath. "Giselle's Sight couldn't be hidden. It was an open secret in Wolvesley. The servants used to come to her quite often for advice or to speak to those they had lost. We had no fear for her, because she had the protection of Tristan. And none would dare move against the mighty Earl of Wolvesley."

Angus held his breath, his mind racing to join the snatches of information and memories he had from this time.

"But then the witch hunts started?" he guessed, causing Morwenna to flinch.

His mother nodded. "A frenzy of fear spread across the North. And Wolvesley was not immune. Especially when Tristan's health began to fail."

"Lucan was still a boy," Angus interjected.

"He had just sixteen years when his father passed." His mother put a hand to her heart as if the memory still pained her. "He was young. And it left us vulnerable." She flicked her blue eyes to Angus. "Do you remember what happened in the village?"

He nodded, nausea twisting in his stomach as he recalled the old woman wrongly accused of murder. "The burning."

Morwenna let out an exclamation of shock and clasped a hand in front of her mouth.

"I'm sorry," he said, turning in his seat towards her. If only he could take her in his arms.

"It was not your doing, Angus," his mother said, her voice steely. "And it was not mine. Nor was it Lucan's. Your brother tried everything he could to restore order, but the judiciary was a weak-willed man, too keen to give in to the mob."

"But Lucan gained control in the end, didn't he?" Angus had always beheld his elder brother as all-powerful. This image of a young man out of his depth did not sit easily with him.

"Aye, he did," his mother said heavily. "But by then it was too late. Esme had already fled from here, taking Giselle with her. I begged her to stay, but she feared for Giselle's life. And she did not want to bring further trouble to our family." She shook her head, as if clearing it of terrible memories. "Esme and I had been careful to remain above suspicion, but if Giselle was publicly accused of witchcraft, it would only be a matter of time before we were considered guilty by association."

The chamber fell into silence at this. No sound from outside could permeate the thick stone walls and the three of them were lost in their own thoughts for a long while. The next person to speak was Morwenna.

"What happened to my mother and grandmother after they left?"

Violetta turned anguished eyes towards her. "That I don't know, my dear. My story ends here." She clutched her hands together in distress. "I tried to trace Esme. I tried to get a message to her, to tell her that everything had settled down and she could come home. Over the years, I have tried many times. But no one could ever find her."

Morwenna bit her lip, her eyes overly bright. "Your messengers mayhap did not look for her amongst the poor folk of Escafeld."

His mother dropped her gaze. "That I cannot say." She fished for a handkerchief and pressed the embroidered fabric to her eyes. "Pray, may I ask you, what happened to Giselle?"

Morwenna cleared her throat. "I never knew her. My grandmother told me she did not survive childbirth."

"And your father?" Violetta asked softly.

"They were married less than a year. He died in an accident bringing in the harvest." Morwenna's voice became quieter. "His leg was cut with a scythe and infection set in. Even my grandmother could not save him."

"Oh, my dear." Violetta pressed the handkerchief to her eyes once more.

Frustration was building up inside Angus. He wanted to help but knew not how. In the end, he stood and edged around the table, which was still littered with the detritus of their refreshments. But standing, he was overly conscious of how he loomed over the seated ladies. Despite his power and wealth, in that moment he felt strangely impotent. He wandered over to the window and gazed unseeingly out at the darkening lawns.

He had brought Morwenna to his mother to see if his wild suspicion was correct. Such euphoria had filled his heart when he first glimpsed the familiar outline of the Ember coat of arms. If it meant what he thought it meant… then there was a possibility for he and Morwenna to be together.

As the granddaughter of Lady Esme of Ember Hall, no longer would Morwenna be a servant in his employ. Down by the river, with the memory of her sweet body still imprinted on his fingertips, this singular fact had blossomed heavily with significance and meaning. But now he saw that there was so much more he hadn't considered.

Her personal history. Her sense of self. His own mother's feelings. *Everything.*

But still, the most important part of the story was yet to be told.

He cleared his throat. "We have items that belong to you, Morwenna."

His mother spoke up. "Yes, my dear. Personal possessions of your grandmother's. I shall look them out for you. They should be yours."

Angus frowned heavily. He was not talking of mere personal possessions. But when he turned to face the women, he saw his mother shaking her head at him and Morwenna blinking away tears. His flare of impatience drained away.

"There is no hurry, I suppose."

"No indeed." Violetta put a comforting arm around Morwenna's shoulders. "I can only imagine how you are feeling, Morwenna. It must be a lot to take in."

Morwenna nodded shakily and Angus knew another wave of frustration, but this time it was because convention prevented him from going down on his knees in front of her and taking her in a strong, comforting embrace.

His mother said quietly, "I should like to hear the end of the story, as you know it, one day. If it will not pain you too much."

Morwenna swallowed. "My tale ends in sorrow, my lady. My beloved grandmother passed from this world last winter."

Violetta's intake of breath was sharp, but she remained still and composed. "I had feared as much," she said.

"There is comfort in knowing she did not suffer overly long."

Violetta passed her a fresh handkerchief and Morwenna dabbed her eyes. Angus folded his arms, his mind searching for a way he could offer assistance. All at once, he grasped it.

"Night is falling," he declared, his voice too loud after the quiet confidences of the chamber. "You stay here, Morwenna. I shall go myself and see to Fauvel." He strode to the door, pleased to be releasing so much pent-up energy.

But Morwenna shook her head and rose to her feet. "Nay." Her voice was strong. "It is my job to take care of Fauvel. I shall take my leave."

Angus shot his mother a look. She needed to tell Morwenna that she had no further cause to continue paid employment. That she was their guest now; no longer their servant. But Violetta only stood up slowly and took Morwenna's hands in her own.

"You will come on the morrow? Or the next day? Whenever you are ready?" There was an unfamiliar catch in her voice. "I should like to hear more about your childhood with Esme."

Morwenna nodded, but Angus could see her desire to leave writ large across her face. "I will."

"Bless you, my dear," Violetta said. "I am mighty glad we have found you."

"Thank you." Morwenna dropped into a small curtsy, the sight of which made Angus bristle with impatience all over again. "My lord," she whispered, taking her leave.

He longed to say something, anything, to delay her departure. But in less than a moment, Morwenna had slipped past him and disappeared from the chamber.

No sooner had the door closed behind her than he turned on

his mother.

"Why didn't you tell her?"

Violetta walked unsteadily over to the window and leaned upon the ledge, looking out. "Whatever do you mean?"

"About the house, Ember Hall. And the land. It is all rightfully hers."

"Of course." Violetta raised her watery blue eyes towards him and with a wrench he saw they were filled with tears. "Do you think I intend to keep them from her?"

He scratched at his beard. "I don't understand why you didn't just tell her? Morwenna is a woman of means and she is out there, right now, rubbing down my horse." Again, a terrible feeling of impotence washed over him.

Violetta's look turned sharp. "I would guess that fact bothers you more than it bothers her. It is more likely the familiarity of the work will bring her some peace."

The validity of her insight stung him, but did not abate his frustration. "It is not right to allow the granddaughter of your closest friend to sleep in a loft above the stables."

He had hoped to shock her, but saw at once he had failed.

Violetta shook her head slowly, as if he were the one who did not understand the situation. "What would you have preferred? Should she have dined with us in the great hall?"

"Aye," he ground out, teeth clenched together. That could have marked the transition from Morwenna being a servant he should not claim, to a lady sitting in her rightful place—by his side.

"Dressed in her groom's livery?"

"You could have found her something more suitable."

Violetta's gaze held him like a rabbit caught in a trap. "You're right, of course. I could have lent her a gown. We are not dissimilar in height or weight. And then that poor young woman could have sat with us on the dais, for all of Wolvesley to see and judge. She would have been quite comfortable there, I'm sure."

Angus sank down onto the cushioned chair and rested his

forehead on his hands. "Mayhap that would not have been for the best."

"Mayhap not. You saw for yourself how she could not wait to get away." Violetta was still looking at him searchingly.

"What is it?"

She came to sit beside him on the couch, her long skirts rustling. "Two things, Angus, that I must say as your mother."

"I am listening," he said, feigning patience.

She put a jewelled hand upon his knee. "Firstly, you must learn to look beneath the surface of things. Life is not all about a public show."

This was so close to Morwenna's earlier comments about putting on a spectacle that Angus was rendered momentarily speechless.

"And the second?" he managed.

She put her head to one side, watching his reaction. "Tread carefully with Morwenna."

"Whatever do you mean?" He all but jumped up from the chair.

"Only that I can tell the girl means something to you." She held up a hand to ward off his denial. "I am not suggesting anything improper has occurred. I hope I know you better than that."

"Nothing has happened."

A half-truth.

She surprised him by leaning closer and resting her hand over his heart. He could feel the warmth of her touch through the thin fabric of his shirt. "I believe a great deal may have happened in here." Violetta leaned back and straightened her shoulders. "I will remind you of point number one."

Angus sighed. "There is little I can say, save that my intentions towards Morwenna are entirely honourable." He got to his feet, unable to sit still while such emotions surged within him. "But how can I proceed when she does not yet know that she is a woman of means?"

"You can't," Violetta answered swiftly. "Because, believe it or not my dear boy, you are not the most important person in this. Morwenna has had a shock. Telling her everything in one sitting would overwhelm her entirely."

He scratched at his beard, pacing from the unlit fireplace to the darkening window. Soon the servants would be coming in to light the candles.

He hated to admit that his mother was right.

Furthermore, what the dowager Countess of Wolvesley had the grace *not* to say, was that he was still betrothed to another.

But for Angus, the greatest impediment towards his future happiness with Morwenna had already been cleared. He would take the necessary steps to break his understanding with Emelia. If he were a gambling man, he would wager that the lady would feel mostly relief at the end of their engagement.

"We don't even know what condition Ember Hall is in," Violetta continued, breaking into his thoughts. "When was it last inspected?"

Angus pulled at his beard, trying to remember. He had long been entrusted with the safekeeping of all Wolvesley property, but these last few months had disrupted his careful routines. "Perchance not since the end of winter."

"What point is there in raising the girl's hopes only to quash them if her family home has fallen into squalor and disrepair?"

"Then we must dispatch someone at once to find out."

"Indeed." Violetta smiled at him. "That is a much more sensible decision."

He was already walking towards the door. "I shall send a messenger, right away."

"Angus?"

He paused, one hand on the door handle. "Yes?"

"The first thing you should do is change out of those ridiculous clothes."

Chapter Seventeen

MORWENNA STAYED IN the circular paddock with Fauvel until long after nightfall. When the temperature dropped and she began to shiver, she crept inside the shelter and covered herself with the thin peasant's cloak which Angus had discarded earlier.

How could so much have happened in just one day?

She sat on an empty sack of oats and pulled her knees to her chin, still feeling the pinpricks of cold despite the cloak. An owl hooted overhead, where a bright, full moon shone in the vast night sky. From here, she could look out over the paddocks towards the dip in the valley and the woodland where they had taken their picnic. Back when it seemed nothing would be more momentous than their daring escapade. His kisses. *His caresses.* His declaration of feeling.

But then the world had tilted all over again.

Out of long habit, Morwenna clutched her fingers over the wristband of the leather cuff and traced the pattern there. Only now she knew it wasn't just a pretty pattern. It was the standard of her grandmother's family.

Her family.

The idea still seemed impossible.

Her grandmother had been an active, capable woman. Her strong hands had rocked Morwenna as a baby, gathered herbs and berries, chopped wood for their fire and stirred endless stews. They were not the hands of a woman accustomed to living in the grand chambers of Wolvesley Castle.

She thought of Esme's habitual grey gown; the rough fabric frayed and worn in places. How could that garment compare to the rich splendour of Violetta de Neville's ensemble? How could her grandmother have borne the drop in status from the daughter of titled nobles to an old woman selling herbs and balms to scratch out a living?

Fortune's wheel never stops turning.

How little Morwenna had realised the meaning of those words!

Part of her couldn't accept that this new slant on her family history could possibly be true. At first, she had thought Angus must be mistaken, but Violetta's tale held the ring of authenticity, not least because of the emotion flashing in the dowager countess's eyes.

A dark shadow loomed out of the paddock and Morwenna's breath caught in her throat, until she discerned the curious form of Fauvel.

"It's only me," she told him, unnecessarily.

Fauvel pricked his ears and swung his head towards her. For a moment she could make out the liquid pools of his eyes, but then he lost interest in his night-time companion and began to crop at the grass again.

She let go of the cuff and linked her hands together instead.

She couldn't deny that the tale rang true for other reasons too. It would explain her grandmother's deep-seated desire for privacy. Her instinct to keep the neighbours at bay. Her strict instructions for Morwenna to always make sure there was no one watching before she communicated with horses.

Her distrust of others, which had gradually communicated itself to Morwenna herself.

Why hadn't she ever told her?

She lifted her face towards the stars as emotion coursed through her heart. If she had inherited any of her mother's abilities to talk with spirits, she'd be demanding an answer now, loud and clear.

Although, what difference would such knowledge have made?

Mayhap Morwenna would have been even more anxious about coming to Wolvesley Castle. The fear she felt when the earl's carriage arrived outside her hut would have increased tenfold.

What a tangled mess it all was.

The cold had settled over her like a blanket and was working its way into her bones. Morwenna didn't want to move, but knew that must, else risk catching a chill. With her limbs shouting in protest, she pulled herself upright and wrapped the cloak more firmly about her shoulders. Pins and needles shot through her feet as she stumbled out of the shelter and found the rabbit path back to the stable yard. Horses paused from their grazing and swung their heads up to follow her halting progress. Twice she stumbled, saved from a hard landing by the long, tussocky grass. At least the night was dry and still, the bright moonlight shining above her like a beacon. A fox slunk silently ahead of her as she rounded the corner towards the stable yard, its bright eyes and white tail gleaming in the dark.

The high archway greeted her like an old friend after the vastness of open land. Torches still flickered from the stable walls and the sweet smell of hay had never felt more welcoming. Here was warmth, comfort and familiarity, after a day of impossible twists and turns. Her legs groaned with weariness as she slowly climbed the wooden steps to her room.

It was a blessing to unlock the door, go inside and fasten it behind her.

She stumbled towards her narrow bed, too tired to worry about undressing, nor even to take off her boots.

With a groan, she fell upon the soft mattress and pulled the blankets over her head, wanting only the oblivion of sleep.

But sleep would not come.

Sounds drifted up from the stable below; the horse moving

around and snorting gently. She tuned into his rhythmic munching of hay, her ears straining for something more. Something she should not want to hear; but she did.

Will he come?

If he did, she would admit him. Aye, and readily so. She needed him more than she needed to protect her heart.

Needed to feel him near, needed his hands on her body, his lips on hers.

And when the sound finally came, she thought she must be imagining it.

But the heavy, steady footsteps came ever closer. She heard them ascend the wooden steps and pause outside her door for the longest time. Morwenna sat up in bed, her whole body tensed for what might happen next. A gentle knock sounded on the wood and her heart threatened to leap from her chest.

Her mouth was too dry to speak. She crossed the chamber, newly conscious of her boots and creased tunic, and hesitated before easing the door open.

There he was. The earl, *Angus*. Who else could it have been? A raft of torchlight illuminated his golden hair and the raspy stubble covering his cheeks and chin. His piercing eyes were bright as a cat's in the darkness.

"Morwenna?" he said. A question. A caress.

She tilted her head. "I hoped you might come."

She stood back to let him enter and he stooped to pass beneath her low doorway. Once inside, there seemed scarcely enough room for both of them, but she already knew that did not matter. Her hands trembled as she lit the taper and a pale, fragile light blossomed between them.

"I wanted to see how you were." His usually booming voice was low and quiet, lest anyone overhear.

"I am better for seeing you."

It was true. She had been bewildered and confused. Now all she felt was warmth and kindness. A certainty that everything would be alright.

"And I you," he breathed.

That was all she needed to set down the taper and move into the enticing circle of his arms, pressing her face into the rich fur of his cloak and inhaling his masculine aroma of woodsmoke and leather. Dressed once more in his own clothes, he was somehow even more attractive than he had been earlier. She had told him that she cared not for riches, and that was true. But Angus was the Earl of Wolvesley; his wealth was part of him, as much as his blue eyes and bright smile.

"I longed to hold you, in my mother's chamber. I could see how her tale affected you. But I could offer you no comfort." He spoke against her hair, warming the top of her head.

"You were there. That was comfort enough."

"Nay." His long fingers stroked her cheeks. "I can no longer creep around and disguise my feelings for you."

The tenderness in his voice unleashed a new trembling that began in her core and spread all the way to her fingers. "You cannot mean…" The remainder of her sentence went unspoken as he dropped his lips to her neck in a series of warm, tingling kisses.

"I mean that I want to be yours, Morwenna. I want you to be mine. And I want everyone to know it."

As if they had minds of their own, her hand travelled over his shoulders to wrap themselves in his thick, golden curls.

"I am still no suitable match for the Earl of Wolvesley," she breathed, clinging onto reality with what remained of her ability for rational thinking.

"Forsooth. That is something I shall decide for myself."

"Nay." She shook her head, even as she closed her eyes and leaned into the warmth of his touch. "We both know it cannot be."

"Everything has changed." His voice was gruff with emotion. "You are the granddaughter of my mother's closest friend."

"The daughter of a witch."

It was the first time she had said the words, even to herself.

Her heart pounded beneath his gentle fingers which were travelling steadily to the laces of her tunic.

"That is not how my mother described her."

A delicious tension unfurled inside Morwenna as he tugged at her laces and the top of the tunic fell away. Still, she could not let the matter pass.

"Are you not afraid of being with me, knowing what you know?"

His hands didn't pause in their languid exploration of her shoulders and neck. "I know that your family and my family have long been intertwined."

"And that my mother was a witch," she said again. She would no longer flinch from her family history.

This time he paused, bringing his forehead down against hers. "Perchance mine too," he whispered. "Besides, that is not a word which I allow in Wolvesley."

Their warm breath mingled in the chill of the chamber. Angus held her close, banishing her fears.

"Are you sure 'tis only the word you forbid?"

"I am sure."

She brought her hands down over his chest, relishing the broad expanse of his muscles beneath the fine fabric. Savouring the sharp, indrawn breath proving his appreciation for her touch.

"Do you have any further questions, Morwenna?" His voice had grown husky.

She could not speak. For an answer, she slipped her palms beneath his shirt and lay them flat against the planes of his stomach.

"Can I kiss you properly?" he breathed.

"I would be glad of it."

This time his lips crashed down upon hers, claiming her mouth with an urgency which thrilled her. After a few seconds he walked backwards towards her bed, seating himself upon it and pulling her down onto his knees. With their heads at a more even height, their kiss gained a new depth and passion. Morwenna felt herself sinking into it, moaning slightly as his tongue touched hers. His fingers inched beneath the fabric of her tunic and without pausing to think, she gripped the garment and pulled it over her head. It had not even hit the floor before his strong hands were stroking the length of her back, pulling her closer and suffusing her with heat.

"You too," she demanded, pulling at the thick brocade of his shirt.

She felt him smile. Then came a chill waft of air as their bodies parted to allow him to take it off. When he reached for her again, Morwenna's bare breasts nestled against the golden warmth of his chest.

"Beautiful," he murmured, one hand sliding up over her rib cage to cup her flesh.

She exhaled hard as his fingers closed around the taut bud of her nipple, letting her head hang forward as he trailed kisses over her shoulder and down. The sensation when his lips fastened onto her left breast was like nothing she had ever known. The core of her began to pulse with wanting, even though she knew she should not want him.

She should not want *this*. Because despite her brave thoughts of earlier, now that he was here, kissing her and making her feel more than she had ever felt before, she knew that she could not give herself to him without also losing her heart.

But heaven help her, she did want him. She always had. Their physical connection was so strong it battered away all reasonable concerns about the morrow. And now, because of this link with her grandmother, it seemed Angus had abandoned his scruples and given in to the fact that he also wanted her.

Everything has changed, he'd said.

The momentous possibilities contained within these simple words rippled through her.

Did great joy hover over her horizon?

Suddenly she was seized with a sense of urgency. If this chance of happiness – almost unbearable happiness – was real; she must grasp it firmly.

Greatly daring, she roused herself from the daze of rapturous pleasure and traced her own hand lower down his abdomen, towards the part of him that strained hard at his breaches. His breath came harder as she circled him, feeling the heat travelling through the fabric. She gasped as his teeth gently nipped her tender flesh, increasing the sharp edge of her desire. Emboldened, she closed her hand around him.

"Morwenna," he breathed.

She stood up shakily, drawing his hands to the waistband of her braccae and holding her breath as he pulled them down. His breath was warm on her belly as he leaned to unfasten her boots. She stepped out of one, then the other, held steady by his warm hands on her bare hips. He lifted his head and looked up at her, blue eyes glinting in the flickering candlelight.

"Are you sure?"

She could no longer speak, she could only nod. Angus pressed a trail of soft kisses on her lower belly, one hand wrapped around her buttocks and the other slowly parting her thighs. When his probing fingers found her curls, her strength ebbed away and she leaned against him. Her own fingers knotted into his hair as he slowly explored inside her.

"I want you," she said in a sudden rush. "All of you."

"And you shall have me."

In one smooth movement he lifted her from the floor and laid her gently on the bed. In another, he whipped off his own breeches and positioned himself on top of her. Reluctant to let any more time pass by, Morwenna wrapped her legs around his waist and drew him towards her, relishing his thrill of surprise as he slid deep inside her.

"Ah, Morwenna."

She arched her back and tilted her head upwards for his kiss. Their fingers entwined as their lips met and his hips rocked slowly against her, gradually increasing the pressure building in her core. He was a large man and he filled up every bit of her; yet somehow it was as if their bodies had been designed to slot against each other, just so. She felt him tense with the effort of self-restraint and in response, she bucked her hips, not wanting him to hold anything back. Panting hard and grasping one another tightly, their passion climaxed in perfect synchronicity.

He tumbled to his side and scooped her towards him, pushing the blankets away from their hot bodies. In the pale candlelight she saw how the sharp angles of his face had blurred with pleasure. Impulsively, she leaned over on one elbow and kissed him again on the mouth.

His response was instantaneous. One hand tightened against her buttocks and with the other, he palmed her breast.

"Are you ready for me again, my lady?"

She chortled; the words sounded even more incongruous amidst the bare walls of her small chamber.

"No one has ever called me that before," she declared. "And most likely none will again."

"We shall see."

Her heart began beating more quickly, but this was not a conversation for now. Not while her head was heavy with the events of the day and her body still glowed from his touch.

"Let us not speak of anything further," she whispered. "Let us just be together."

"We can save further discussion until the morn," he allowed, reaching down to pick the blanket from the floor and spread it over their entwined bodies.

"Until morn," she agreed. And safely nestled against him, Morwenna finally found the sweet welcome of sleep.

Chapter Eighteen

T HE MORNING LIGHT was too bright, and his back was pressed inexplicably against a cold, hard wall.

Angus emerged from a deep sleep feeling cramped and uncomfortable. He put up a hand to shade his eyes from the unaccustomed light and immediately encountered something soft and warm by his side. A smile broke over his face as he realised where he was.

Morwenna shifted on the pillow, drawing long strands of blonde hair away from her face.

"Good morrow," he whispered.

For an age, he had wanted to be close to her. Now they were so close on Morwenna's narrow bed that not an inch could separate them.

"You're finally awake," she teased. "I thought I would have to get up and leave you here."

He placed a hand on her cheek and rose up to press a kiss against her parted lips. "Now why would you do a thing like that?"

"Some of us have work to do," she retorted, pulling the thin blanket so that it covered the parts of her Angus most wanted to see.

Her bantering words hit him like a pail of cold water, banishing the last remnant of sleep. "Nay," he said, mayhap too forcefully given the tense expression that came over Morwenna's sea-green eyes.

She answered steadily. "Fauvel is yet to be ridden. My work is not complete."

"I can find another trainer to work with Fauvel."

But he saw at once that he had said the wrong thing.

"I would prefer to finish what I have started. Fauvel trusts me, but he is not yet ready to trust others."

Angus felt frustration building inside of him. Morwenna should be a guest in the castle with her own chamber and an allocated lady's maid. Instead, she was sleeping in a draughty room above the stables, which let both daylight and chill winds in through any number of cracks.

After all she had learned yesterday, *after all that had passed between them*, she was still preparing to dress in her groom's livery and attend to his horse.

"Morwenna," he began, trying to soften his voice. "It is not proper."

Her green eyes gazed right into his soul. "You are embarrassed."

"'Tis not that."

But he could not deny that she was right. The impropriety was inside his mind, rooted in his long-ago vow to steer clear of relationships with anyone not of his social class.

She turned to face the bare wall. "Yet I did not ask you to come here. And I did not demand that you stay."

The situation was slipping beyond his control. He tried to take hold of her hand but she snatched it away.

"I came willingly, and I stayed willingly, and I would do it all over again." He spoke from his heart and hoped he was reaching her. "I want to give you everything, Morwenna. I want to restore you to your family's rightful place. And that is not in the stables."

Morwenna hugged her knees, her face still turned away from him.

"I would like to court you," he continued, a note of desperation creeping into his voice. "I want to sit by your side in the great hall. I want us to be together."

He had ne'er opened his heart to anyone before and now he felt weak with the possibility of rejection.

But Morwenna's small hand crept slowly over his. He grasped it like a lifeline.

"And you cannot court a woman wearing your groom's livery."

He found himself laughing, partly with incredulity but mostly with relief at this acknowledgement of their shared future. "I have oft said that the Earl of Wolvesley should be able to do as he pleases. Mayhap I could try it."

Although even the Earl of Wolvesley could not court two women at once. He must write to Emelia before the day was out.

Morwenna sighed, tilting her head so her beautiful eyes looked straight into his. "You are right. I see it, though I do not like it. But there is one thing I must have."

"Name it."

She held his gaze. "One more day."

He didn't want to agree. But he could see by the resolution in her face that he had little choice.

"How do I know that at the end of this one day, you will not ask me for another?"

She shrugged her slender shoulders. "Fauvel is ready to be ridden. After today, if I have not done so, then I will have failed in the task you set me. Either way, my work here will be all but finished. If it pleases you, I will select one of the grooms to continue working with Fauvel."

Aye, it pleased him very much.

"One more day." It felt like a lifetime. "But you must promise me that you will come to the keep and meet again with my mother. There are things we must discuss."

"Afterwards," she promised, squeezing his hand.

He nodded, resigning himself to the sequence of events. "May I watch your work with Fauvel?"

She looked surprised. "You are welcome of course. Come to the circular paddock at noon. Though I am not sure it will be of interest."

He leaned closer to her. "Everything you do is of interest to me."

Morwenna blushed prettily. "I hope that is not true. I must rise up and dress. Will that be of interest?"

"Most definitely," he growled, part of him very interested indeed. Alas, the sound of the horse below whickering for his morning oats stopped him in his tracks. He groaned out loud, dragging a hand through his tousled hair. "I have stayed overly long."

"I could find some more groom's livery and you could leave in disguise?"

"Nay," he smiled, approving of her ingenuity. "I have already said that we will not creep around in disguise again." He sprang from the bed, aware and uncaring of his nakedness, although he was not expecting the sharp autumnal chill which quickly clamped around his body. "God's Bones, it is like the depths of winter in here."

Her laugh was like a tinkle of chimes. "Winter is much colder, I assure you. Especially in a wooden hut."

He had located his clothing and was in the process of pulling on his shirt, but he paused to consider her words. In the cool light of morning, he could see more of her room than he could last night. The room was sparsely furnished, with a simple washstand and a small wooden closet in one corner. But the walls and door were solid and strong. Unlike a hut, he imagined, where both the elements and ill-intentioned intruders could wander through at will.

"Is that truly where you live, Morwenna? In a hut?"

She nodded. "Aye. And I make no pretence otherwise." She averted her eyes from the part of him that was still unclothed; the part most directly within her eyeline. "So you see, my room here above a stable is grand indeed."

He grunted noncommittally, quickly stepping into his breeches and fastening his mantle about his neck. He had never before tried to picture her life before she came to Wolvesley and now he felt humbled by what he had learned. Morwenna spoke nicely and had undoubted skills with horses. He knew, of course, that she would not have been raised with fine clothes and comfort, but this new knowledge sliced into him.

Once decent, he perched again at the end of her bed and took hold of her hand. "Your past has made you who you are." He chose his words carefully. "And I would not change that. But the future can be different." He swallowed. "I want it to be different."

Silently, he willed her to accept.

A smile broke over her face, making his heart glad. "I begin to believe you may be right." She flinched as a tuneful whistle floated up from the stable yard. "The grooms are already up." Her green eyes widened. "How will you return to the keep unseen?"

He had already thought about this. "I do not need to make it all the way to the keep; merely to get away from here without being spotted." He leaned forwards and kissed her cheek, reluctant to leave but knowing he must. As he glanced out of her small window, he saw the yard already springing into life. Horses looked over their half-stable doors, ears pricking to the sound of buckets being filled with feed. "'Till noon, Morwenna."

"'Till noon."

Angus slipped quietly down the wooden stairs, hoping with every fibre of his being that he would not encounter the stable boy attending to the horse below. Happily his luck held; the horse stood alone in the stall, looking only mildly surprised to encounter such a grand visitor before receiving his morning oats.

Angus took a deep breath and peered out into the yard. The morning sunshine was battling a greyish mist which clung stubbornly to the chilly air. If he could emerge from here without being seen, then Morwenna would be saved from suspicion. He saw no one about and took his chance, striding out and swinging the half wooden door closed behind him. He set off at a jaunty pace, his cloak billowing around his calves as he cut through the yard making a beeline for the archway. With every stride he took away from Morwenna's quarters, the safer he felt she was.

He had all but reached the archway when Jacob bowled through it, startling in surprise to see his lord and master at such an hour. He jumped to the side and bowed.

"Good morrow, milord."

"Good morrow, Jacob. I'm just out for an early morning walk."

"Very good, milord."

Angus nodded curtly and strode past, cursing himself for explaining his presence. Mayhap Jacon would have thought nothing of the encounter, but he might be more prone to pondering it now.

Angus was unused to subterfuge. He did not enjoy deception, and his heart sang to think that after today, he would have no need of it.

He bounded up the stone steps to the keep, relieved to be stepping inside, away from the clinging mist and ominous grey light. He had intended to go straight to his chamber to wash and change, but the enticing aroma of freshly-baked bread lured him instead to the great hall which was already filling with people. Just through the doorway, he encountered Sir Henry.

"Henry," he boomed jovially. "Come and break bread with me."

"My lord." Henry gave a small bow.

"Come." Angus urged him towards the dais, where the table was already laid with fresh bread, figs, honey and soft cheese.

Once seated, he turned to his friend and ally. "What plans do you have for the day?"

Henry was spreading a hunk of bread with sticky honey. "Gerrault and I had planned to ride out towards the Darkmoor borders with a few of the men."

Angus paused, a fig part-way to his mouth. Gerrault was the tall youth who had feelings for Morwenna. But Angus felt more inclined to forgive him for this, now that his own future with

Morwenna felt more secure. "What takes you to Darkmoor?"

"We've heard reports of unrest. A few skirmishes. Nothing too serious."

Angus chewed ruminatively. "Those are Otto Sarragnac's lands."

Henry nodded. "I have already sent messengers to the Earl of Darkmoor to ask for his assistance, should we need it."

"He will give it freely."

"That I know." Henry took a swig of ale. "It is not from the North that we look for threat, but to the West."

"And how are our friends in Powys?"

"Quiet." Henry grinned, tearing off another hunk of bread. "And by the look of the morn, they will remain so for a while at least."

Angus frowned. "How so?" He spoke through a mouthful of bread and cheese.

"The weather is changing. A storm is expected before night-fall. I am already re-considering our plans. Perchance we will train with the men as usual today, and journey to Darkmoor once the bad weather has passed."

Angus clapped him on the back, hastily apologising when the experienced knight half-choked on his food. "Whatever you think is best, Henry. I would not want you caught out in the open in a downpour."

"Nay, my lord. I am not as young as I once was."

"Nonsense." Angus reached for some customary banter, then reconsidered. He took a mouthful of ale and then spoke quietly. "I owe you a debt of gratitude for taking on the leadership of my men." He stumbled a little over the words, still thinking in his own mind that the Wolvesley army belonged to Lucan.

"It is an honour, truly." Henry surprised him by grasping his arm. "I will lead your men for as long as you wish."

"Forever then," he quipped lightly.

"Nay, not forever." Henry shook his greying head. "Do not forget that I rode out alongside your father."

"I do not forget it." Angus felt a twinge of guilt. "Would you prefer to be sitting by your fireside on a damp day like today?"

Henry laughed out loud, making several men below turn their heads towards the dais. "Not in the slightest. But there are two things I know to be true. May I speak freely?"

Angus nodded and waved a hand for him to continue.

"The first is that my strength will not last me many more years. The second is that in times of peace, your men are happy to follow my orders. But in times of war…"

A beat of silence fell between them.

"They would prefer to follow the Earl of Wolvesley," Angus finished for him.

"Exactly so." Henry paused and said emphatically, "They would prefer to follow the man whose standard they bear."

Angus made a noncommittal noise, his head beginning to pound. "I need a little more time, Henry, to secure things here. Are you telling me that war is coming?"

"Nay, my lord." Henry answered quickly, then lowered his voice. "But we both know that our King has seen more years of battle than even myself. Moreover, he is still grieving the Queen's death. Times of unrest may be coming to our land."

"If so, we shall be ready for them." Conviction grew within Angus. He had found the woman he wanted to marry. He and Morwenna would secure the de Neville line at Wolvesley.

He and Morwenna would keep his mother safe from suspicion.

With a warm thrill of recognition, he realised he could have no better ally in that goal.

"I do not doubt it." Henry dabbed his lips and pushed his plate away. "If you will excuse me, my lord, I will be about my day."

"Good day to you."

Angus left the great hall just moments after Henry. Having satisfied his hunger, he was now impatient to see if the messenger he had sent to Ember Hall had returned.

And impatient also to despatch another messenger to Emelia.

He may be confident in his suspicions that the lady also wished to be freed from their long arrangement, but he could not countenance the idea of her arriving in Wolvesley before he had a chance to forewarn her of his intent.

That would be poor treatment indeed, of an old and important friend.

He bounded up the staircase and all but ran along the gallery to his mother's chamber.

Nella opened the door after his first knock.

"Milord." She bobbed into a stiff curtsy.

"Nella," he greeted her. "How is Lady Violetta faring?" he asked quietly, glancing behind her to check his mother was not lurking nearby.

"Much more herself," Nella whispered. "Her nightmares have ceased and she is held less in the grip of her visions. I begin to hope that the danger has passed."

Angus smiled in genuine relief. "That is what I too hope."

"I will leave you to talk." Nella curtsied once more and then stood back to allow him inside.

"Good morrow, Mother."

"Angus." Violetta turned towards him, pleasure stamped on her face. "What a surprise. Will you break your fast with me?" She gestured to a silver tray laden with the same fare Angus had already enjoyed in the great hall.

He pursed his lips regretfully. "I have already eaten."

"No matter." She brushed aside his apologies and took a place at the small round table. "Join me, at least."

"Of course." He sat down in the cushioned chair by her side, noting his mother's steady hand as she cut into the cheese. She was dressed in a beautiful gown of grey silk, with pale green flashes at the sides. Her long white hair was pinned into a neat chignon and, as always, jewels flashed on her fingers and about her neck. "Did you sleep well?" he asked politely, knowing it would not do to launch straight into his questioning.

"Very well." Violetta flashed him a dazzling smile. "Lucan

came to see me."

All of Angus's hopes and certitude drained away. He felt diminished by her words, as if a heavy weight had descended from the sculpted ceiling and landed directly upon his shoulders.

"Really, Mother?"

She nodded happily, taking small bites of bread. "He came to tell me that everything would be alright."

Angus took a steadying breath. "In what regard?"

The dowager countess pressed her lips together. "He was not specific," she said reprovingly.

"I see."

Angus did not see at all. But then he gave himself a little shake. He had told Morwenna last night that he had no qualms about her ancestry. Yet here he was, fearful of his own mother's announcements.

"I am glad you take comfort from it," he added quickly.

Violetta treated him to a smile. "What have you really come to see me about?" She held up a hand and continued before he could speak. "Let me guess. Could it be a beautiful young woman named Morwenna?"

Despite himself, Angus felt a flush of embarrassment, which he pushed away as ridiculous. "Her beauty has nothing to do with it."

"You're right, of course." Violetta reached for a handful of fresh berries. "Although I do believe her beauty has a great deal to do with your particular interest in this matter." She popped the berries into her mouth, feigning a deep interest in the dull view out of the window.

He held up his hands in surrender. "If you must know, I have some feelings for Morwenna."

"Some feelings?"

"Strong feelings," he corrected. It was as if the years had been stripped away and he was sitting before his mother as a distraught youth, confessing to unrequited love for Johanna the tanner's daughter.

He pushed the memory away. Back then, Violetta had correctly divined that he would eventually recover from that particular heartbreak. But if she made the same pronouncement now, he would counter it.

The dowager countess fixed him with a steely blue gaze. "And what are your intentions towards my friend's granddaughter?"

"Entirely honourable," he spluttered, taken by surprise.

"You intend to marry the girl?"

"I do."

His heart pounded as he waited for her judgement.

Violetta smiled and patted his arm. "I am delighted for you both."

Angus frowned in bewilderment. "That's it? You're delighted?"

"Esme was once my dearest and most loyal friend. Why would I not be pleased?"

Angus cleared his throat. "There is the matter of my existing betrothal…" his words trailed away.

Violetta inclined her head. "I was never convinced that was a good match. And Lucan himself was too young and inexperienced at the time to judge well." She fixed him with a piercing stare. "My expectation is that you will deal with this situation in a manner which leaves Lady Emelia with her dignity intact."

"Of course." Angus nodded emphatically.

"The Foxtons have long been allies of the de Nevilles. The lady must not be treated ill."

"I will do all I can to alleviate any awkwardness."

"Well then." His mother's smile was serene.

Angus hesitated, his mind leaping back to the person who most occupied his thoughts. "And you have nothing to say of Morwenna's lineage?"

Violetta shrugged. "You forget that I was once merely the daughter of a knight. Your dear father was distant cousin to an earl. Lineage did not loom large for either of us, not until the terrible Battle of Cadfan, when losses were great and Tristan was declared the last surviving heir to the Wolvesley estate."

He swallowed, his mouth suddenly dry. "I begin to believe it might all be possible. I might marry Morwenna and we might be happy."

Violetta patted his arm again. "You are right to value happiness. Tristan and I were happy together, right until the end. So were Lucan and Angelique." Her brow clouded with sorrow.

"But what of Ember Hall?" Angus pushed on, not wanting to revisit such painful memories. "I must see if we have received news from the messenger."

"Angus, my dear, your impatience does you credit. But you forget, Ember Hall is many miles distant. Even riding all through the night, our messenger has no hope of returning until much later today."

His hand thumped gently on the table, making the dishes tremble. "I do not enjoy waiting."

"You never have," his mother observed drily. "But are some things not worth waiting for?"

His lips curved into a smile. "You may be right." The distant rumble of a carriage rolling into the courtyard made him prick up his ears. "What is this? We are not expecting visitors today?"

"No indeed." Violetta pushed back her chair and went over to the window, craning her head to the right so she could see the sweep of driveway.

Angus impatiently ran through his list of jobs for the day. The first thing he must do was write to Emelia. Once that was done, he could visit Morwenna in the paddocks to witness her finally proving that Fauvel was a horse that could be ridden. Next, he must ensure she came back here to speak with his mother about Ember Hall. Even if the messenger had not yet returned, he decided, the news of her inheritance was too important to wait.

Once Morwenna was fully furnished with all the details of her family's past, he would ask the question he longed to give voice to.

If Morwenna will do me the great honour of becoming my wife.

Angus could not deny the thrill of excitement which gripped him. He was as giddy as a boy in the school room. The last thing he wanted right now was an unexpected guest.

As if from a great distance, he heard his mother's sharp intake of breath.

"What is it?"

Violetta cleared her throat and turned to face him. "It is a carriage."

He made an impatient gesture. "I could have guessed as much, Mother."

"A carriage bearing the Foxton standard." She put a hand to her heart. "Angus, I believe your unexpected visitor is Lady Emelia Foxton."

Chapter Nineteen

AFTER DAYS OF unseasonal sunshine, the day that meant so much to Morwenna was drab, grey and oppressive. The morning mist refused to lift from the lower paddocks, cloaking the distant trees and trapping the usual daytime sounds in its eerie fronds. Morwenna found it strange to work without the familiar backdrop of birdsong and the hum of activity from the castle grounds. Fauvel, however, was unperturbed.

She haltered him, groomed him, inspected his hooves and pulled his mane free of tangles. Throughout it all, he stood stoically, resting one back foot and blowing gently through his nose.

"You're ready," she told him, shivering a little in her green liveried tunic and wishing she had thought to bring a cloak.

She cast an eye towards the incline leading from the stable yard. At any moment she'd been expecting to look up to see Angus striding towards her, but so far there was no sign of him. She ignored the tug of disappointment. Mayhap he had other matters to attend to, especially after a day playing truant yesterday.

"What does an earl do all day, anyway?" she asked Fauvel, who showed little interest in the question.

She rested a hand on the horse's shoulder. He was warm, despite the mist, but she could not leave him standing here much longer. Soon he would grow impatient, and her chance of riding him successfully would diminish.

"Will you let me ride you, Fauvel?" she murmured, patting his neck.

His ears flicked backwards, listening, thinking.

"Is that a yes?"

She moved to his head and placed her palms at either side of it. Exhaling heavily, he leaned into her belly and half closed his eyes. She bent at the waist and planted a kiss between his ears.

"Thank you."

She had already brought tack up to the paddock and placed it in the shelter. In a matter of minutes, she had carefully placed a saddle on Fauvel's back and adjusted the girth. Next came the bridle, which she had to stand on tiptoes to get over his ears.

"You're a beauty," she told him, standing back to admire the handsome horse in his gleaming tack. What a shame there was no one else here to show him off to. Then again, the last thing she wanted was an audience.

Unless it was an audience of just one man.

She bit down on her lip, pushing all thoughts of Angus away. She had no cause to doubt him. He had never let her down. And in truth, she had not been overly taken with his desire to watch her ride Fauvel. Mayhap Angus had picked up on that and stayed away? Oft-times now he had displayed surprising sensitivity, especially for an earl.

She couldn't help a smile as her mind conjured images from the night before. Aye, he had been sensitive indeed. Kind and thoughtful of her needs, despite his taut muscles and obvious strength. He had held back to ensure she took her pleasure first. A gentleman in every sense of the word.

Fauvel's ears flicked back, as if sensing her wayward thoughts, and Morwenna pulled herself back to the present.

"You're right," she told him soothingly. "One man at a time. I shall concentrate on you."

There was no mounting block out here in the paddocks, so Morwenna led Fauvel over to the fence, banishing the memory of how just yesterday she had done the same with the grey horse before galloping across the meadow with Angus in hot pursuit. Before then, they had spent so little time in one another's company, but now, somehow, she missed him.

Fauvel tensed as if realising both her intentions and her wandering attention. This would never do. Morwenna got a fierce grip on her emotions and took the reins in her hand. She clambered to the highest rung of the fence and balanced against Fauvel's withers. The horse's back was still some inches above her. Not for the first time, she wished she were taller.

Morwenna put the toe of her boot into the stirrup and lightly sprung into the saddle. The horse gathered his powerful hindquarters beneath her and threatened to rear, but she soothed him with her voice and her thoughts. Projecting calmness and quiet, scarcely moving her hands on the reins.

Fauvel snorted and swung his head up and down. This was make or break time. He would either toss her from the saddle, or accept her mastery of him.

Morwenna took charge, wrapping her legs around his belly and squeezing until he moved off into a slow, reluctant trot. She shortened the reins and forced him into a tight circle. Round and round they went, until she felt him become restless again. Then she motioned for him to trot in the opposite direction. Gradually, Fauvel's demeanour relaxed. He dropped his head and pricked his ears, listening to her instructions. At the head of the next circle, she urged him into a canter, breaking into a smile when he acquiesced without any hesitation.

Fauvel's stride was long, balanced and flowing. He would make the perfect charger for Angus.

She had done it.

"We have done it," she corrected herself, reaching down to pat Fauvel's neck as she slowed him back to a walk. They had both learned to trust again.

A smattering of applause rippled through the heavy mist, startling both her and the horse who shied to one side.

"Steady," she murmured.

Fauvel recovered his stride and Morwenna exhaled with relief. She strained her eyes to see who was watching them, but the fog was too dense.

It must be Angus, though she would have thought better of him than to applaud like that without any warning. He must have known a sudden noise exploding through the mist would alarm even the steadiest of horses.

"Wonderful, truly wonderful," a refined female voice spoke through the grey haze.

Morwenna felt her heart tense, as if she had been doused with cold water. Fauvel sensed the change in her mood and became instantly fearful; halting in alarm with his body rigid and his head high.

"You're alright," she told him, soothingly. Although it was the last thing she felt.

Two figures stepped forwards. One of them tall and broad, unmistakably Angus. The other was a woman dressed in a fine cloak of sapphire blue. Morwenna could see no more from this distance. What was it about a woman in a blue cloak that could make her heart hammer so in her chest?

Still speaking words of reassurance to the horse, Morwenna dismounted, dropping on heavy feet to the ground which turned out to be surprisingly far away.

Oh, how she would love to press her face against Fauvel's warm shoulder and ignore the sharp pull of reality, for she already knew this woman was bad news.

Fortune's wheel never stops turning.

She pulled up her stirrups, loosened the girth and urged Fauvel to walk closer to the shelter. If she could have busied herself longer with mundane activities, she would have.

Angus cleared his throat. "Congratulations, Morwenna. That was an impressive display of horsemanship."

"A display which still continues," the woman added, opening her arms disarmingly. "See how the wild horse is entirely in your control."

Morwenna found her voice. "He is not wild. And he is only in my control for as long as he chooses to trust me."

There was an awkward silence. Now that they were closer, Morwenna could make out a strain across Angus's open features; frown lines at his brow and an anxious light shining from those piercing eyes. His companion stood an entire head taller than Morwenna. She had blonde hair which framed her face with ringlets, and eyes a deeper shade of blue than even her sumptuous cloak.

"Lady Emelia Foxton," she introduced herself with a gracious smile. "I was the one to send the horse to the earl."

Morwenna's gaze skittered to Angus. "Your friend?"

Angus nodded. "Emelia, may I introduce Miss Morwenna of Em...," he froze mid-sentence. "Morwenna has trained the horse, made him rideable," he concluded lamely.

"So I have seen." Lady Emelia gave a tinkling laugh like a peal of bells. "You have done an excellent job," she said to Morwenna with real feeling.

"Thank you."

Morwenna couldn't pinpoint what it was about Lady Emelia which put her so on edge. The woman was polite and spoke with true warmth in her voice. She radiated neither hostility nor disinterest, and despite the rich fur on her hood, she conversed with Morwenna quite readily, putting on no false airs.

Still, something about her sent tingles racing up her spine.

"You have, Morwenna. Truly magnificent," Angus added, gazing down at her in something like desperation.

"Thank you," Morwenna said again. She began to feel a little desperate herself. "May I?" She indicated the shelter.

"Of course." Angus stepped back and motioned for Lady Emelia to do the same. Morwenna couldn't help but notice how her gloved hand caught at his elbow.

She led Fauvel over to the fence and looped his reins over a post, then worked quickly to remove his saddle before the tension growing in her belly should communicate itself further to him.

All the while, she murmured to him gently, pretending her insides were not writhing like a basket full of snakes.

She offered him half an apple and when he lowered his head, she lifted the bridle over his ears, sending up thanks that her actions still managed to be smooth and swift, despite her newly trembling fingers.

"Allow me." Angus stepped forward quickly to take the bridle from her. She flinched as his warm hands closed over her own.

Morwenna patted Fauvel's shoulder. "You can go now," she told him, although she longed for him to stay.

The horse exhaled heavily and moved away, though after a few strides he flicked up his tail and broke into a joyful canter.

"A transformation," Lady Emelia remarked. She smiled again at Morwenna before switching her gaze to Angus. "And so, dear Angus, you have completed my final challenge."

Morwenna watched as his eyes widened in alarm. His voice, however, was smooth and calm. "Your final challenge, Emelia? Forsooth, the days will grow dull without them."

"Oh, I doubt that, very much." Her gloved hand again tapped at his elbow. "I'm sure you recall that the stakes for this particular challenge were high indeed?"

Angus nodded mutely, his lips pressed together.

He doesn't want me to hear this, realised Morwenna.

She spoke up, her voice high and wavering. "What were the stakes?"

Lady Emelia's cheeks tinged with pink and she gave another tinkling laugh. "Well, I hardly like to say, although considering you played such a part in helping the earl succeed, perchance it is only right you should know what, exactly, he has won." She nudged at Angus as if asking him to speak up on her behalf.

The earl's face had turned ashen. "Something so long ago discussed, that I fancy it had become almost entirely theoretical between us."

"You're right," Lady Emelia mused. "In truth, dear Angus, it was something that my younger self rebelled against."

He took a breath as if to say something significant, but then his eyes met Morwenna's and he froze once again.

Morwenna now felt strangely calm. The crisis, whatever it was, was coming, whatever she now said or did.

"I most likely owe you an apology. Any number of them. The lute, I fear, was impertinent." Lady Emelia smiled up at Angus. "And then the horse." She gestured towards Fauvel and her voice dropped. "I didn't know the circumstances of Lucan's death when I arranged for the horse to be sent to Wolvesley. It was a terrible misstep." She shook her head, pursing her lips together. "But e'en before I learned what had happened, I felt sure you would refuse."

"Mayhap I should have refused." Angus sounded as if someone were strangling him.

Morwenna looked from Angus to Lady Emelia. The wispy mist lent an air of unreality to the unfolding scene. "What were the stakes?" she asked again.

Lady Emelia looked expectantly at Angus, as did Morwenna.

His face was now as grey as the fog, but his voice regained its steadiness. "Lady Emelia wagered our wedding date on my ability to master the unrideable horse."

Morwenna's heart plunged into a lake of ice, but she was not entirely sure she had heard correctly. Her head swam. "Your wedding date?"

"Angus and I have been betrothed for many years. Since we were so high." Lady Emelia flattened her palm and held it below shoulder height, smiling at Morwenna to ensure she understood.

Morwenna understood. As if in slow motion, her memories of the strange conversation she'd had with Molly and Isaac shifted into a new and terrible light.

There's no sign of a new countess coming any time soon.

'Twas not the case that the earl had no interest in courting, as she had assumed. *It was that he was already spoken for.*

"A contract drawn up between my brother Lucan and Lady Emelia's late father," Angus interjected shakily. "We had no say in the matter."

"None," Lady Emelia agreed, a smile on her lips. "And so, Miss Morwenna, I have been testing his lordship's determination to see the contract through with a series of challenges."

"Challenges," Morwenna repeated. Her lips were dry. She recalled that first conversation with Angus in the stablemaster's room.

"I've been set a challenge, and it is very important I succeed."

All at once the full meaning of those words reached her. She gasped as if for breath, fearing she might topple to the ground. Angus loomed out of the mist towards her, placing a large hand on her shoulder. A hand which just minutes earlier might have offered comfort.

"Morwenna, are you well?"

She shook his hand away and lifted her chin. Never had she needed her grandmother's strength and wisdom more.

"That is why you needed me to tame the horse?" She fixed Angus with a steely stare.

He nodded. "That is why I first summoned you to Wolvesley. It is not why I asked you to stay," he added through clenched teeth.

Morwenna gave a little shake of her head to show how disinterested she was in any such explanations.

"I am pleased to have helped you answer your challenge."

Angus flinched as if her words had wounded him. Lady Emelia raised her blonde eyebrows a notch.

"You really have done a magnificent job," she murmured. "I felt sure you would admit defeat on this occasion." She inclined her head towards Angus, who looked utterly stricken.

"I am sure the Earl of Wolvesley will succeed at whatever he sets his mind to," Morwenna said bitingly, uncaring of the look of surprise passing over Lady Emelia's lovely face. "I wish you both a good day."

She nodded to both in turn, resisting the urge to dip into an elaborate curtsy – and resisting a stronger urge to slap the Earl of

Wolvesley across his lightly stubbled cheek.

He was betrothed.

To a beautiful wealthy woman.

She, Morwenna, had believed his words of affection. She'd placed her trust in the instinctive connection between them. *She had taken him to her bed.* And all the while, he'd been *betrothed.*

Even in her rage, she acknowledged that he had never lied to her, not explicitly. But his actions had always implied that their relationship meant something to him. He had allowed her to believe in the possibility of *more.*

Albeit, that tantalising prospect had never been properly spelled out.

Her cheeks burned with a mixture of shame and rage as her feet pounded up the rabbit path and she crested the hill.

He was betrothed.

And she had helped him win the challenge that would see his wedding date named.

Nay, she had not helped him. She had delivered his victory.

"I want you to be mine, and I want everyone to know it."

The memory of his fine words in her room last night made her skin flush pink. Not with embarrassment, but with a red-hot rage.

He had seduced her. He an earl, and she an impoverished village girl.

She should have known better. She had seen off more than one unwanted advance from uncouth youths in the past. Youths who saw her unprotected status and thought nothing of pushing their advantage. The difference, she realised, stumbling to a halt, was that she hadn't wanted to stop him. On the contrary, she'd been longing for his touch and his kiss for endless days.

Tears blurred her vision as she turned into the stable yard, her booted feet readily finding their way over the familiar cobbles.

"Morwenna?" A light touch on her arm made her startle. "What ails you?"

She knew even without turning her head that it was Gerrault. The very last person she wanted to see right now.

Or was he?

She lifted her tear-stained cheeks and heard him gasp in surprise.

"Gerrault." She choked back a sob, noting how his grey eyes had clouded at her visible distress. He was a kind soul.

Not a man who would ever lie and deceive.

"Tell me what has happened?" he urged.

She clutched at his sleeve, anchoring herself to him. He was wearing a clean shirt and pale breeches, not his usual groom's livery.

"Why are you dressed like that?"

He glanced down. "Sir Henry has given me the afternoon off."

An idea began to form in Morwenna's muddled mind. She sniffed in a most unladylike fashion as her tears cleared and the cobbled yard came into clearer focus. "Do you have plans?"

He shook his head. "Nay. The plans I did have were cancelled. Sir Henry thinks that heavy weather is on the way."

Morwenna pushed back her shoulders and lifted her chin, meeting his anxious gaze. "Then will you help me?"

Chapter Twenty

THE RAIN STARTED slowly at first, but by the time the torches were lit in the great hall, it had become a deluge. Angus stood at the arched windows and watched as enormous puddles formed in the courtyard. His stone lions were half hidden by a curtain of rain; the musical splashing of the fountain entirely drowned out by the staccato drum beats of rain falling upon granite walls.

He turned to Emelia, who had silently drifted to his side. "It is just as Sir Henry foretold."

She raised a perfect eyebrow. "Heavy rain?"

"More than heavy." He let go of the drape, allowing it to fall back into place. "You will have to stay here overnight."

Emelia pursed her lips. "That was not my intention. I had planned to continue to Foxton Hall."

"That will not be possible." He was gruff with the inevitability of it all.

"The rain may yet ease."

He pulled back the drape and pointed towards the grey sky, thick with cloud. "Not likely."

"But Foxton Hall is not far away."

"'Tis far enough in weather such as this." Angus folded his arms in an effort to quell his impatience with the situation, but it rose up inside him and could not be denied. "God's Bones, Emelia. Do you imagine I plan to sneak into your chamber and ravish you?"

She surprised him with another tinkling laugh. "You forget, I have spent many a summer in the debauched halls of Cheltenham Castle. Mayhap I have grown accustomed to sneaking around and ravishment."

Angus was speechless with surprise. His eyebrows disappeared beneath his thatch of hair as he regarded his former playmate. As children, they had been evenly matched for height and strength. Now he towered above her, but Emelia was nonetheless a tall, competent woman. Her blue eyes sparkled with determination. She was not, as he well knew, one to back down from any situation.

"Are you serious, Emelia?"

She put a hand on his arm and leaned close. He caught his breath, half expecting a confession.

"I am not."

He couldn't help but bark with laughter as a servant came near with a silver platter holding two goblets of wine. He took one for himself and passed the other to Emelia. Behind them, rain-drenched men-at-arms filtered into the great hall, shaking out their cloaks and pulling benches closer to the roaring fire.

"You are full of surprises," he said.

She sipped steadily, her eyes dancing over the rim of the goblet. "Am I correct, Angus, in thinking that the notion of me sneaking around Cheltenham Castle has rather unsettled you?"

He swallowed a large mouthful of wine, feeling more relaxed as the heady liquid ran down his throat. "It was not what I expected to hear," he hedged.

"You anticipate a more innocent wife?" The challenge was implicit in her voice.

Angus shook his head, slowly. "You know as well as I do, Emelia, what our betrothal was all about."

She held his gaze. "An heir for the Earl of Wolvesley."

He inclined his head. "Indeed."

"And your brother considered me a suitable mother for this future heir." She tossed her blonde head, apparently unconcerned with the perceived propriety of their conversation.

Angus cast his eye about the hall, satisfied that no one was within hearing distance. "As did your father."

Emelia nodded slowly before draining her goblet and holding it out towards him. "More wine, please, your lordship."

"Our wine is strong," he warned.

"As am I, dear Angus." Emelia smoothed her silken skirts. "Though I should like to sit."

"Of course." He offered his arm, as etiquette dictated, and together they ascended the steps to the dais. He pulled out a wooden chair for Emelia and held it as she lowered herself gracefully down, unable to help admiring her slender neck and the golden-hued slope of her shoulders.

Lady Emelia Foxton was a beautiful woman.

But she is not the woman I want.

He heaved out a breath as he sat beside her and waved for more wine.

"What ails you, Angus?"

Her question took him by surprise, as did the proximity of her deep blue eyes.

"Nothing at all. I am quite well." He nodded his thanks to the servant who delivered a flask of richly-coloured red wine to their table.

"You were surprised to see me, this morning?"

"I was, I do not deny it. Your last letter said to expect you before All Saints Day." He poured a generous measure of wine for each of them. "That is still some weeks hence."

"Are you not pleased to see me, Angus? Have you not missed me dearly?"

He kept his voice level. "It has been more than ten years, Emelia."

"I know it." Her face became still and watchful.

"Much has changed," he ventured.

"Much." Her blue gaze seemed to hold him in a trap.

His hands shook as he was suddenly taken by an unaccountable urge to tell her the truth.

I love another.

The clatter of booted feet and conversation around them diminished as Angus played the scenario out in his mind. Emelia had always been honest and straight-talking, but had the years changed her?

Even if they had, would she not prefer the truth?

But when he looked at her, the words died on his lips. The woman seated beside him may appear to flout convention, but she was the daughter of one of the oldest families in England.

He could not offend her.

"We were little more than children when last we met." Emelia's elegant fingers traced a line around her goblet. "Now I see that the tousle-haired boy with a liking for honey cakes is a man grown." She nudged him gently. "A *fine* man grown."

His lips quirked into a smile. "I believe that is usually what happens." He suppressed a comment about Emelia's own lovely appearance. She had turned from a tall, long-legged girl into a woman of beauty and poise. The only thing unchanged was her air of bright, unfaltering courage. A trait he had long admired. "I will not compliment you, Emelia," he declared, beginning to feel the effects of the wine. "I suspect you received compliments enough down in Cheltenham."

"I will not deny it." She looked at him again over the rim of her goblet. "And I am not surprised by your rough manners. I have always found company in the south to be far more polite than that of my cousins in the north."

He snorted with laughter when he realised she was teasing him. "Were you always this outspoken?"

"Yes," she answered shortly. "I believe it was one of many things you liked about me."

He was instantly sober. "Mayhap you are right." There were many things he liked about Emelia.

As a friend.

He found someone had placed a trencher full of food beside

them. He must eat and soak up some of this wine.

"So tell me, Angus." Emelia forked some roast meat delicately into her mouth. "Were you pleased to see my carriage arrive?"

His mouth was full of food which he suddenly could not chew. Long moments passed until he swallowed. "Why should I not be?"

"That is my question to you." Emelia's voice had lost some of its gaiety.

This was his moment. He could appeal to the long years of friendship between them, and the equally long years of little contact. Emelia herself had agreed that neither of them had input into their betrothal.

He could speak up now and declare his love for Morwenna.

The words were upon his lips. In another moment he would give voice to them, moving one step closer to claiming Morwenna as his bride.

And then Emelia hiccupped.

"Excuse me." Her blue eyes opened wide with surprise.

"I warned you the wine was strong." He heard his own words slurring against each other.

"Mayhap it is stronger than I am accustomed to." She put down her fork with deliberate care. "Forgive me, Angus. We must continue this conversation in the morn."

"I shall have someone escort you to your room." He waved to the Seneschal.

Heads turned as the lovely Lady Emelia walked from the great hall on the arm of his grey-haired Seneschal. Her skirts flared around her slender ankles and her golden hair shone in the candlelight, but Angus was immune to her beauty.

He loved Morwenna.

God's Bones, he should not have spent the day showing Emelia about the castle and making well-mannered conversation about their mutual friends and acquaintances. True, he had stopped by the stable yard and tried to find Morwenna just after luncheon; but no one knew where she was and within minutes, the heavy rain had chased him back indoors. But he should have tried harder.

Nay, he should have gone after Morwenna the very second she turned away from them in the paddocks. Instead, he had taken the coward's way out; standing as if rooted to the spot while Emelia voiced her polite admiration of Fauvel's condition and the sweep of land down to the woods.

She had been easing an awkward moment, he realised belatedly.

And with that insight came another, hot on its heels.

Was Emelia's peculiar line of questioning tonight aimed at prompting him to tell the truth? To confess he no longer wished to marry her?

His head swirled and against his better judgement, Angus poured himself another goblet of wine, pushing his unfinished trencher to one side.

He put a hand to his forehead, steadying himself against the solid wooden table as fragments of conversation came back to him. He saw Emelia looking over at Fauvel, soon after Morwenna dismounted.

"I felt sure you would refuse," she had said.

Had she *wanted* him to refuse?

Angus drained his goblet and gripped the edge of the table, seized with new determination. He would go out to Morwenna now and tell her what had happened. What he *suspected* had happened. He would reassure her that he would find a way for them to be together.

He realised, like a slap in the face, that the very worst thing he could have done was stay away from Morwenna all day.

He had been like a man in a dream. A nightmare, more like. So consumed by the twists of fate that he had done nothing to unravel them.

It was time to put it right. He rose from the table, then immediately sank back into the chair as the great hall began to spin around him.

Just like Emelia, he had underestimated the richness of the wine.

With the last of his sensibility, Angus knew that he needed a clear head for this conversation with Morwenna.

It would have to wait until morning. And morning could not come quickly enough.

THE STIRRINGS OF the fortress roused him from a deep but troubled sleep. His head pounded as if it had been beaten; even his limbs felt heavy. But as soon as his eyes opened, Angus knew he must rise from his bed. There was much that he had to put right.

He stumbled to his nightstand and splashed cold water onto his face, wincing at the chill but relishing the punishment. He left the drapes closed, fearing that any sharp light would hurt his eyes and slow his progress. There was no time to wait for his manservant to help him dress; instead he pulled on yesterday's emerald green shirt and breeches. His hair, he combed roughly. Never had he been less concerned with his appearance; but for Morwenna's sake, he must make an effort.

An effort that was mayhap several hours overdue.

He groaned inwardly when a knock came at his door.

"What is it?"

Whatever it was, he would not be delayed.

A young serving boy shuffled into his chamber, head down, cheeks red.

"I have a message for you, milord."

"Give it here." Angus held out a hand and nodded his thanks.

He unfurled the parchment with uncharacteristic haste, his anxiety only increasing when he recognised Emelia's sloping hand.

Dearest Angus,

I do not know if you have ever realised how fond I am of you? Have you?

Either way, I dare to believe you also hold me in some affection.

It is this affection that I now appeal to.

Angus, my friend, I write to release you from our betrothal.

Do you want to be released? I suspect you do. Your face, at the table last night, told me what you could not bring yourself to say.

And I too have my reasons. Perchance one day I will tell them to you.

For now, I have sufficient experience of the world to realise that I may have misjudged the situation. If I am wrong, Angus, you must tell me. Meet me at Foxton Hall before noon today. If I see the Wolvesley carriage approach, I will know that my destiny is to become the Countess of Wolvesley. It is a role that I will perform with dignity and the greatest respect.

Your friend,
Emelia

Angus read the note a second time, the words blurring and reforming before his eyes.

God's Bones, Emelia had surpassed his expectations yet again. She had done what he could not bring himself to.

His first feeling was one of admiration for her courage and honesty.

His second was one of relief.

But both paled when he realised the implications of this letter. He was now free, entirely free, to marry Morwenna.

He didn't pause to grab a cloak or consider his next move. It was imperative he reached her. Already it seemed as if he had been gone from her life for too long, when in reality it was her bed that he had woken in just yesterday.

Yesterday, when his life had taken such an unexpected twist.

But now he was back where he wanted to be; with the sole exception of taking Morwenna's hand in his.

He had never told her he loved her.

He had yet to tell her she was a woman of means. His messenger had returned last night, reporting that Ember Hall was clean, comfortable and in a solid state of repair. It wanted only the addition of servants and furniture, and Morwenna could take up residence there whenever she pleased. It was her family home, after all. The estate had passed to Esme upon the death of Lord and Lady Howell. As Wolvesley Castle was Esme's last known address, the de Nevilles had been keeping it safe and maintained ever since.

But Angus didn't want Morwenna to live in Ember Hall. He wanted to marry her with all possible haste. She would live in Wolvesley Castle, by his side, always.

He skittered down the stairs and plunged out into the courtyard, wincing at the drizzle which immediately dampened his shirt. Few servants were about at this time; Angus met no one on his journey to the stables, not that he cared.

He was ready to shout from the rooftops that he loved Morwenna.

The drizzle became a fine rain which had slicked back his hair and ran down his face by the time he came to the old stone building which housed a stable below and Morwenna's room above. Two young grooms looked at him curiously, before quickly walking away towards the low-slung barn where they took their meals.

Angus paused, breathing hard. What if Morwenna was in there with them, breaking her fast?

He would willingly walk in and demand an audience, but she would most likely not appreciate the public spectacle.

With luck, she would still be in her room. His heartbeat quickened as he pictured her rising from her narrow bed, yawning and dressing for the day ahead.

He ran up the wooden stairs with the energy of a young

child, hardly pausing to catch his breath at the top.

"Morwenna?" He knocked on her door, uncaring of being overheard.

The door remained stubbornly closed. No footsteps sounded within.

He put his head to the wood, listening hard.

"Morwenna?" he tried again, rapping hard.

Slowly the truth dawned upon him. *She was not there.*

She would be eating then, in the barn.

But no, deep down he knew that this battle, so carelessly played, would not be so easily won.

A terrible suspicion had lodged deep in his chest, but he had to make sure.

He raised his foot and delivered a swift kick to the door, which splintered easily. He stepped into the gloom, his eyes razing over the neatly-made bed as he took two strides towards the closet.

It was empty.

His suspicion was correct.

Morwenna had gone from Wolvesley.

Chapter Twenty-One

H E STALKED OUT of the empty room and found himself face to face with Jacob, concern writ large across the older man's face.

Concern which rapidly morphed into surprise when he recognised the earl.

"Milord." He bowed low, his grey cloak falling forwards over his emerald green tunic.

Angus ran a hand through his sodden hair, too distracted to worry about propriety. "I am looking for Morwenna."

Jacob politely averted his rheumy eyes from the splintered doorway. "Morwenna appears to be missing." He bit down on his lip. "One of my stable boys brought me the news at first light."

Angus couldn't bear to remain on the narrow confines of the stairway for a moment longer. He edged past Jacob and pounded down the wooden stairs, oblivious to the startled horse which skittered out of his way.

Once outside, he placed his hands on his knees and breathed deeply. The air was cool and damp, helping to restore him to his senses.

I must find Morwenna.

But there was one thing he didn't understand. He swung back around to Jacob, who had followed him more slowly down the stairs.

"Why was Morwenna missed so early in the day?"

Jacob removed his cap, scratched his head and replaced it,

looking very much as if he would rather be anywhere but here. "'Twas not Morwenna that was first reported missing." His mouth clammed shut.

With a sinking heart, Angus realised what he was about to hear.

"Who then?" he barked.

"Sir Henry's personal groom. A boy named Gerrault." Jacob fixed his eyes over Angus's shoulder. "One of my lads, young Isaac, shares a room with him."

Gerrault.

Angus had seen Gerrault's affection for Morwenna and foolishly, he'd done nothing about it.

Angus cursed silently. Now a gangling groom had offered Morwenna the future that he had been poised to provide.

"I then discovered this had been pushed under my door." Jacob handed over a scrap of parchment onto which was inscribed a short message.

> *Thank you for your kindness towards me.*
> *I am sorry to leave without warning.*
>
> *Morwenna*

Rage unfurled in his stomach. Rage at himself as much as the young groom who had taken the opportunity Angus had been too blind, and too arrogant to seize for himself.

Holy Hell, he swore under his breath.

Jacob gave a small shake of his head and Angus raised his eyes in surprise. But Jacob's gesture was aimed at a gaggle of stable boys coming out of the barn who promptly turned and retraced their steps. Nonetheless, Angus understood that if they remained here in the yard, they would soon have an audience.

Holding his emotions in a firm grip, he nodded sharply to the stablemaster. "Thank you, Jacob. If you hear news of either Gerrault or Morwenna, please bring it to me directly."

"Very good, milord."

Angus took his leave, ignoring the curious eyes following his departure through the yard from the barn doorway.

His early morning search for Morwenna would be all around the castle by noon.

So be it.

He cared only that she was found.

Servants paused in their work and bowed low as he strode past, but for once Angus did not acknowledge their presence. His thoughts went round and round in a tight spiral. Morwenna had left without knowing the true depth of his feelings, nor the true extent of her family's wealth.

And it is all my fault.

He was a fool.

His feet had brought him back to the keep, where he was not at all sure he wanted to be. He was too restless to sit amongst his men and break his fast in the great hall. Instead, he veered towards the staircase and made a beeline for his mother's chamber.

Nella blanched when she saw who it was outside the door.

"Lady Violetta has not yet risen from her bed," she said pointedly, blocking the way in.

Angus ignored her. "Mother, may I enter?" he shouted past the maid.

"Let him in, Nella," came the reply.

With obvious reluctance, Nella moved her stout frame to one side so that Angus could barrel into the chamber.

Candles had been lit but the drapes were still closed and Angus had to blink in the artificial brightness after the grey gloom outside.

Lady Violetta was sitting up in bed, with a beautiful pale green shawl draped over a white nightrail. Her long hair was loose about her face; her blue eyes alert with interest.

"Whatever has happened?" she asked mildly.

Angus knew he should sit down, but he could not stop pacing. "Did Morwenna come to see you yesterday?"

His mother shook her head. "Nor did you," she added.

"Sorry," he managed.

"How was Lady Foxton?" His mother straightened her shawl, watching him like a hawk.

"In good health." Angus finally sank down onto a chair.

"I am pleased to hear it."

"You did not come down." He raised his eyes to her, accusingly.

"No. At my age you can get away with such things. And I thought it best to leave you two alone." She paused. "To see how events played out."

Angus let out a mirthless bark of laughter.

"Lady Foxton is a very beautiful, very wealthy woman," Lady Violetta observed.

"I agree on both counts," he said hollowly, fixing his gaze on the leaping flames of the fire. "She has gone."

"Gone?"

"Gone." He nodded. "She has released me from our betrothal."

"I see." Lady Violetta clutched at her shawl. "And Morwenna?"

"She has also gone."

His mother surprised him with a low chuckle. "Perchance I should have come down after all."

"It is no laughing matter, Mother."

"No indeed." She sat up straighter in bed. "And what are you going to do about it?"

"I will write to Lady Foxton, of course." He was growing overly warm in his mother's stifling chamber. "But first I must find Morwenna."

Lady Violetta settled herself back against the pillows. "When you find her, bring her to me. We have much to discuss."

Angus kissed his mother's cheek and left the airless room, nodding to Nella who waited in the passageway.

His stomach rumbled as he descended the stairs. Mayhap

some food would restore his temper and prepare him for the day ahead. But once in the marbled entrance hall, he was confronted with a stern-faced Henry standing beside a shame-faced youth who looked all too familiar.

Angus halted in his tracks, his mind racing to put these facts together.

Henry spotted him and bowed. "Good morn, my lord."

"Sir Henry." Angus stepped closer.

"You remember young Gerrault, my lord?"

"I do." His voice reverberated around the muralled walls.

Gerrault flushed a darker shade of red, but to his credit, he lowered himself into a low and steady bow.

"Well?" Angus barked, crossing his arms over his shirt.

"Jacob advised that you might like to speak to Gerrault," Henry said mildly.

"You were missing." Angus turned to him accusingly.

"Aye, milord, and I'm sorry for it." He swung his gaze desperately towards his master. "I will make up my work. I have already promised Sir Henry."

"That is not my concern." Angus cut through his bluster. "What do you know about the whereabouts of Morwenna?"

The boy swallowed, his Adam's apple moving in his throat. "I know naught."

"Do not lie to me." Angus moved closer, menacingly. "Morwenna left a note."

"I am not lying, milord."

"I will have you thrown into the dungeons." Angus ignored the worried look Sir Henry was giving him.

Gerrault began to visibly tremble. "I swear, milord Wolvesley, Sir Henry. I don't know where she is now."

Henry laid a restraining hand on Angus's arm. "Why don't you tell us what you *do* know?"

The boy looked as if he might drop to the floor with fright. "Morwenna came to me yesterday and asked me to help her."

"Help her with what?" Angus's voice was icy cold.

"She wanted to leave Wolvesley," Gerrault blurted out.

A passing group of serving maids heard his outburst and looked up in surprise before veering off into the great hall.

"Should we go somewhere more private?" Henry asked mildly.

"Nay." Angus couldn't bear to waste another second, even though Gerrault's tale made him sick to the stomach. "Carry on," he barked.

"She asked if I could get her a horse from the stables after nightfall." The boy's voice had become little more than a whisper. "And I said I could."

"So you stole a horse?" Angus raised his eyebrows, remembering the last time Morwenna had attempted such a stunt.

"Nay, milord." Gerrault pulled himself together. "I was going to," he admitted, "but I couldn't, because of the rain. It wasn't safe for anyone to be out last night."

"Quite right," Henry spoke up.

"And then this morn, I went to see Morwenna at first light, but her door was bolted, and I feared she was gone."

"Gone?" repeated Angus, aware of the echoes of the conversation he had so recently had with his mother. "Gone where?"

Gerrault shrugged helplessly. "That's why I left the castle. To see if I could find her. But there was no trace." His voice shook.

"Can you think of anywhere she might be?" Henry was looking from Gerrault to Angus, as if searching for a clue as to why this girl might matter so much to both of them.

"Only one place, my lord. And it's most unlikely."

"Tell us," Angus ordered.

"She might've gone back to Escafeld. It's where we were both raised. Though she wasn't happy there." Gerrault sniffed.

"Escafeld." Angus drummed his fingers against his sleeve. "That's half a day's ride from here?" He looked questioningly at Henry, who nodded his agreement.

"I will go after her." Henry was already edging towards the door. "Gerrault, you must come and show me the way."

"Nay." Angus strode past them both. "I will go there myself."
It had to be him who put this right.

But before he reached the open doorway, reality gripped him by the shoulders. There was something he must do before he raced away from Wolvesley. Never again could he allow unfinished business to come between him and Morwenna.

"Saddle my horse," he barked at Gerrault, before turning towards his solar. "We will leave as soon as we are able. I will meet you in the yard.

But first, he would write a reply to his friend Emelia.

MORWENNA SLEPT LATE. When she awoke, the sun was already high in the sky and streaming through the half open drapes. She lay still, dazed and confused, unable to recall where she was.

How could she be resting on such a comfortable mattress? It felt as if she was floating on a cloud. The pillows beneath her head were soft, the blankets drawn over her were cosy and comforting. Even her toes were warm.

She glanced around the spacious chamber, noting the beautiful carvings on the wooden closet in the corner and the fur rugs spread out on the floor. She was laid upon a high, canopied bed, positioned directly opposite an arched window. Through the opening in the drapes, Morwenna could make out an elegant sweep of lawn.

The rush of memory made her squeeze her eyes tightly shut.
She was at Foxton Hall.

A flood of shame brought heat to her face and neck.

She shouldn't be here. In fact, this was the very last place she should be.

But here she was. Not only taking shelter in the hall, but sleeping in one of the best chambers, dressed in a nightgown trimmed with lace.

Lace.

Morwenna drew her knees to her chin and pressed her head against them, holding her legs tight as she relived the tumultuous events that had brought her here.

She had crept from Wolvesley Castle when the first rays of morning sunshine brought a slight orange hue to the dark sky. The day had dawned damp and chill, so instead of dressing in her poor gown from home, she'd pulled on her usual groom's livery, adding a cloak for good measure.

She no longer felt that she owed the earl anything.

She packed her own belongings in a small cloth bag, together with a half-loaf of bread and several hard apples. She had not been able to bring herself to eat anything since the scene in the paddock, but still had sense enough to realise that the situation could not continue for long. Lack of food was already making her vision blur at the edges.

She slung the bag over her shoulder, and marched out, locking her chamber door behind her.

The more time she could buy before she was missed, the better.

The guards on the main gate stood aside to let her pass and Morwenna slipped through, marvelling at how easy it all was. She would make faster time with a horse, but theft was theft. And she didn't want to drag Gerrault's name into the mud. His star was still rising at Wolvesley. Nay, 'twas better this way. She raised her head high and moved forward, choosing to follow a narrow cart track through the trees rather than the open paved road.

Last night, despair had twisted into her heart at the relentless rain which conspired to keep her imprisoned in the castle. But now she could see that all would be well.

She would walk as far as she could. Then she would find shelter for the night. One day at a time. The faith that she had so recently learned to place in the earl was far weaker than the faith she had finally learned to place in her own abilities. Never again would she stay in a place that made her unhappy, for want of the courage to leave it.

But the damp air made her sneeze and hot tears squeezed from her eyes as she thought of all she was leaving behind. Fauvel would miss her. Mayhap Gerrault too. And the earl.

She no longer thought of him as Angus.

She no longer allowed herself to dwell on his piercing blue eyes and that wonderful feeling of safety and protection he had exuded. Though she was the suspected witch, 'twas as if he had weaved a spell over her. A spell which caused her to abandon all sense and proper caution.

Morwenna paused to gather her composure and remind herself that thinking like that would not aid her progress. The rumble of carriage wheels came from behind her, and she looked from right to left, unable to see a safe place where she could stand aside and let the vehicle pass. The pathway was rutted, even more so because of the recent downpour. Morwenna stumbled a little in her haste to clamber out of the way. Surely the carriage driver had seen her and would slow down?

Alas, the carriage did not slow. Morwenna's stomach churned and she flung her arms out towards a tree trunk, but it was too late.

As she fell into the mud, she could hear a high shout of alarm followed by the whinny of a startled horse. Then her head hit the ground, and all was still.

A gentle knock on the chamber door brought her back to the present.

Morwenna looked askance at the door. *How should I answer?*

"Hello?" she tried.

The door nudged open, and a familiar face peeked through the gap.

Morwenna's heart sank like a stone as she struggled to sit up. "Lady Foxton," she managed.

The tall, elegant young woman stepped into the chamber and closed the panel behind her.

"How are you feeling?"

"Better."

"I am pleased to hear it." She stepped closer to the bed. "There is more colour in your cheeks, but I am still not sure we shouldn't send for the physician."

"Nay, please don't," Morwenna begged. "I have already put you to enough trouble."

"Nonsense," Lady Foxton tutted. "It is no trouble at all." She folded her hands across a rippling gown of blue silk. "It is pleasant, after all, to have company. Foxton Hall is a vast and empty place, and I have been used to the chatter and bustle of Cheltenham Castle."

Morwenna pressed her lips together. "I fear I have not been good company, my lady."

"You had a nasty knock to the head, for which my carriage driver is to blame. If he had not been half asleep at his post, none of this would have happened."

Morwenna had no wish to heap blame on a man who had made an honest mistake. "I feel stronger now." She swung her legs to the floor, testing her theory.

"There is no hurry." Lady Foxton's voice was soft. "But if you are ready to get out of bed, I shall send a maid in to help you dress."

Morwenna gave a strangled little laugh. "You are too kind, honestly. But I have no need of a maid." She raised her eyes to meet the concerned gaze of Lady Emelia Foxton, noting her elaborately coiled hair and the jewels gleaming at her throat. "I am only a servant, my lady. I am unused to such luxuries."

Lady Foxton bit down on her lower lip. "You are my guest, Morwenna. And I would not see your strength overly tested." She took a breath. "I have no wish to make you uncomfortable, but I feel there are things we should discuss."

Morwenna took a deep breath, trying hard to keep panic at bay. She could not discuss Angus with Lady Emelia Foxton. *His betrothed.*

And what else could it be?

Mayhap Lady Foxton had discerned her feelings for him.

Mayhap Morwenna had even said something in the delirium which had seized her for most of yesterday.

She shook her head, resolved to show dignity today at least. "I should not take up any more of your time."

Lady Foxton came closer and laid a hand on Morwenna's shoulder. Her grip was gentle but firm and she smelled faintly of rose petals. "I will send in a maid and once you are dressed, we will talk in my parlour." She smiled slightly. "There is much you need to know."

MORWENNA HAD KNOWN many strange outfits in her time. Poor gowns long outgrown, which she had squeezed into to save her grandmother the labours of making or sourcing a new one. The unfamiliar tunic and braccae which had been her uniform at Wolvesley.

But never had she been so uncomfortable as she felt in the beautiful cream dress which Lady Foxton's maid had unsmilingly laced her into that morning.

Once finished with the dress, the maid had combed out the tangles in Morwenna's long hair and pinned it back from her face. The pins had scraped against Morwenna's scalp, but she was too overwhelmed to cry out.

She hardly knew what to think, much less what to say.

The maid was wise in the ways of ladies and how they should behave. She would know that Morwenna was no such thing.

Morwenna herself was under no illusions. She was a peasant from Escafeld. One skilled at training horses. That was all she had ever wished to be. It mattered not that her grandmother was once a titled lady. That was not how Morwenna had known her, and it was not a life to which she had been raised.

So why was Lady Foxton so insistently treating her like a member of the nobility?

Morwenna had followed the maid down endless stairs to a small parlour overlooking the gardens. The parlour was distinctly feminine, filled with fur throws, candles and morning sunlight. Lady Foxton sat at a small round table, eating daintily from a platter of cut bread, soft cheese and glistening grapes.

"Come and join me, Morwenna?" She beckoned towards the chair pulled up beside her.

Morwenna hesitated in the doorway and bobbed into a small curtsy.

Lady Foxton flapped her hands. "I do not like to stand on formality, my dear. Especially not so early in the day."

Swallowing her anxieties, Morwenna stepped forward. Lady Foxton had been nothing but kind to her, she reminded herself. It would not hurt to pass the time politely in her presence, then make her escape as soon as possible.

"Sit," she urged.

"Thank you, Lady Foxton."

"And call me Emelia."

Morwenna lowered herself as gracefully as she could into the chair. She was unused to such a long, restrictive gown which nipped her at the waist and caught under the polished legs of the chair.

Lady Foxton followed her gaze and tittered slightly. "The gown, of course, is much too long. I'm sorry I had nothing more suitable."

Morwenna's cheeks burned and she folded her hands together to stop them from trembling. "It is beautiful. I shall return it at my earliest opportunity."

"Don't give it another thought."

Morwenna's stomach rumbled, betraying her hunger. Lady Foxton hid a smile.

"Please, eat." She pushed a trencher towards her. "You must regain your strength."

Morwenna opened her mouth to apologise yet again for causing so much inconvenience, but instead she found herself reaching for the freshly-baked bread and chewing with enthusi-asm.

"I am truly sorry for the trouble I've put you to," she said, after she'd swallowed.

Lady Foxton frowned. "Morwenna, if we are to become friends, I must insist that you refrain from this endless thanking and apologising. It's exhausting."

Morwenna paused, another serving of bread raised part-way to her mouth.

"Are we to become friends?" she asked, startled.

Lady Foxton spread out a roll of parchment on the table before her. It was angled so that Morwenna could not read the flowing hand, even though she tried.

"I rather think that depends on you."

Morwenna put the bread back into the trencher. "Lady Fox-ton. I don't understand."

"Emelia," she corrected sternly. "And neither do I, not entire-ly." She rolled the parchment back up. "There are two things which you should be made aware of." She pursed her lips. "But I do not believe I am the correct person to tell you about either of them."

"Please." The room was becoming unbearably warm. "I should like to know."

Emelia's blue eyes danced. "The first, you must know al-ready. God's blood, I knew the moment I saw you together."

Morwenna pressed her hands together. "Knew what, exact-ly?"

"There is no need to be coy, my dear. I am a woman used to spending time amongst women." Emelia let out a peal of laughter. "I am talking of Angus, of course. That rather beautiful man who we now must call the Earl of Wolvesley." She paused. "You are in love with him."

Morwenna thought she might faint clean away. "I'm sorry," she whispered.

"Sorry? Whatever for now?"

She gripped the edge of the table. "I did not know about your betrothal." Her mouth had become as dry as straw, but she managed to force out the words.

Emelia leaned forwards. "Our betrothal no longer stands."

The world tilted, Morwenna braced herself against a fall. "How so?"

"Because Angus is in love with you."

Morwenna took a deep breath, then another. She had all but allowed herself to believe Angus loved her once before. And heartbreak had swiftly followed.

"It cannot be."

"Why ever not? Angus and I have wealth enough to guide our own destinies. Why shouldn't we take action to ensure our own happiness?" She gave Morwenna a wry smile. "There is no cause for shame. People fall in love with one another all of the time."

"Not where I come from." Morwenna put a hand to her aching brow.

"Ah, you should spend time in Cheltenham, my dear. The place positively rings with declarations of devotion. Some of them are even true." Emelia's voice took on a different quality. "I did not break off our betrothal purely for Angus's benefit."

Morwenna said nothing. She had no words left to her. She simply waited for Emelia to continue.

"Take a sip of ale, my dear. You look as if you need it."

Morwenna closed her fingers around the cup and moved it automatically to her lips. Drinking did make her feel marginally better.

"I have been looking for a way out of our betrothal for some time. Not that Angus isn't a wonderful man. He is. You know it as well as I. Any woman would be lucky to be his wife. The Countess of Wolvesley. Although, when my father agreed on my betrothal, he never guessed I would rise so high. We always thought Lucan's heir would inherit." Emelia paused. "There is no rational way to explain why I would not embrace such a life. Only the truth makes sense. And the truth is, my heart beats for another."

Morwenna sat back in her chair, cradling her cup and digesting this revelation. "So you are not displeased?"

"On the contrary, I am delighted." Emelia plucked grapes from the bunch as if her words hadn't altered absolutely everything.

"How did you know?" Morwenna whispered.

"About you and Angus? I could sense there was something between you two when we were in the paddocks with that wild horse I had challenged Angus to tame. I felt sure he would refuse that particular challenge." She shook her head, amusement flickering in her eyes. "But any doubts I had about the two of you were removed by the message I received just this morn."

"The message you have there?" Morwenna eyed the parchment. She would dearly love to read it.

"Quite so." Emelia sighed thoughtfully. "Angus has explained a great deal. I had to read it twice to make sense of it all. But I still think that I am not the right person to speak on this."

Morwenna's heart pounded.

"And so one question remains, Morwenna. Will you come to Wolvesley with me to speak with Angus?"

Chapter Twenty-Two

HOW HE REGRETTED his impulse to ride to Escafeld now that his legs and back were aching, the weather was dull, and his quest had proved futile.

Angus tried to swallow his frustration as Gerrault made enquiries at a ramshackle inn some miles from the poor wooden hut which his beloved Morwenna had once called home. He was standing with their horses, both of whom were exhausted from hours of galloping. A drizzle of rain was running down his neck, towards a chilly gap between his shirt and his now filthy mantle. He could not remember when he last felt more miserable.

"They can offer us accommodation for the night or a change of horses," Gerrault declared, walking tentatively back towards him.

Angus knew he had been glowering at the boy for the best part of the day. Glowers which were mayhap excessive. After all, none of this was young Gerrault's fault.

All of it was *his* fault, and his fault alone.

He harrumphed in response, attempting to sort through his muddled thoughts. Their horses were too tired to continue back to Wolvesley, that much was undeniable. As much as he wanted to be home, preferably in a hot bath, with this whole regrettable incident behind him; Angus had to admit that he too was tired.

And hungry.

And the boy looked fit to drop.

"So be it," he growled. "We will stay here until the morn."

He took a breath, about to order Gerrault to see to their horses, but then he reconsidered. "Where are the stables?"

Gerrault hid his surprise. "Back there." He pointed to a weed-strewn courtyard through which a gaggle of chickens were clucking and scratching for food. "I can see them settled, milord."

"Nay, I shall settle my own horse." Angus forced his tired legs to start walking. "Mayhap I should tend to your horse as well, Gerrault. 'Tis my fault you are out here in the cold, instead of at Wolvesley where we both belong."

He flicked a gaze over his shoulder, somewhat gratified to see the youth speechless with astonishment.

Gerrault scratched at his head as he led his horse into the stall alongside Angus. "It has been an honour to ride with you."

Angus laughed out loud, wincing at the smell of old hay and horse manure. "I have been nothing but rude. When in truth, your directions were invaluable." He summoned his inner steel. "Thank you."

The boy almost dropped his saddle onto the cobbles. "Any time, milord."

Angus laughed again, but mirthlessly. "I do hope there will not be another time." He settled his saddle against the wall and began to rub down his horse's coat with a twist of straw. It was many years since he had done this, as a young knight at the Lindum training academy, but the actions were somehow soothing.

"I hope we find Morwenna." Gerrault's pale cheeks coloured as he worked.

"Aye, me too, lad." Angus paused, remembering the cold, hard shock of coming up against the empty hut. Grass had grown over the path to the front door, which clearly hadn't been opened in many weeks. An air of abandonment hung over the small shack. Standing back, Angus could see holes in the roof and ivy entirely covering one wall.

His resolve had hardened. Morwenna would *not* come back here.

But where was she?

Please don't let her be sleeping outside, exposed to the elements, he begged, silently. *Don't let her be injured, or afraid, or have fallen amongst rogues.*

He rested his forehead against the horse's warm shoulder, all too aware that those outcomes were mayhap the most likely.

Morwenna was not in Escafeld. And she was not to be found on any of the paths leading to Escafeld. Angus had dispatched riders in every conceivable direction. No one had seen her since she left Wolvesley.

If only he had gone to her that night.

If only he had stopped her walking away from the paddocks.

If only, if only, if only. The refrain beat around his head like a caged bird.

"She will be alright, milord."

Gerrault's hesitant voice cut through his spiralling thoughts.

Angus jerked back to the present to find Gerrault's grey eyes fixed upon him.

"What makes you so sure?"

Gerrault's smile transformed his face. "Because she's Morwenna. I've known her all my life and she's always found a way to survive. She's stronger than she looks."

"That I know," Angus agreed. But no matter her inner strength, he hated the idea of Morwenna being in trouble; either here in the present or back in the past. All he wanted was to protect her from harm. Which was a bitter irony, considering the pain and upset he had caused her.

And to think his ire had risen against this blameless boy.

"I believe that Morwenna may be lucky to have you as a friend," he said slowly.

Gerrault blushed again, busying himself scooping out oats for the horses.

"She helped me, after my parents died. It's only right that I look out for her."

At one time, Angus may have questioned the lad further,

intent on finding out to what extent Gerrault wished to look out for Morwenna. But now he was weary to the very bone.

"The horses will do well now until morn. Let us now go inside." He scratched at his beard then fished in his cloak for a bag of coin. "Here." He tossed it to Gerrault who caught it neatly, his face a picture of surprise. "Make sure you get a good meal inside you," he advised. "We have another long ride ahead of us tomorrow."

ANGUS SLEPT LITTLE on the hard, narrow bed in the inn. The floor sloped dramatically to one side and all night he had the feeling that he might roll off his mattress. The next morn, however, dawned bright and it was such a blessed relief to see the sun once again that he felt his mood improving.

He broke his fast with a bowl of thick, gloopy porridge. If his stomach had not been growling with hunger, he would have set it aside. But the innkeeper made it clear that there was no alternative.

He strode through the thin entrance hall to the courtyard, ducking his head under a low beam and blinking as he emerged into the light.

A new day, he thought, resolved to make the best of it.

Gerrault was out before him, making their horses ready. He could hear the lad chatting away as he worked.

For the briefest of moments, Angus tilted his face to the sun and believed that he may yet find solace.

But how can there be solace without Morwenna?

He paused in the middle of the cobbled yard and closed his eyes against the onset of despair. Chickens clucked around his feet and horses whickered to one another, but he closed his ears to these normal, everyday sounds.

How could he sleep and eat and talk without knowing she was safe?

"Good morn, milord." Gerrault banged the half stable door shut behind him and ducked into a hasty bow.

Angus opened his eyes and regarded his travelling companion. The boy had a healthy colour in his cheeks and a streak of dirt on his green tunic. In one hand he held a horse brush and in the other a hoof pick. Highly aware of his own dishevelled appearance, Angus disregarded the dirt. He could hardly order Gerrault to go and change, either way. They had not thought to bring a change of clothes with them.

"Good morn, Gerrault. How are the horses?"

"Well rested, milord. I will have them ready before long." Gerrault hesitated. "Will we ride straight back to Wolvesley?"

Angus raised his eyebrows. "Unless you can think of anywhere else Morwenna might have gone. Had she friends, or family nearby?" A jolt of hope surged through him, making his knees weak.

But Gerrault shook his head. "Nay, milord, I cannot think of any. I have been thinking hard, all night." His voice broke and Angus saw how worried he was.

"Steady, lad," he advised, putting his own fears and worries to one side and putting a reassuring hand on his shoulder. "You told me yesterday that all would be well," he added, almost accusingly.

"Aye. Morwenna can look after herself." Gerrault dashed at his eyes, leaving another streak of dirt across his youthful face.

"We will find her," Angus promised. "We will ride back to Wolvesley. But then I will send out every man I have." His hand closed into a tight fist. "I will allow no harm to come to her."

Gerrault nodded, relief shining in his grey eyes. To him, the word of the Earl of Wolvesley was as good as law.

Angus clapped him on the shoulder and went to heave up his saddle. Tacking up his own horse would provide a welcome distraction and give him something to do with his hands while his mind raced.

Gerrault had believed his fine words. Words which Angus

meant with every fibre of his soul.

But how could he track down Morwenna if she didn't want to be found?

∞

MORWENNA FELT MORE uncomfortable with every minute that passed.

She had allowed Lady Foxton to persuade her back to Wolvesley.

Now she was sitting in the vast, echoing great hall; dressed like a lady and feeling like a fool.

But she did not regret her decision to come. She had to give herself this chance of happiness. Aye, she could have returned to Escafeld, as she had planned. Emelia would have willingly given her use of a carriage for the journey. But Escafeld did not feel like home anymore. It hadn't since her grandmother's passing.

Morwenna had always put faith in her instincts. And her instincts told her, quite pressingly, that Wolvesley was where she needed to be.

Near Angus.

Albeit, this was a side to Wolvesley she had never grown used to. The great hall was a far cry from the paddocks and woodland, where she had felt like she belonged. And Angus was not here.

"Gone for two days," the Seneschal had declared, bowing his head politely to Lady Foxton and glancing curiously at Morwenna, who he no doubt recognised.

Every time she glimpsed a passing serving girl, she wondered if it was Molly. But even though there was no sign of Isaac's sister, Morwenna couldn't shake the notion that everyone here recognised her and knew that her place was with the grooms and stable hands. Not beside the refined and lovely Lady Foxton. Not wearing cream muslin and a fur cloak which made the back of her neck overly warm. "He will come, Morwenna," Emelia declared serenely, sipping from a goblet of wine.

"How can you be sure?"

"He rode to Escafeld to find you. When he discovers you are not there, he will return." Emelia twisted in her chair to look out of the high arched window and consider the angle of the sun. "Before nightfall, I would wager."

Morwenna bit down on her lip, wanting to keep her anxieties locked up inside. If Angus had found her hut in Escafeld, he would have seen with his own eyes how poorly she had lived there.

The tapestries hanging on the plastered walls seemed to leer down and mock her plight. The marble columns had never seemed so smooth; the wooden carvings so intricate. Morwenna leaped to her feet, ignoring the chair which clattered onto the stone-flagged floor behind her.

"What is it?" Emelia leaned forward in concern.

"I must take a breath of air."

"Morwenna, wait." Emelia half rose from her chair, but Morwenna had already turned and walked briskly from the hall.

Her skirts flared out behind her as she rushed down the marbled passageway towards the entrance hall. The gleam of golden light from the courtyard shone to her like a beacon. Once outside, she would be herself again.

But her pathway to freedom was barred by a vast dark shape which moved in front of the sun, blocking the light. Unwilling to pause, even for a moment, she ducked to one side, but two strong hands reached out and gripped her shoulders.

"Morwenna?" The familiar voice was raised in wonder. "Is that really you?"

She didn't have to raise her head to know that she stood beside the earl. The sound of him, the height and breadth of him, the very *presence* of him all soothed her soul. Like a frantic hammering that had ceased, allowing birdsong to flourish in the sudden silence. Once more, she could breathe. Once more, she was whole.

He had lied to her.

But then he had ridden out to find her.

Slowly, she lifted her gaze to meet the full force of his piercing blue eyes. They were fixed on her face as if they would never look away again.

"It is," she said, entirely unnecessarily.

"You are here."

"Aye."

She couldn't tear her gaze from his. As if they had a will of their own, her hands crept up towards his stubbled cheeks. At her touch, he closed his eyes.

He looked tired and dirty. Mud smeared his rich cloak and a film of dust coated his golden hair. But no dirt could dull the intensity of his inner light. Nor his energy which hummed from every pore.

"I am so glad you are here," he whispered. "I was so worried."

"I was with Lady Foxton."

His eyes jerked open. "Emelia?"

The sound of her name on his lips caused Morwenna a twinge of discomfort. "She is waiting in the great hall."

"It is not Emelia that I have been longing to see." He reached up to clasp her hands in his own, his eyes travelling over her beautiful gown with some surprise. A smile quirked at his lips. "While I was racing around the countryside looking for you, you were at Foxton Hall?"

"'Tis true."

His face sobered. "Safe?"

"Aye." She nodded again. "Safe." She wanted to say more. To tell him that although she had been safe in body, her spirit had been most troubled. But before she could form the words, Angus had dropped to his knees before her.

"I have never been gladder of anything."

"What are you doing?" she asked in alarm, conscious of the curious eyes of passing servants. Through the open doorway she spied two men-at-arms striding past the fountain on their way to the keep. In another moment, they would be climbing the steps. "You must get up," she hissed.

"Nay." He pressed her fingers firmly. "I will stay here, on my knees, until I have said all I have to say."

"People are staring."

"I care not." Resolution shone from his eyes.

"But I do." She could feel heat travelling up her neck towards her face.

Angus angled his head over his shoulder. "Get out," he roared towards the courtyard. "Leave us," he ordered a group of servants on the stairs. He raised his eyebrows at Morwenna. "Better?"

"Not really."

She was still held in his grip, but for the first time ever she was now looking down at the mighty Earl of Wolvesley. The top of his golden head did not quite reach her shoulders.

"Marry me," he said. The momentous words tripped from his tongue so easily, she could not believe she had heard him correctly.

Struck dumb, she could only stare down into his beautiful eyes.

"Marry me," he repeated, more forcefully this time. He tilted forwards until his forehead pressed against Morwenna's belly. "Please."

"Angus." She wrapped her arms around his head, pulling him closer to her. "I cannot marry you," she whispered, half furious. "You are the Earl of Wolvesley. And I am a nobody."

"You have lands and property of your own," he said, steadily. "Ember Hall stands on the northern fringes of the Wolvesley estate. It is a fine house. Your ancestral home. Your rightful inheritance."

She reeled backwards, unable to make sense of it.

"You do not need to marry me," he continued, his words falling over one another. "You do not need to marry anyone. You are a woman of means, Morwenna. You can do entirely as you please."

"I don't understand." She tightened her grip of his hands, seeking his strength. When that didn't stop the hall from lurching, she also fell to her knees.

Angus put his hands on her waist and held her steady. "Lord and Lady Howell came to regret their cruel behaviour towards your grandmother. She was their only heir and they left her everything. Alas, upon their death, Esme had already fled from Wolvesley and despite our very best efforts, we were not able to find her." His voice rose with passion. "Just think, Morwenna, how different things could have been."

"That is in the past," she whispered, unable to contemplate an upbringing so markedly altered from the one she had known. Unwilling to wish away those happy years she'd known with her grandmother. The future though, that was different.

As Angus spoke, the future spread out before her, glittering and inviting.

"I will show you the deeds. They have long been in our safe-keeping."

She opened her mouth but no words came out. She cared naught for deeds. Angus carried on talking, naming a yearly sum of income from tenant farmers. Morwenna put her hands over her ears and silenced him with a shake of her head.

"Stop, please. It is too much to take in."

"I kept things hidden from you. And then you disappeared. I vowed I would never do that again." Angus stroked her face gently. "You are a strong, intelligent woman, Morwenna. I am telling you that from this day forwards, you need never be dependent upon anyone, ever again."

She swallowed hard. "My grandmother's house?"

"She grew up there, aye."

"I never knew."

"It is yours. All of it. I have checked and re-checked." Angus paused. "Though Ember Hall is not your only option. If I have understood correctly, there is also a young groom out there who very much admires you." He cocked his head towards the stable yard.

"Gerrault?" She felt her face break into a smile.

"A fine young man," he declared.

"The finest."

His face creased in concentration. "There. I believe that is it. I have told you all I know. But tarry a while, for there is more I must say.

"More?"

"I am a judiciary. I have long put my faith in books and learning. But in the short while I've known you, Morwenna, you've taught me that instincts are more important than knowledge. When I am with you, my heart fills with happiness. I have longed for the chance of a future side-by-side with you. I have longed for *you.*" He took a ragged breath. "I love you."

A strange emotion unfurled in Morwenna's heart, sending tingling sensations all through her limbs. Was it hope, she wondered?

Nay, it was something stronger than hope.

It was *joy.*

She rose to her feet, resting her hands on his shoulders, gazing down at the face of the man she loved.

"Does your original offer still stand, my lord?"

His brow creased into a frown. "To train my horse?"

"Nay," she laughed. "To be your bride?"

"It will always stand."

She dropped a kiss onto his golden head. "Then I am delighted to accept."

Chapter Twenty-Three

Seven years later...

T HE GOLDEN-HAIRED LITTLE girl stood in the centre of the long gallery and waited, as still as a statue made of stone. After many seconds had passed, she closed her eyes and opened her arms, palms facing up to the vaulted ceiling. For a long while, nothing happened. The house stood silently watching, the air thick with anticipation. A silvery light filtered into the gallery from the high arched windows, illuminating the wooden carvings on the panelled walls and giving the whole scene an ethereal glow.

But ethereal glow or not, a woman pregnant with her fifth child could only crouch beneath a banister for so long without running out of patience.

Morwenna was just about to stand up and stretch her aching legs, when she realised the light had changed. It was no longer silvery and faint, now bright patches of gold blazed from torches affixed to the walls. Lively music filtered up from the hall below, not quite drowning out the excited whisper of young children. She breathed in the heady scent of cloves, roasting meat and smoke from the fire. Then she blinked, and the scene dissolved.

Morwenna steadied herself against the cold banister as she stood upright and caught her breath. She could only see Frida, her oldest child, stood in the centre of an otherwise empty gallery. Ember Hall was now unoccupied and unfurnished. The torches which had once blazed from these ancient walls had been long extinguished. There were neither rugs nor rushes on the floor; no children to whisper excitedly to one another.

But before her eyes, Frida rose onto her tiptoes. Her face was tipped upwards, her rosy lips partially open.

Morwenna had seen enough.

"Frida de Neville, are you up here?" she cried, pretending to have just ascended the wide, creaking stairs.

Frida came back to the present quite readily. "I'm here, Mama. I'm exploring." She skipped to a circle of light by a window and twirled in the dust motes.

"And what have you found?"

The child shrugged. She had Morwenna's green eyes and slight build, but her father's easy air of confidence. "Not much. It's just a lot of empty rooms."

"Well, that is to be expected, daughter, in an empty house." Morwenna smiled indulgently. "The family who lived here since you were but a babe have moved south to join the court of the new King."

Which was why they had come; to inspect the property now that it was no longer tenanted. That and to fulfil one of Violetta's last requests. In her final days, she had urged her beloved daughter-in-law to return to her ancestral home.

"My grandchildren should run in the fields above Ember Hall," she had breathed.

Morwenna blinked away salty tears at the memory. Violetta had provided kind and unfaltering support as Morwenna navigated her first daunting days at the helm of Wolvesley Castle. Her presence had shone like a gentle light, guiding them ever forward. The dowager countess had found deep pleasure in her role as a grandmother; the chortling laughter of her grandchildren keeping her sharp mind tethered to this world. She had passed from them peacefully, just days after the Twelfth tide decorations were taken down.

"But Esme says there's something far more exciting on top of the hill outside."

Morwenna came back to the present with a frown. She was

still not fully comfortable with hearing her daughter casually evoke her grandmother's name; but to Frida, Esme was not an old lady but a fun-loving six-year-old.

The same age as Frida herself.

An imaginary friend, Angus would laughingly explain to anyone who heard Lady Frida de Neville chattering away to a little girl that no one else could see.

Mayhap he was right, Morwenna sometimes mused. Or mayhap little Frida really was conversing with the returned spirit of her grandmother.

Morwenna folded her arms across her chest, drawing her cloak closer to ward off a slight chill. Outside, the first green shoots were beginning to poke through the frozen ground, but winter had not yet released them from its grip.

"Where is this hill?" she asked lightly, crossing the gallery to stand before a window.

Frida came to stand beside her, slipping her small hand into hers. "There." She pointed eagerly at a small incline heading east towards the distant glimmer of the sea. "Can we go and look? Please?"

Morwenna smiled at her enthusiasm. "Let's find your father and Tristan first. Then we can all go together."

Frida ran down the stairs eagerly and Morwenna followed at a more sombre pace, trailing her hand down the smooth wood of the banister and imagining the generations of her family who had walked here before her.

Her grandmother for certain had grown up within these walls. One of the chambers so quickly dismissed by Frida would have been where she slept.

Ember Hall was not large or grand, certainly not by the standards of Wolvesley Castle. But it was sturdy and welcoming; standing four-square and strong against winter storms and battering winds. When Angus first brought her here, weeks after their wedding, Morwenna had felt instantly at home. She'd wandered around the overgrown rose garden, inhaling the fragrant aroma and imagining her grandmother's arm around her shoulders as she fingered the soft petals.

Such strong fancies she would once have banished, fearfully, but now she simply acknowledged and enjoyed them.

Her own daughter's undeniable Sight might once have made her weak with fright; but now she had learned to have faith in the future.

The heavy front door creaked in complaint as Frida shoved her slight frame against it. The sound of her little boots clattering across the courtyard was soon followed by a shout of pleasure.

"Father. Come quickly. We're going up a hill."

Morwenna increased her pace, closing the front door carefully behind her and shielding her eyes from the glare of noon-day sun. She grunted softly as a small, warm body barrelled into her.

"Mama, I've been riding," her son, Tristan, announced proudly.

"Really?" She reached down and swung him into her arms, entirely consumed by a sudden rush of love.

He nodded, planting a wet kiss on her lips. "Papa says I can be a knight one day."

"Oh, does he?" Morwenna tightened her arms about him protectively. "I'm not sure I shall let you."

Five-year-old Tristan laughed in delight, the very image of his father. "You can't stop me, mama. You'll be an old lady by then."

She laughed in spite of herself. "Old ladies can be very powerful, I'll have you know."

Tristan shook his head doubtfully and Morwenna was ready to further argue her cause, when her attention was fully taken by Angus coming out of the barn. He was holding hands with Frida and leaning down to listen intently to whatever she had to say.

If anything, she loved him more now than she had the day they married.

He glanced up, as if aware of her thoughts, and treated her to a radiant smile. He was still a tall, handsome man. His blue eyes could still see directly into her soul. One calm word from him could steady a storm of doubt in her heart.

"I hear we are walking to a hill," he announced, leading Frida towards them. A few strands of grey were woven amongst the gold on his head, but the years had not altered his strength or bearing.

"It's that way." Frida pointed behind her, pouting slightly.

"Why don't you run along then? Show us where to go," Angus suggested.

"Take Tristan with you," Morwenna added, lowering her son to the ground and flexing her aching wrists.

The two children skipped off through the overgrown paddocks and Angus drew her close.

"Happy?" he asked, his voice against her ear.

"Very." She looped her arm around his waist and rested her head briefly against his shoulder. How could she not be? In seven years, she had known naught but love and stability. Wolvesley grew stronger and more prosperous with each passing summer; her children were healthy and flourishing. Morwenna was truly blessed.

Even her role as countess, which she once approached with trepidation, had brought her a sense of fulfilment. She had not forgotten her early days in the castle, nor the hungry days before that. Soon after her marriage, Morwenna had taken Molly to one side and asked her to take charge of distributing leftover food amongst the needy in the village. And each year, she ensured that local boys were offered apprenticeships in the castle; many of them training as grooms under the expert guidance of Gerrault, the new stablemaster at Wolvesley.

"Are you pleased we came back here for a visit, as my mother wished?"

"I am," Morwenna sighed. "But I can't help feeling we should spend more time at Ember Hall. It's my ancestral home, but I still hardly know it."

"We could make it a summer retreat?" Angus suggested, helping her over a patch of muddy ground. "It would be nice to be near the sea in the warmer months."

Morwenna smiled up at him. "That's perfect. Then all of our children can run in the fields, just as Violetta wanted."

They walked in companionable silence for a while, both keeping a watchful eye on Frida and Tristan who clambered on ahead of them. The ground began to rise steeply and Morwenna had to slow down. She was in her fourth month of pregnancy and grew tired easily.

"Should we rest here?" Angus hovered over her, concerned.

"I'll be fine in a moment," she panted, pulling down the hood of her cloak so the spring breeze could cool her warm cheeks. "Just look at that view."

Angus swivelled around and whistled in appreciation. "Beautiful."

Far below them, sparkling waves rolled onto a small strip of sand, bordered with rocks. Gulls cried out from the headland and a soft breeze carried the tang of sea salt.

"A far cry from the elegance of Cheltenham," Morwenna observed. They had visited Emelia and her husband before travelling to Ember Hall.

Angus laughed. "A splendid place which suits Emelia very well. I have never seen her so content. But I much prefer to feast my eyes upon the hills and the sea."

She nudged him playfully. "There was much beauty to be enjoyed there."

His blonde eyebrows raised. "There was? I did not notice." He leaned closer. "I have all the beauty any man could ask for in my lovely wife."

Morwenna laughed easily. "Let's go." She took her husband's arm, leaning into his strength and warmth.

"I could carry you, if you like?" His blue eyes glinted with amusement.

"Mayhap on the way down."

A sudden shriek made them both look up in alarm. Tristan was chasing after his long-legged sister, his right arm stuck out at right-angles to his stout body.

"I think he is being a knight," Angus said fondly.

Morwenna smiled, pushing away a twinge of discomfort. The only cloud on her sparkling horizon was the ever-present threat of unrest. With a new king on the throne, who knew what the future held for them all? And loyal Sir Henry was becoming too frail to lead the Wolvesley army as he had done so unfailingly these last years. The duty – the honour – had passed once again to the earl; to Angus. And one day, god-willing, it would pass to Tristan.

Morwenna huffed up the final stretch of slope. "I only hope he'll be kinder to his sister when he is old enough to be a knight."

"He will be." Angus was serene. "And to his brother and sister at home, as well as this little one." His hand rested lovingly on the slight curve of Morwenna's body.

"Another girl," she reminded him.

"Come and see," Frida demanded loudly. She had successfully outrun Tristan and then come to an abrupt halt just over the brow of the hill. Only the top of her silvery blonde head was visible.

"What is it?" Morwenna asked, still catching her breath.

"Oh." Angus stopped and Morwenna walked into his broad back. "Standing stones," he declared, slipping his arm around Morwenna's shoulders.

Ahead of them, an uneven circle of tall granite stones reared towards the sky. Each of them climbed vertically upwards from a narrow base, giving them an oddly human appearance.

"Seven of them," Frida counted. "See, they're taller than me." She danced to the centre of the circle and twirled around.

"What is this place?" Morwenna put a hand to her heart, clutching at the folds of her cloak. Part of her wanted to gather up her family and run from yet another reminder of sorcery. But she reminded herself that her days of running were over.

She was safe. She need not run from anyone.

Unable to deny her curiosity, she moved closer to the golden-hued stones which seemed to exude some ancient energy. She put out a hand to the rough granite, sucking in her breath when she felt its warmth.

"They have been soaking up the sun all day." Angus soothed her with his practical wisdom.

"But why are they here?" She looked around her, perplexed. This was no accident of nature.

Angus lifted his shoulders. "They must have stood like this since ancient times."

"I like them," announced Tristan.

"So do I." Frida put her hands on her hips and glared at her brother. "I found them first."

"You can both play amongst them," Angus ruled.

He guided Morwenna to a long flat stone nearby and they sat down together, watching the gulls swooping and their children playing. Morwenna laughed as little Frida clambered to the top of a particularly wide standing stone and elaborately knighted her younger brother.

"She is entirely at home," Morwenna said, feeling her heart squeeze with happiness. Part of her wished that her grandmother was still alive to see this; but another felt sure she was here, watching and smiling.

"And what about you?"

"I'm at home here too." Morwenna linked their hands together. "Happy at Ember Hall. Happy at Wolvesley Castle." She laughed. "You're very fortunate in your contented wife."

"That I know." Angus pressed a kiss to the top of her head.

Morwenna leaned against him, taking familiar comfort from his warmth and broad strength. "But happiness is about people more than places. My grandmother made a wooden hut into a happy home."

"She was a very special lady."

Morwenna tipped back her head so she could look into her husband's eyes. "She was. And at one time I thought I would be forever lost without her. But the truth is, Angus, that I'm at home wherever you are."

"And I you." He kissed her upturned forehead. "And I promise to make sure that is true for the rest of our lives."

THE END

About the Author

Elizabeth grew up in a rambling old farmhouse high on the Yorkshire moors, where a sense of history was never far away. She studied English at university, specialising in mythology and folklore and often bemoaning the lack of sword-wielding heroines. After graduating, she spent several years moving between northern France, southern Germany and London, where she worked in travel publishing and PR.

She now lives a stone's throw from her childhood home, with her husband, children and a feisty black cat who enjoys interrupting her writing. She plots most of her novels while walking in the rugged Yorkshire countryside, finding endless inspiration in the rolling hills.